TAKEDOWN

TAKEDOWN

ALI BRYAN

DCB

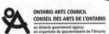

We acknowledge financial support for our publishing activities: the
Government of Canada, through the Canada Book Fund and The Canada Council
for the Arts; the Government of Ontario, through the Ontario Arts Council,
Ontario Creates, and the Ontario Book Publishing Tax Credit.

Library and Archives Canada Cataloguing in Publication

Title: Takedown / Ali Bryan.
Names: Bryan, Ali, 1978- author.
Identifiers: Canadiana (print) 20230591590 | Canadiana (ebook) 20230591604 |
ISBN 9781770867406 (softcover) | ISBN 9781770867413 (EPUB)
Subjects: LCGFT: Novels.
Classification: LCC PS8603.R885 T35 2024 | DDC jC813/.6—dc23

United States Library of Congress Control Number: 9781770867406

Cover and interior text design: Marijke Friesen
Manufactured by Friesens in Altona, Manitoba in March, 2024.

Printed using paper from a responsible and sustainable resource,
including a mix of virgin fibres and recycled materials.

Printed and bound in Canada.

DCB Young Readers
An imprint of Cormorant Books Inc.
260 Ishpadinaa (Spadina) Avenue, Suite 502, Tkaronto (Toronto), ON M5T 2E4, Canada

Suite 110, 7068 Portal Way, Ferndale, WA 98248, USA

www.dcbyoungreaders.com
www.cormorantbooks.com

for *Pips*, always a fighter

also for Coach Dan (rugby), Coach Greg (football),
Coach Pam (ringette), and my own coach, Jackie Nicholl
(gymnastics), who coached me with humor, kindness,
and unflappable patience. I'm sorry I kicked you.

CHAPTER 1

He snaps me down, hand pawing the back of my head, my braids a tangle of rope, blond and frayed and doused in sweat: mine, his. He goes for my leg, reaches, reaches, misses. I snatch his wrist and we circle, foreheads crashing into each other like a pair of animals locked in a violent dance. The kind of beasts you'd see headbutting on some undisclosed hilltop, all horns and hooves, their every move narrated by some old British dude with composer-era hair, speaking in whispers.

He tries to snap me down again. Fails. We end up in a clinch, chest to chest, arms over and under. His breath is hot against my ear, his shirt soaked and smelling of breakfast. I step in for an inside leg trip. Stall. He launches me onto his hip, up and over. I'm weightless long enough to flinch, long enough to anticipate the landing. Hard. We grapple until I feel his ball sack squished against the back of my neck and I regret only putting a half-assed effort into recruiting more girls at the beginning of the wrestling season.

I try to bridge and escape but get nowhere. Leo is sixty-five kilos of farm chores and male siblings and meat and potatoes. I turn my head, expecting to see the referee on his knees assessing the pin, ensuring my shoulders are flush with the unforgiving blue mat. Instead, I see my father's legs, the white of his sports socks, and his pristine sneakers, balancing on the footplates of his wheelchair. I hear the robotic lilt of his text-to-speech device call to me, *Rowan, get off your back, get up!* I can't. No matter how hard I try to buck Leo off, no matter how hard my brain tries to direct my body into action, regardless of my will, I can't get off my back.

And my dad can't get out of his wheelchair.

The ref thumps the mat with his hand and blows his whistle, signifying the end of the match, even though it's just an exhibition. Leo wastes no time getting off me. He extends his hand to help me up, and I accept. He's being decent, not chivalrous. Besides, I'm tired as fuck. Six rounds of live wrestling, all with guys.

Leo fist-bumps me. "Good job," he says, wiping his brow and adjusting himself.

I nod and step off the mat. Pia tosses me my water bottle, and I drink sloppily, my hand trembling.

"Nice whizzer," she says, cradling her arm. "You almost had him."

"Almost," I reply, catching my breath. "You see the doctor yet?"

Pia holds up her left arm, which is casted from her knuckles to her elbow. "Three more weeks," she sighs.

"You made a new sleeve."

"You like it?"

I slide down the wall, collapse onto the floor, and start untying my wrestling boots.

"Better than last week's."

"Right. The fur. Then you'll appreciate this." She waves her broken arm. "One hundred percent vegan leather. And for the record, I salvaged that fur from a theater trunk sale. It was worn no less than three hundred times by three different actresses."

"No doubt," I reply, stuffing my boots into my bag. "But I'm more impressed that you managed to sew it with one arm. I can't even thread a needle."

"I do have a gift," she says, admiring her handiwork.

Pia looks like an influencer — 50k followers, pictures with palm trees in the foreground, skin so glowing it looks nuclear — because she is. Fifty-three thousand followers to be exact, all of them enthralled by her thrifting genius, her DIY style, and now her cast sleeves.

"So are you coming to Tate's party?"

"Look at me!" The neck of my shirt is stretched so wide it hangs off my shoulder, and though I can't see it, a scratch stings below my left eye.

"I think you look kinda hot."

"Yeah, well. I don't smell so hot."

"Go shower. I'll wait."

"I have to go see my dad."

Pia nods and looks over at him. Her face turns to pity. I hate that look. I don't want anyone looking at my dad that way. Like he's poor, or sick. Like he's dying. I wonder if she sees it. The increased tilt of his head. It's only a few degrees, but I know my mom saw it too, at breakfast this morning. She didn't say anything. One minute she was lifting her fork to her mouth, and the next it was in the sink, her pancake untouched, the whipped cream a murky runoff.

"Pia!" I shout.

She flinches. "Sorry, I was just thinking about … I found this dress at Goodwill …" Her voice drops off.

"Who's going to this party?"

"Everybody."

"Let me talk to my dad."

Pia nods and sits cross-legged on a bench, cruising her phone with one hand. It's weird to see her as she appears online, coiffed and assembled, and not as my training partner, my shadow, hair ripped from her ponytail, shirt soaked and smelling of debauchery.

My dad waits near the gym's entrance reading a *National Geographic* clipped to a mechanical arm on his wheelchair. The magazine he's brought from home. It's all climate change: fires, floods, flus. Where are the features on ALS? *Lou Gehrig's* disease. *His* disease. What good is saving the planet if he won't be around to enjoy it?

"Rowan!" my coach calls.

I jump over the slick band left by the mop Leo uses to clean the wrestling mat. My socks leave behind a trail of prints.

My coach grabs my wrist. "Next time he takes your arm like that, you have to circle in, not out. Circling out leaves you vulnerable. That's how he was able to get under your hips."

I nod. He makes me do a few reps before slapping me on the back.

"Good work," he says.

I shake his hand. The look on his face reminds me of my physics teacher, my middle school softball coach, and the guy running the whack-a-mole game. A look that mixes pride and surprise as if they're still getting used to the idea that girls can solve complex equations, pitch, or get the high score in a game that calls for savagery.

"Thanks."

He runs through the drill again until his face starts to redden and he has to hike up his sagging track pants. "There's a huge girls' tournament in New York next month. Tons of recruiters'll be there. Teams from all over the world. You're going."

"Sounds good." I should be more enthusiastic, but recruiters make me nervous, New York makes me nervous. All those musicals and cabs. Times Square. Ozzy is going to be so jealous.

Coach pauses to look at my dad. Sunlight pours in from the glass front windows, illuminating his hair, the sheen of his magazine. "Your dad doing okay?"

Don't notice the head tilt, don't notice the head tilt. "Yeah, he is." I brave a smile.

The bell above the gym's front door jingles. My dad reverses his wheelchair to make room. The guy who comes in looks like a *Call of Duty* character, head shorn and neck covered in tattoos, cinder blocks for shoulders. He might be thirty.

Coach nods sympathetically and gestures toward the entryway.

"Who's that?" I ask.

"That's Axel 'The Fist' Barrett."

Axel wears gold aviator sunglasses and clutches the kind of leather portfolio you'd expect with a lawyer. His sneakers are expensive.

"The *Fist?*" I reply. "What kind of fighter name is that?"

Pia sidles up beside me.

"I'm not fussed about the name if he pays rent." With his foot, Coach nudges the industrial-sized bucket being used to collect water from the leaky ceiling. "If we don't fix this place up, we'll be wrestling in the parking lot next to the KFC." He smiles and then looks at Pia. "Hurry up and get the cast off, eh?"

Pia lifts her arm. Coach runs the oldest wrestling club in the city. It *smells* like the oldest wrestling club in the city. He owns the building too — if you can still call it that. It has more issues than a high school senior.

We watch him hustle over to Axel and follow behind. Outside, I see my mom back the van toward the door. You'd think she'd be good at this by now. Wheelchair parking spots are wide for a reason, but she always finds an angle.

"Hey, Dad." I bend to kiss him.

Nice practice, he types into his device. *Stance was looking great. You were moving fast.*

Not fast enough, I think, a mystery pain blowing up my knee.

Mom suggested we go for Italian. You coming? He looks at Pia. *You're welcome too.*

The last thing I want to think about right now is eating. Especially something as heavy as pasta. I just want water. And a massage. And physio. And a nap.

"I think I'm going to go to Pia's. We might hit up a friend's house later."

Okay, he types. *No drinking.*

"I know, Dad. Elite athletes don't drink."

Or vape.

"Yes, Dad." I roll my eyes.

Mom rushes through the door, her hair a bird's nest, heels clicking on the tile floor. "Sorry I'm late." She kisses my cheek and then wrinkles her nose.

"I know, I stink."

She waves and grabs the handles of my father's chair. "How was practice? Your brother's game went into overtime. They lost in the final three seconds."

She has a nice whizzer, Dad replies.

A nice whizzer's not going to get me to college.

"Good job, Rowan," Mom says.

I hold open the door, and she wheels Dad up the ramp into our converted van. It seems like yesterday Dad was lifting our mountain bikes and backpacks into it. Now it looks like a hearse.

Dad attempts to glance over his shoulder. *You and Pia want a ride?*

"We'll walk," I say, airing out my shirt.

Pia drapes an Adidas jacket over her shoulders. The print reminds me of a circus. Her followers love it. Behind the front counter, Axel and Coach shake hands.

"Looks like 'The Fist' is moving in," Pia says.

"But who is he?"

Pia holds her phone up to my face. She's already googled him.

Axel Barrett is an NCAA wrestler, American mixed martial artist, and former UFC Bantamweight champion.

"Bantamweight," I repeat.

"Perfect," Pia says, sticking her phone in her pocket. "If my arm doesn't heal, you have a new training partner."

"Ha." I shoulder my way out the front door. The air is humid, like the gym, the sky a blazing flamingo pink. We pass an Audi the color of champagne, a pair of miniature boxing gloves dangling from the dash, and walk the length of the strip mall parking lot toward Pia's.

"You know if we go to this party, I'll have to borrow something."

"I got you, Row," Pia replies as if it wasn't completely obvious.

And I know she will because Pia's *got me* since sixth grade.

CHAPTER 2

Halfway down 32nd Street, Pia drags me into some dirty vintage shop. A pair of straggly chaps hangs in the window beside a trio of mannequins dressed like Disneyland. Neon shirts and fanny packs. Inside it smells like a camper van that hasn't been opened in a decade. I cringe and cover my nose with my shirt, but all I can taste is Leo.

Pia touches everything. She runs her fingertips along cuffs, checks tags, and traces seams. I just want to get to her house and shower, but she's happy here. I can't stop her. Every time we go on a wrestling trip, she scouts out the local thrift and convinces Coach to let her check it out. *I promise I'll only be fifteen minutes.*

When she finds the denim, I realize we're going to be here for a while. I pull out my phone. Ozzy Snaps me, asks me how practice went. I look for Pia, who is buried in a pair of overalls. "Hey," I call. "I'm going to wait out front." She nods, brings a pair of jeans to her cheek and starts filming a TikTok.

Outside, I lean against the front window. A mannequin in ridiculous fuchsia earmuffs looks over my shoulder. Ozzy sends me a pic of himself wearing a face mask and holding some sort of demolition tool. A claw hammer? Drywall dust blankets his dark hair.

What are you doing? I type, laughing.

Dads got me working.

No kidding. Thought you had rehearsal.

I did. Finished early. Mr. B. was sick.

Where r u?

I'll show you.

I move to the store's front step, waiting for Oz to FaceTime. Seconds later, we connect. He pans the camera in a room with ten-foot ceilings. One of his dads is perched on a stepladder in the corner, safety goggles strapped to his head. The other kneels on a paint-splattered drop cloth littered with swatches. Ozzy looks hot in basketball shorts and a white ribbed tank top.

"Whose house is it?"

Ozzy shrugs. "Some rich people. Where are you?"

"A thrift shop with Pia. She wants to go to some party tonight. You should come."

"If I ever get out of here." He nudges a pile of curled wallpaper with his foot.

I hear his Tall Dad say, "Is that Rowan?"

I wave into the camera. "Hey, Mr. Spencer."

He holds up two paint swatches that look identical.

"Granite gray or drizzling mist?"

"Uh, mist," I offer.

Before Mr. Spencer responds, Ozzy walks into another room. "Get me out of here," he whispers.

I peer into the shop window and spy Pia, wrapped in a crocheted shawl the color of egg yolk. *Ugh. Me too.*

"I love you," I say.

Ozzy holds up the crowbar. "I gotta go whack some shit. Love you too."

I hang up. Across the street is a bubble tea café. I have a sudden hankering for honeydew. Pia will want mango. I weave through traffic stopped at a red light. My legs are heavy from practice. My hip hurts. The bubble tea place is flanked by a laundromat and an alleyway covered in graffiti, some of it good, some of it fit for a dumpster. As I pass the narrow opening, something catches my eye. A dog, face scrunched and fur matted, limps toward me, whimpering. I stoop down to call it, reaching, just as a brick whizzes by my head. The brick clips an electrical box, bounces, and lands beside my foot. *What the hell?*

I stand. The dog staggers. There's blood on its face. Down the alley, a bag of garbage tumbles from behind a bin. Someone mutters. I stare down at the red brick. I should run. Get the heck out of here. Call 911. But I can't. My feet feel petrified. My fists are clenched so hard they might shatter. The dog can't be more than a year old.

I charge down the alley. Past aluminum doors, graffitied tongues, and filthy vents. A guy, my age, maybe older, sprawls on a wrought iron railing smoking a cigarette, trash and chicken bones at his feet.

"You do something to that dog?"

He blows a flimsy smoke ring in my face. "Did I hit it?" He gestures to a pile of broken bricks against the wall. "That was with my left hand."

I don't think. I don't hesitate. In wrestling, you can't. The moment you recognize that you're thinking about what you're going to do, it's too late. You're on your back, shoulders pressed into the ground, pinned. Match over.

I strike him with my own left, a hook punch, right into the black hole of his pockmarked smug face. His head flings back, his posture caves, and then he comes at me. *Circle in.* We stumble over trash bags and buckets of road salt. A party of seagulls squawks as my heel skids across an oil spill. I throw him down, jam my knee into his hard belly. Blood trickles from his mouth. Footsteps reverberate from the walls and close in.

A pair of gold sunglasses lands on the ground beside me as I'm hauled off the dog abuser.

Axel, "The Fist," bends and holds a finger to the boy's face. "Get outta here."

The boy scrambles away, vaults over a dilapidated sawhorse, clears the alley, and disappears.

I look toward the street. There is no sign of the dog. My phone buzzes from my pocket. My hands tremble. Tears swell in my eyes. Axel retrieves his sunglasses from the ground and brushes them off with scarred fingers. I step away, adrenaline caught in the back of my throat.

Axel stares. "You okay?"

I nod and wait for the lecture. Unless it's for self-defense, combat athletes aren't supposed to fight outside the gym.

"Rowan?" Pia calls from the front of the thrift shop, a bundle of jeans under her arm. I forget about bubble tea and run to her.

"What happened to you?"

I exhale a wild breath, my chest still heaving.

"Is that blood?" Pia motions to the splatter dotting my shirt like cities on a map. She ushers me toward the thrift shop so we're not blocking the sidewalk as a weary mother trudges by pushing a stroller. Her kid's asleep, mouth open, head heavy. And tilted. I think of my dad and crumple to the steps.

"Rowan." Pia's voice is stern now, her eyes worried. "What the hell happened?"

"I got in a fight."

Pia surveys both sides of the street as if my opponent might be just grabbing a few swigs of water and some coaching tips before the next round. She spies the champagne Audi parked in front of the bubble tea café. Axel fiddles with his keys. A grass-colored drink balances on the hood of his car.

"I went to get us a drink and this dog comes out of the alley, limping and injured. Some guy threw a brick at it. Almost hit me."

"So you went after him?"

I shrug.

"Rowan, he could've had a knife or something."

"Well, he didn't and now he probably has a black eye."

She shakes her head, causing her cinnamon curls to bounce. "You gotta get out of that shirt." She leads me back into the thrift shop, to a rack of vintage T-shirts. "Pick one."

I rifle through the wire hangers, my hand aching. I can barely make a fist. *Who would pay five bucks for these?* I study a Guns N' Roses concert T-shirt, screen-printed and faded. 1991. No thanks. Vintage Mickey Mouse, vintage tractor, vintage can of sardines? WTF. I settle on a ripped *I Love New York* tee and head to the makeshift changeroom in the corner.

Pia waves her receipt from the cash. I mouth, *Thank you* before drawing the velvet dressing room curtain closed. I yank the soiled shirt over my head and replace it with the new one. My stomach churns as I think about the upcoming tournament there. I was supposed to go last year but it was cancelled because of coronavirus; the whole state shut down. There's not a lot of time left to get on the radar of college recruiters. I stuff my old shirt in my bag.

Outside, the temperature has dropped. I shiver. Pia orders delivery from her phone: butter chicken for me, pad thai for her.

"What happened to the dog?" she asks as we cross the last set of CTrain tracks before her neighborhood.

"Dunno," I say. "Axel kind of pulled me off the guy and when I looked back up the alley, it was gone. Like, who throws a brick at a dog?"

"Did he say anything?"

"Not really. He just kind of stared."

"How's Ozzy gonna react?"

We turn onto Pia's leafy street, the homes mostly urban infills, modern, beige, and towering. The kind of house I lived in before Dad's diagnosis, when ramps and accessibility didn't matter. Pia would be happier living in one of the squat throwbacks dwarfed beside hers. She takes out her key.

"He'll probably say I'm nuts for going after the guy, but he won't be surprised. You know he'll be secretly impressed."

"He will," Pia agrees.

We toss our stuff in the doorway. Pia's parents are at a fundraiser, her brother is at a sleepover. "You can shower first," she says. "You know where everything is."

I jog up the stairs, grab a towel from the linen closet, and strip down in the kids' bathroom. I crank the hot water so it's almost unbearable and cower under the stream. What's left of my makeup melts down my face. I examine my swollen knuckles and make a fist. My phone chimes from the heap of clothes on the bathroom floor. I quickly wash my hair and turn off the tap, wrapping myself in one of the Choudharys' luxurious towels. It's like drying myself with a bearskin.

Dripping, I dig for my phone. Ozzy wears safety goggles that resemble scuba gear, his face still so coated with plaster or drywall dust or whatever kind of home-reno powder turns you into a ghost.

You still at it? I type.

It's kinda fun, he replies. *I got to sledgehammer the kitchen.*

He sends a picture of splintered cupboards and a wall with holes and severed wiring. *I swung so hard. It was awesome.*

I flash back to the alleyway. The whoosh of my fist traveling through the air, the pleasing crack of his cheek, the way his body went slack as a broken hair elastic. The feeling of being on top, heavy and ruinous. Fear converted to power. And then: shame. Street fights are for thugs.

I beat up some guy in the alley by the bubble tea on thirty-second.

Huh? He immediately FaceTimes, blushing when he sees me in a towel. "You did what?"

"I smashed this guy in the alley."

"Why?"

"He threw a brick at a dog, so I hit him."

"And then?"

"This fighter guy — former UFC champ — kind of intervened."

"And?"

"That's it."

"You hit some junkie in an alleyway and you're happy about it?"

"You should have seen the dog."

"Rowan, that neighborhood's sketch. It's full of crackheads and pimps. The hell were you thinking?"

"Never mind then." I put my phone face down on the granite sink and squeeze the excess water from my hair. When I pick it up again, Ozzy's taken off the goggles. His short dad drinks a beer in the background. "I thought you'd at least be … I don't know … proud of me."

"Well, I'm glad you're not hurt, but fuck. I worry about you."

"You should have seen the dog," I repeat.

Pia's fancy doorbell rings.

"I gotta go. Food's here. Call you later."

I gather my clothes and dump them on Pia's floor, then throw on fresh underwear and a pair of her jogging pants before fishing the *I Love New York* shirt from the tangle. Downstairs, Pia has already emptied our food onto plates. My rice looks like a sandcastle. We sit at the island.

"You feel better?" she asks.

"Yeah," I reply, coiling my hair into a topknot. "My hand hurts a bit. And my hamstrings." I jab my fork into the butter chicken. "Ozzy seemed pissed about the fight."

"Of course he's pissed. He can barely watch you wrestle in a gym with referees and rules without worrying that you're gonna get hurt, and you went after some guy in an alleyway who was actively throwing bricks."

I shrug. "Whatever. I can't change it now."

Pia sets down her fork and straightens. "You know what? I'm having a beer." She slides off her stool, marches matter-of-factly to the fridge, and hauls out a can, its muted artwork resembling an event poster.

"That's craft beer. Your parents will notice."

She studies the can, puts it back, digs through the trough on the door, and pulls out another. "This one then. Tsingtao."

"Since when do your parents drink Chinese beer?"

"They don't. That's why we are."

She finds another, pops off both caps, and buries them deep in the garbage. She sets the beer in front of me. I trace the label with my pinkie.

"We have practice tomorrow."

She holds up her cast and takes a long drink. Foam races up the bottleneck as she swallows hard.

"*You* have practice tomorrow," she corrects. "Come on, Rowan. It's one beer."

"God, you sound like a public service announcement."

She laughs. "Sorry. No pressure. It's just … I'm having one. It's hard, not being able to wrestle."

"Now you sound like an alcoholic."

She takes another swig, wipes her mouth, and pinches a piece of fried shrimp from her plate.

One sip. I flatten my rice with my fork. "You know, I kind of enjoyed hitting that guy."

"I'm not surprised. You're a fighter."

My dad's a fighter.

"Is that wrong?"

Pia shakes her head. "If you're into combat sports, you're into combat sports. Just remember, you're not the one who got hit. It's different when you go full-on MMA. Once you're in that cage, pretty much anything goes."

True.

"On the flip side, if you win, you can make a shit ton of money."

I think of Axel's Audi. Not that I'm into cars. Though his sneakers were kinda cool. His gold aviators.

"Way more than you'll ever make from wrestling," Pia adds.

"But the UFC doesn't offer science degrees."

"That they don't." She winds a noodle around her finger. "But think of all the vintage *I Love New York* tees you could buy."

Or a cure for ALS. I pick up the bottle of Tsingtao and tip my head. It burns my throat.

CHAPTER 3

Pia wraps a blue recycling bag over her cast. I help her cinch it with KT tape.

"I'm gonna shower."

I sink into her couch, bloated. "Do we have to go to that party?"

"I'd like to." Her eyes beg. "Please? We never go to parties."

"Parties always disappoint."

"Then tell Ozzy to come."

"He's working with his dads."

"This party will be different."

"Why, because the whole rugby team won't be passed out on Tate's pool deck?"

"God, that was a mess." Pia's eyes shine. "No drunk rugby players. It'll be chill."

And no blow jobs in the boathouse either.

I roll my eyes. "Do I have to dress up?"

"You don't have to do anything you don't want to."

I finish the lukewarm remains of my beer. *That's it. No more.*

"But can you at least let me do your makeup?" she asks.

"Fine."

Pia skips excitedly upstairs. I follow and climb onto her queen-size bed.

"I'll be quick," she says. "You can find something in my closet. I know you probably just want to wear jeans but that dress I picked up from Goodwill last week would be perfect on you. It has twenty-two thousand likes. Just sayin'."

She turns to go down the hall. I bury myself in her red comforter and read a text from my mom.

Did you make it to Pia's? Did you get something to eat?

I text back a thumbs-up emoji.

Call if you need anything.

Another thumbs-up. I drop my phone into the pillow and then pick it up again. *What was that new treatment for ALS called?*

Tofersen? she types.

Yes.

Why?

Is that something Dad can do?

It only works for familial ALS. So far.

Not Dad's kind. I drop the phone back into the pillow and will myself to get up, rolling off Pia's bed to the floor. My head feels buzzed. I search her closet for the dress. I remember it being pink in the post she tagged me in. Or coral. I find it wedged between two suede coats. The texture is awful, like the kind of artificial grass you find on a mini golf course, but she's right about the shape. It'll show off my waist, narrow my shoulders, and highlight my battered collarbone.

"You like it?" Pia stands in the doorway, hair wrapped in a spiraling towel that looks like soft-serve ice cream. She wears the same robe she's worn since grade six, with the smiling cupcakes and happy pizza slices. It barely grazes her knees.

"I might need to borrow a bra."

She combs through her top drawer and tosses me a push-up, Victoria's Secret. I wrestle it on. I'll get stuck if I attempt to pull the dress over my head, so I strip down and step into it. Pia slips on a pair of wide-leg jeans and returns to zip me up.

I stare at myself in the mirror. "What kind of weird-ass time period is this even from? It looks like something my grandma would wear."

"Well, if your grandma grew up in the late sixties or early seventies, then she probably did."

"Where would you wear this? A bake-off? A cult meeting?"

Pia giggles. "Here, throw this over top." She hands me a faded jean jacket. It's better, but still a no.

"Can I just borrow the leggings I really like?"

"Bottom drawer." She unzips me and we dress on opposite sides of her bed. "Wait here," she says, examining my shirt. "If you're going to wear that T-shirt, let me at least make it better." She disappears down the hall and returns with a pair of blue scissors. "Can I?" she asks, the shears hanging perilously close to my stomach.

She snips the bottom from my shirt so the edge curls up above my belly button. I look like an American Eagle ad.

"There. Now for your makeup."

I sit cross-legged on her bed and she goes to work, an entire aisle of Sephora spread across the desk beside her.

"You've got a scratch under your eye."

"I know. Leo."

She dabs around and I close my eyes. I barely feel the beer. Really, how bad is it to have just one? Half of our team drinks. I'm pretty sure both Leo and Reese were hungover last Sunday. Johnny's a nic addict, and Hugo smokes some salvia hippy shit.

"Open," Pia says holding a mirror in front of my face.

I nod, impressed. My lashes look double their normal length and my cheekbones glow without looking like they belong to a figure skater. Pia swipes lip gloss across her mouth and orders an Uber. We hustle downstairs. She opens the fridge and holds up a Tsingtao.

"One more?"

I hesitate.

"We'll split it."

She flips off the cap, hides it with the others in the bowels of her kitchen garbage, and takes a sip. We pass the beer back and forth, pounding it down until the Uber is a block away.

"What about the empties?" I gesture toward the others.

Pia collects the bottles and carries them to the laundry room. "Uber's here." She locks the door and we parade down her walkway to the Prius idling out front. Our driver is Punjabi. Pia says a few words to him, but it's not her best language. He smiles, popping a mint in his mouth. He talks about the girl featured in the handmade portrait dangling from his rearview mirror. I don't know what he says.

Tate's house is in the rich part of the city, where the NHLers and the oil and gas mavericks live. His mom works for some huge PR firm and his dad is a lobbyist. A new-agey sculpture of a buffalo guards the front lawn. We pull up and Pia thanks the driver.

Inside we lose each other. Not intentionally. I run into one of Ozzy's former teammates from when he played AA bantam hockey and not Benvolio. We chat until his girlfriend slinks over and demands his attention. She wears more makeup than a corpse. I catch my reflection in the fridge door. Then again, so do I. I barely recognize myself.

A guy from my biology glass hands me a drink. "What is it?" I shout over the music that pours from a speaker on the counter.

"Vodka and something red."

"I don't drink," I tell him.

"Right," he says, taking a sip for himself. "You're some kind of athlete. Boxing? Karate?" he slurs.

"Wrestling."

"Isn't that just for lesbians?" His drink sloshes from his limp wrist and splashes down my arm.

"Yep, one hundred percent. Lesbians only. You'd be perfect for it." *I shouldn't have come. I shouldn't have drank. I should have gone to the gym.* I blow by him toward the backyard. The pool's closed but the hot tub is an amusement park, two girls for every running back. Gross.

I wander the yard looking for someone I know. There's a cooler on the lower deck. Not the shitty Coleman kind our family's used for the last hundred years, but one of those fancy Yetis. I flip the lid, run my hand through the ice. I pull out a hard lemonade, snap the cap off with the bottle opener, and take a sip. It stings my teeth.

The pool is surrounded by lounge chairs and landscaping. It's the closest thing I've seen to an all-inclusive resort. I choose a striped chair and flop down, legs straddling the metal frame. I think about my dad. How hopeful his face looks when I wrestle. As if my muscles are the only things keeping him alive. I Snap Ozzy. He doesn't answer. Instead, I open Instagram, search #MMA. Frame after frame, it's the same thing: dudes in gis, chokes, strikes, blood, injuries, half-naked chicks with tattoos, Tiger King. WTF?

At the top of my feed is a picture of Pia, her leg in the air and arms around a guy who used to go to our school. The hot tub is in the background. I spin around to see if she's still there. I move too fast and feel sick. I stand, dizzy, and knock over what's left of the lemonade. The bottle rolls, clinking haphazardly, and lands in the pool.

"Shit." I fish out the bottle and stumble toward the upper deck. "Pia," I call, barfing a little in my mouth. She waves. The slats between the deck boards blur. I can't focus. I use the handrail to navigate the stairs. I nearly make it to the landing when I trip, slamming into a guy from my LA class. He stumbles, spilling his beer into the hot tub. Some stereotype, with blond hair and cleavage, squeals.

"Watch it," the guy says.

"You watch it," I mutter.

Pia grabs my arm, her grip strong. She whispers, "Are you drunk?"

"Maybe? A little? No."

The guy stares at my shirt. Then looks at Pia. "The dyke party's across the street."

"Excuse me?" I slur. Before he has a chance to answer I shove him back toward the hot tub and swing, same arm I used in the alley. This time, I miss. My elbow cracks. Someone pulls out their phone. Pia drags me away, back down the stairs and around the side of the house before anything goes viral. "Homophobe!" I shout.

"Give me your phone."

"I don't know where it is," I say, leaning up against the siding.

Pia snatches it away. It was tucked in my bra strap. She calls Ozzy. I can hear his voice as she paces up and down the walk. I can hear his disappointment. My head feels like a kettlebell, what I should have been swinging tonight instead of my fists that I can now barely feel.

"He's coming to get you," she says, folding my phone into my hand. "Can you try not to hit anyone else tonight? Please?" She puts her arm around my waist, half-carrying me to the front yard. I collapse under the bison with its shiny billiard eye. "The fuck are you looking at?" I pass out.

CHAPTER 4

When I wake up, Ozzy and Pia hover over me, the string from Ozzy's favorite gray hoodie grazing my chin. Above, the sky is black and pricked with hundreds of pulsating stars. The grass is damp against my skin. I rise up onto my elbows. Ozzy stares down at me, his expression mixed. All I can do is reach for his hand. He pulls me to my feet.

"What's going on, Row?" he asks.

I shrug because it's too big a question. I steady myself on the bison and swallow, hoping the sour taste in my mouth will disappear.

Ozzy runs his thumb across my cheekbone. "You're cut."

"From practice," I say.

Pia stands on the edge of the sidewalk next to Short Dad's company van. The ladder fixed to the roof shines in the moonlight. The lettering on the side is blue fuzz.

"Where's your car?" I ask.

Ozzy brushes a twig from my shoulder. "Out of gas."

"Short Dad let you take his van?"

"He drove."

"You brought your dad? Oh my God, Oz." My head spins.

"I didn't exactly have much of a choice. Pia said it was urgent."

"Urgent as in come get me, not urgent as in bring your dad on a ride-along. What if he tells my parents?" Adrenaline surges through my limbs, the way it does before a match. I take a deep breath, sucking in a piece of my hair. I frantically spit it out.

"Well, next time you randomly decide to get drunk and pick fights I'll make sure I have a full tank." He turns toward Pia and throws up his hands.

"Come on." Pia waves.

Tears start to well. I'm shivering. I take a step and nearly face-plant, my foot catching on a sprinkler hidden in the grass. Ozzy rips off his hoodie and tosses it to me. His tank top looks fluorescent in the glow of the van's taillights. I wrangle the sweatshirt over my head and sink into its familiarity, the frayed cuffs, faded logo, and wild scent. It reminds me of his hockey days when we first started dating and everything was new and perfect. The late nights we spent on the phone, the sushi dates, the first time he told me he loved me on the Center Street Bridge. Before wrestling and wheelchairs.

Short Dad gets out of the van.

"Shit." I will myself to walk a straight line across the yard. When I reach the sidewalk, Pia, Ozzy, and Short Dad stand in an arc like Hollywood chauffeurs. Do they think I'm so drunk I need three people to help me into the van?

"I'm fine." I reach for the door handle, but miss. Short Dad opens it instead. Pia crawls in first and then muscles me in. Her lipstick looks the same now as it did hours ago. The van smells like turpentine and glue, like my dad's workshop when it was still in use. Ozzy closes the door behind me. I touch the window and mouth *sorry* but have no idea whether he sees.

I buckle my seat belt and exhale. Ozzy sits in front of me. A cardboard air freshener that no longer freshens whips around from the rearview mirror. R&B plays on the radio. Short Dad turns the music down and clears his throat.

"Let me know if you're going to get sick," he says.

"I'm fine," I repeat. "I only had two drinks."

"And a half," Pia corrects.

"You should have had no drinks," Ozzy mumbles.

What, are you my dad now? "I'm just tired."

Short Dad says, "You can sleep it off for a bit. Then I'll take you home."

I lean forward in my seat. "Mr. Howard …"

"Gareth," he interrupts.

"Gareth. Please don't tell my dad."

Short Dad sighs. There's a spot of green paint on his driving hand. He wears one of Ozzy's old winter coats. Beside me, Pia twirls a hardened paintbrush.

"Let's just focus on getting you sober."

"It will kill him," I say.

The van goes silent, jerking over a speed bump as we pass a Shell and pull onto a thoroughfare. Pia reaches for my hand. I ignore her. When we get to her house, she gives me a sympathetic smile. "Text me in the morning," she says.

I want Ozzy to move to the back, take Pia's place. But he remains distant, head in his hand, occasionally fiddling with the vents. I brace for the bump at the end of his driveway. Sure enough, it makes me puke in my mouth. I swallow it down. As if he knew it was going to happen, Ozzy hands me a bottle of water without even turning around. I unscrew the cap and drink half. When I unbuckle, I notice Tall Dad in the window. "My God," I whisper. "Who next?"

Ozzy opens my door. I feel a bit better now and navigate the winding front steps of their house with ease. Inside, Tall Dad has set the table. It's eleven o'clock. Fresh flowers droop in a vase.

"Are you hungry, Rowan?" Tall Dad asks. He's bent over the stove, moving a skillet back and forth over a tiny blue flame. "Omelets are a great hangover cure."

Food suddenly seems appealing. "That would be great." I muster a smile. Ozzy kicks off his slides behind me and pilfers a handful of cheese from a bowl on the counter.

"I had that all portioned out," Tall Dad sighs. "Hand me the green onions."

Ozzy rummages through the fridge and places a bundle of onions on the counter.

"Do you know where my phone is?" I ask.

Ozzy pulls it from his pocket and goes to the living room where Short Dad has made a bed on the couch. I sit on the end. Ozzy lifts the remote from the coffee table and punches buttons. Short Dad clears empty glasses from an end table and disappears into the kitchen.

"Are you mad at me?" I ask. "You won't even look at me."

He stops on a cop show and tosses the remote. "No," he says, plunking down beside me. "I'm not mad at you. It's just been a long day. I kept messing up my lines at rehearsal, had to spend five hours demoing that house with my dads, and then Pia calls to say you're drunk and throwing punches."

Ozzy reaches over and massages the permanent knot beside my left shoulder blade. He could find it blindfolded. I close my eyes. Instant relief.

"You okay?" he asks.

"I don't know. Just … I have this big tournament coming up

in New York, which my parents probably can't even afford. Same one I was supposed to wrestle last year during Covid. There's going to be a ton of recruiters there. I have to do well."

"That's awesome, Row. You will." He drapes his arm around me and pulls me tight to him, like a safety harness on a rollercoaster.

"I'm not ready. Pia's out because of her arm, I have no good training partners, and my dad's getting worse."

Ozzy places his hand over mine as a police chase unfolds on screen.

"No new treatments?"

"Nothing. There're more treatments for Ebola than for ALS."

"That sucks," he says.

I wipe a tear from my cheek. He knows not to say everything will be okay. He knows my dad will die. In months. A year if he's lucky.

"Just focus on training," he offers. "You want to get a scholarship to some big American school, you gotta go after it. You gotta work hard every day. You can't be going around getting trashed and starting fights at parties. You're better than that, Row. You're different."

"I don't want to be different."

He kisses the top of my head. "It's too late for that now."

I lay my arm across his chest and settle into the shape of his body. On the TV, a helicopter joins the police chase. The guy running for his life wears boxer shorts and dress shoes. We both smile at the absurdity of the scene and for a moment I feel at peace. That everything's going to be fine.

My phone chimes and I jump. It's my mom.

You good?

I type back, *Yep. At Ozzy's. One of his dads will drive me home.*

You have practice at ten, don't forget.

Yes, Mom. I've had practice at ten every Sunday for the past two years. I'm not going to forget. I text *I know* and then a heart so she'll leave me alone.

Tall Dad raps on the door somewhere behind us. "Hangover cure is served. Greek quinoa omelets with feta and tzatziki. Kidding," he waves. "That one's mine. The rest of you get the ham and cheese."

I sit at my regular spot in front of Ozzy's growth chart, which is penciled into the wall. He was adopted when he was two. The first little mark etched into the paint always makes me smile. Tall Dad holds the skillet in one hand, a spatula in the other. He pauses. "You're not cutting weight, are you?"

"Nope. Weighed in at one thirty-seven this morning." Though I'm probably pushing one forty by now.

"I'm not cutting either," Short Dad says patting his beer belly.

"Perhaps you should be." Tall Dad winks, serves me an omelet, and returns the pan to the stove. One of them has left an Advil by my fork. I down it and pluck the garnish from my plate.

Ozzy rubs my leg under the table but pauses to check his phone. He texts madly on his lap.

"No phones at the table, Oz," Short Dad says, dabbing his chin with a cloth napkin.

I try to see who he's texting. "Who's that?"

"Juliet," he replies, sliding his phone under his leg.

"Right," I nod. Juliet. Of course she's named Juliet.

"We were going to go over some lines. That's what I was doing when Pia called."

"Right," I say again, my appetite waning. I just want to go home, crawl into my bed, and dissolve beneath my weighted blanket.

CHAPTER 5

At midnight, Short Dad drops me off at my house. He waits until I've cleared the ramp he and Tall Dad helped build before he pulls away. In the front room, my brother, Ike, is perched on the end of the couch, shoulders erect, Xbox controller glued to his hands.

"What are you playing?" I ask. "Mom still up?"

"Mom and Dad are both in bed. *Call of Duty.*" He jerks the controller with a sharp flick of his wrist. "Asshole," he mutters. "Should have covered me."

Larry, our lumpy blond cat, jumps from the sideboard and meows. He slinks over. I rub his head.

"Heard you tried to hit Mitchell Cummings," Ike says without taking his eyes off his game.

"Seriously? Who said that?"

"Who *hasn't* said that?"

Fuck. I sit down next to my brother.

"Come on, I totally had that guy!" He grits his teeth and toggles the controller. "You were drunk too?"

I ask, "What do you think of MMA?"

"It's all right. Title fights are fun to watch. It's not as fun when they go to the ground."

"As a career."

"Depends. What are you comparing it with? I'm sure it's not bad for the ones who make it to the UFC. Win a few big fights, retire, open a distillery, launch a clothing line. For the ones that don't, my guess is it's pretty shitty. Flipping tires in a warehouse basement between shifts at Arby's and getting on some garbage fight card sponsored by the local plumbing store." Ike pauses and really looks at me for the first time since I walked in the door. "Why?"

I pour myself some water. Ike turns off his game and joins me, rifling through the pantry. He finishes a bag of chips standing and opens another.

"Those are Dad's," I say, noting the flavor, sour cream and onion.

Ike stops, a potato chip pinched between his fingers. "He hasn't been able to eat chips for over a year. Did you see the last time he tried?"

I reach in and grab a handful. My brother is a year younger than me and half a foot taller. He has Dad's hair, wiry and brown. Under the track lighting, it looks red.

"What did you drink?"

"Beer and vodka."

"Row, you *never* mix. That's like the first rule of underage drinking. Don't mix drinks."

"And the second?"

"Don't get caught."

"Well so far, I'm one-for-two. Let's keep it that way."

Ike opens a Gatorade. "Practice is going to be so shitty for you tomorrow." He laughs.

"You're such a douche."

"Just kidding." He peels the label off the plastic bottle. "Actually, no. Practice is going to suck. Make sure you drink lots of water."

"You're speaking from experience?"

Larry chases a cat toy, batting it between our legs. At one point it might have been a mouse. Now it's a felted ball with a crimped tail.

"I'm pretty sure that's why we lost our first game this morning." I notice he's still wearing his team shorts.

"You were hungover?"

"We all were."

"Don't drink, Ike."

He hands me the Gatorade. "*You* don't drink. You're the athlete. Don't mess things up by being average."

"What if I want to be average?"

"You don't and you're not." He jams his hand into the chip bag, vaults over the couch, and returns to his game. Larry sits on a chair and contemplates the plant stand under the window. I scoop him into my arms to use as a decoy in case one of my parents wakes up. Mom cashed in some investments to widen the hallway, making our house feel like a hospital. I tiptoe to my room, turn the knob with measured precision so it doesn't make a sound, and slip inside.

I don't bother to brush my teeth. I ditch my dirty clothes in the laundry bin and pull on one of Ozzy's old T-shirts, worn to perfection. Larry massages the pillow beside me, circles, and then chooses the foot of my bed to settle on. I plug in my phone and crawl under the blankets.

Juvenile glow-in-the-dark stars gleam from the ceiling. No one had the patience to pick them off when we moved in. It was months before I realized the stars had been painstakingly mapped to mimic actual constellations: the Big Dipper, Orion's Belt, Hercules, Cassiopeia. My dad loves the stars. He always wanted one of those thousand-dollar telescopes to drag camping so we could "view the sky as it was intended to be seen." Not from the city, not from my bed.

I roll over, my back to the moon and Canis Major, the dog constellation. I think of the pup in the alleyway, wishing upon a star that it's okay. That everything is going to be okay.

* * *

The smoke detector goes off at eight thirty. I stumble out of bed to the kitchen where my mom waves a piece of burnt toast in the air. The sliding patio door is open, causing the curtain to billow. My head pounds. Dad is wedged against the table with a bowl of oatmeal.

Good morning, he says through his device.

"Morning." I grab a dish towel from the counter and flap it under the smoke detector. Mom mutters obscenities under her breath. Ike sleeps through it all.

"You want some oatmeal?" Mom dishes herself a bowl.

"Not hungry."

"You can't go to practice on an empty stomach."

I'm already triggered. I try to keep my voice calm. "Practice isn't for over an hour. I have lots of time to eat before then." Mom takes her bowl to the table and sits across from my dad. She's missing a slipper. I root through the cupboard above the sink, pop an Advil, and wash it down with tap water.

Do you have a headache? my dad's typed.

Oh my God. Why do parents ask so many questions?

"Yes, I have a headache. Didn't sleep well." I wait for a lecture on athletes and the importance of sleep, but none transpires. My parents are distracted by the nature show my dad's watching, in which a pair of lemurs tussle in an empty lot, drawing crowds and upending clouds of dust. I pour myself a coffee and go back to my room.

It's too early to text anyone, so I search up the latest ALS news. At any given time, some lab in some American city, San Diego, La Jolla, Boston, Baltimore, is starting a new clinical trial, testing another new drug on another desperate patient. Because ALS doesn't affect that many people, not like cancer or diabetes, the drugs are ridiculously expensive. I screenshot the abstract from a European medical journal to read later.

Leo texts, *Need a ride to practice?*

I type back, *Yes.*

Be there at 9:30.

I grab the towel from the back of my door and go to my parents' bathroom. The walk-in accessible shower with the seat works as well for hungover wrestlers as it does for disabled dads. I scrub at my eye makeup and wash my hair with my mom's peachy drugstore shampoo.

Remembering that I left my wrestling boots at Pia's, I dig through the front hall closet for my spares. My hair drips.

"Are you sure you don't want some oatmeal?" my mom hollers.

Holy shit. "No thanks," I reply. "I'm going to make some toast."

I quickly dress, brush my wet hair into a painfully high pony-tail, and throw a piece of bread into the toaster. My mom changes out of her single slipper, plunks onto a chair, and starts putting on sneakers.

"Leo's giving me a ride," I say.

She kicks off her shoes and relaxes back into the chair while I butter my toast and gather my belongings. "Do you need a ride home?"

I shrug. "I'll text if I do."

Have a good one, Dad says. His head is tilted again. I convince myself it's because the nature show has switched to bats that are hanging upside down like socks on a clothesline, and he's trying to get a better view of them.

"Thanks, I will." I go to leave and then turn back. I hip-check Dad's chair. He pretends to roll over my foot. We both laugh.

Get out of here, he types. *Go rip someone to shreds.*

"Scott!" Mom says. "Don't encourage her."

Outside, Leo's massive diesel truck rumbles. It's covered in crop dust. He tosses his bag into the rear when I climb into the front seat. He's drinking a fast-food smoothie. His eyes are bloodshot.

"You look like shit," I say.

"So do you."

We laugh. I sit on my hands to stave off the morning chill. "What happened to your cheek?" There's a bruise the size of an Oreo floating below his right eye.

"Your elbow," he says, opening and closing his jaw as if the bruise might impact his bite.

"Sorry."

He offers me a sip of his smoothie. I like Leo. He works hard and he's kind. In the chaos of the wrestling room, of eleventh grade, and of the totally fucked up twenty-first century, these virtues, simple as they sound, are wildly underrated.

"Thanks." I take a long haul from the straw.

The wrestling club occupies a squat building at the end of the strip mall. Someone has changed the alphabet sign belonging to the garage at the south end so that it reads *fuck oil*.

"Why's the lot so full?" Leo parks a good ten spots from the door beside a roofing van. We get out in front of the 7-Eleven and watch a pair of bearded dudes unload a heavy bag through the gym's front doors. "Is Coach getting us to take up boxing? Da fuck?"

"You ever hear of Axel 'The Fist' Barrett?"

"Hell, yeah. Legend. Trained with GSP."

"Coach rented him some space."

"Since when?"

"Since yesterday after practice."

"And he's moving in already?"

"Looks like it."

We pass the back of the truck where the equipment is being un-loaded. There are a couple more bags, a laundry basket of gloves and shin guards — Muay Thai gear — and some free weights. Leo opens the door and motions for me to go first. Coach hovers behind the front desk, shoving back an Egg McMuffin, some-thing his wife would chastise him for if she were here. When we go on tournaments, he indulges in breakfast sandwiches. A roofing contractor hands him an invoice. In the back of the gym, Axel stands on a stepladder, a yellow drill in his hand, installing a ceiling mount. The bearded men deliver the heavy bag there.

I hit the locker room. It's half the size of the boys', but Coach let me paint it. Pia picked the color, *liquid blue*, like how our legs feel after a session. I dump my bag on the floor and tighten my hair elastic. I take a sip from my water bottle. My stomach churns. Ike was right. Practice is going to suck.

I join my teammates for warm-up, jogging around the mat's perimeter, my feet uncomfortable in my backup boots. Coach wipes a spot of egg from his shirt and cues up some music. He'll alternate between terrible eighties rock and a clusterfuck of hits from the nineties. I'm pretty sure we're the only wrestling club in the world that practices front headlock position to the Spice Girls. I shuffle side to side, circling my arms and imagine a room full of Kazakhstanis drilling to Baby Spice.

"Rowena," Coach yells.

I hate that nickname.

"Something funny about Sunday mornings?"

"Nope," I reply, changing directions with the masses. "Just excited to practice."

"Well, good" — he smiles, adjusting the volume on his Bluetooth — "because we got a lot of work to do today. I want to see a better gut wrench in New York."

Gut wrenches. Because there's no better move when you're hungover than getting the living shit squeezed out of your stomach. He plays AC/DC. We're two minutes in, and I want to kill myself.

Coach organizes us into groups of four and uses Leo to demo a move. The faint scent of vodka leaches from my pores. I try to distance myself in the corner. The sound of the drill grates my skull.

"Forty push-ups, slow, on my count."

Huh? I wasn't paying attention. Neither was someone else on account of Coach's command. I drop to the mat, spread my arms, feet together in plank.

"One."

I lower my chest to the floor, forgetting to breathe.

"Two."

Repeat.

"Three. Four. Five. Luke, you call that a push-up? My grandma can go lower than you. Drop your chest to the floor. I see one more lazy push-up and we start over."

A stream of drool dangles from the corner of my mouth. I suck it back and lift my chin. My shoulders shake. Axel's finished hanging the first heavy bag. He drags the ladder across the concrete and lines it up under another beam.

"Fifteen."

Keep going, I tell myself. I think of my dad. On the mantle, there's a picture of me balancing on his back while he does a push-up. He wears a hideous tracksuit while I'm in a princess dress, smiling hysterically. He will never do another push-up. I remember this when the workouts get tough.

"Thirty-four."

When I don't feel like I can do another rep.

"Thirty-nine."

When I want to quit.

"Forty. Everybody up."

I exhale, pull myself to my feet, and shake out my arms. Axel gives me a nod. Not in a creepy pervert way, but in an I-wish-you-were-my-athlete way. I get this look all the time at training camps and tournaments. I smile and turn my focus back to my coach.

We spend an hour on gut wrenches and leg defense. The music goes from bad to worse. Ricky Martin, Right Said Fred, the frigging Pet Shop Boys. During our last water break before live wrestling, I hole up in the girl's bathroom, drinking and spitting alternately. I feel like I need to puke, but nothing comes up.

I'm the last one to return to the mat. I try to file into the group discreetly. Coach calls me out.

"Rowan, what were you doing in there? Getting your nails done? Puttin' curlers in your hair?"

I think about saying I had to change a tampon. It shuts him up quickly, but I used that excuse last week. If he's paying attention, he'll know I'm full of shit.

"Forty more push-ups. The rest of you, find a partner and get started."

I drop back to the floor, flick a hairball out of the way, and grind through another set. When I get back up, my whole body is Jell-O. Axel stands mat-side, a link of chain draped on his arm to hang another bag. "You're very strong," he says.

I've heard this before. A typical response might be a simple "thank you," an appreciative smile, a playful flex, a fist bump. Instead, I burst into tears. I wipe my face in my shirt, now a mix of sweat and snot and tears. Coach catches me crying. He furrows his brow in confusion, but his eyes are sympathetic. He's still trying to figure out how to coach a girl.

He clears his throat. "You okay?"

I nod and take a deep breath.

"Do you need a minute?" He cautiously places a hand on my shoulder.

I shake my head.

"Okay, then. Get in there. Proper wrestling stance."

I pair up with a fifty-kilo boy a fraction of my size. We hand fight. I do an arm drag and take his back. We drill, going hard until the timer goes off, signifying a partner change.

"Leo, go with Row."

Leo narrowly avoids getting in the way of a teammate's rogue shoulder throw. We shake hands and lock foreheads. He tries to take a two-on-one, but I circle away. Coach watches. I sense it. Leo takes my back. I break his grip and we tie up again, face-to-face. After a grueling ten minutes, neither of us scores. My heart beats out of my chest. Only a sprig of hair remains in my ponytail.

I rotate my way through two more partners before the final chime. Coach instructs us to "cool down, ten easy laps, stretches on your own." I finish the laps, collapse into a straddle at the back of the mat, and empty my water bottle.

The heavy bags hang from the rafters like carcasses in a butcher shop. Axel and the rest of his team gather by the back door in a tangle of ropes. I'll get out before I have to face him. *Who gets complimented by someone with a trademark name and bursts into tears? God.*

Leo shakes Coach's hand and calls to me, one foot already in the boy's locker room. "Row, you need a ride home?"

"I'm good. Think I'll take transit." The train station is twenty minutes away, but the walk takes me by the river, a place for just me, not connected to my father or Ozzy or anyone else. No memories.

I refill my water at the fountain. Coach sorts singlets behind the front desk.

"Is mine there?" I try to read the screen-printed names on the backs but he's too fast.

"These are the boys," he says. "Girls are over there."

He points to a sad pile on the counter. Two singlets.

"You can take yours if you want."

"Pia's too?"

He nods and circles something on a crinkled packing slip. I gather our plastic-wrapped gear and head back into the main gym. In the corner, Axel playfully strikes one of the heavy bags. Jab, cross, hook. The chain rattles from the swivel.

"You want to try?" he calls. "It needs to be worked in."

I look back at Coach, seeking his approval, but he's bent over a cardboard box. He pulls out a hoodie the width of a small car. Definitely Jared's, our heavyweight. Or Coach's.

I set my stuff on the floor, and kick it under one of the benches so it's out of the way. Axel holds the bag. At his feet is an array of gloves, fanned out like shoes in a closet. He points to a hill of hand wraps. I grab a camo pair.

"You know how to put them on?"

"Sort of." I stick my thumb through the loop. Axel gets me started. When I've finished wrapping my left hand, he inspects my work.

"Good," he says touching my fingertips. "Now the right." He selects a pair of gloves. They feel heavy on my hands, tugging at my shoulders.

"Give me a simple one-two. Nice and light."

I line up in front of the bag, mimic a boxing stance, and unleash. The bag wavers pleasingly. Axel steps back, smiling.

"I said *light*." He laughs.

My shoulders relax and I feel an intoxicating rush zip through my limbs, as if all the chaos from the last twenty-four hours has been flushed from my body. An oil change. *Dog, beer, vodka, Juliet, head tilt.*

"How about a hook?"

"I don't know how."

"Oh, I assure you, you know how to throw a hook punch. Go back to the alley. But keep it tight." He demonstrates.

I adjust my stance and throw a hook. Then another. I think

of the dog, the blood clumped on its face, its awful limp. The hissing sound of the flying brick. Five more hooks. My lungs and lats feel like they're smoldering, ready to catch, explode from my body. By my eighth strike, Axel intercepts, grabbing my wrist.

"Never compromise form."

"Hey!" Coach calls.

We both turn. I stumble and have to brace myself against the bag.

"What are you doing with my wrestler?" Coach has his hands on his hips. A cliché. His tone is joking, but his red face suggests otherwise.

"Your wrestler is a natural-born striker," Axel says.

"Yeah, well the NCAA ain't giving out scholarships for mixed martial arts anytime soon." Coach looks at me, eyes serious. "Go home, Row. You need to rest. Keep hitting like that you're gonna get injured. Focus."

"She's strong," Axel says.

"I know she's strong. And as her coach, I also know she's got a lot going on right now and can't afford any more distractions."

I undo the Velcro straps of my gloves, pull them off, and begin to unravel the wraps. My hands are sweaty.

"All good," Axel says, hands up disarmingly. "We were just testing out the bag." He takes the gloves and wraps and sets them on a chair. "And based on what I just saw, I'd say that it's working just fine. Thanks for your help, Rowan."

I duck away while Coach and Axel continue their conversation. They've moved on from talking about me to the sprinkler system, but I can feel the underlying tension. After my parents used to get in a fight, all of their actions would become sharper.

They'd load the dishwasher louder, set their plates down harder, and speak in clipped, one-word sentences. So annoying.

I take a quick shower, keeping my hair out of the water, and throw on a change of clothes. The singlets take up a lot of room in my backpack and I have to kneel on my bag to zip it up.

I step outside and shield my screen from the sun. I scroll through my phone. Ten messages from Pia. *Are you okay? How r u feeling? How was practice? Did you get my singlet?* The fresh air feels good on my skin. I text her back: *Fine. Tired. Hard. Yes.* Nothing from Ozzy. It's almost one. He should be up by now.

Hey, I Snap sending him a pic. No response. *Did he have a rehearsal today?* I assume he does. The play's at the end of May. That's in a month. Shit. I scroll through my calendar. It's the same weekend as the New York tournament. I've never missed one of his performances. *Why won't he Snap me back?* I think about texting Tall Dad, but he'll think I'm a stalker and he'll be right.

Pia sends me a pic of a new sleeve she's made for her cast. It looks like a metallic Wonder Woman cuff, a cosplay prop. *Nice*, I reply, before checking the latest ALS news. There's an article on misfolded proteins and gene mutation with more acronyms than an online chat. A second story announces that a drug developed by Swedish researchers has moved to phase two testing — the phase where most promising new ALS drugs go to die. I need to clear my mind and shove my phone in my pocket.

I round the corner of the strip mall and take the trampled grass path downhill through the abandoned baseball diamond where my brother and I both played T-ball. Dad coached both of our teams. He wasn't very good, not the way he was at coaching soccer or basketball, but he tried hard.

I climb through the broken chain-link fence onto Seventh Avenue, cutting through a lineup outside a dim sum. Traffic seems heavy for a Sunday. Across the street, the river is high, the banks spotted with runners and cyclists and gangs of geese, their necks like field hockey sticks.

I cross at the lights, my backpack tugging at my shoulders. The river smells crisp as a cold shower. I edge down the bank toward a rocky recession where people feed the ducks despite the sign that says DO NOT FEED THE WILDLIFE. On cue, a mallard paddles over, eyes pleading for a piece of stale bread.

"I got nothing." I show my empty hands. The duck eventually swims away convinced, but three more replace it.

Trees and trails line the opposite bank. A freight train, red and majestic, lumbers into view. The rail cars strung behind it are covered in wheat logos and graffiti. I scramble back up to the main pathway and replay the leg defense techniques covered in practice. *Hip pressure and angle, fall to the lead leg, push the head away.* But my mind wanders to the heavy bag. Just walking I can still feel the power in my fist.

A man at the LRT station struggles to carry one of those folding shopping carts old people use up the stairs to the platform. The elevator is out of order.

"Need a hand?"

I don't know if he speaks English because he meets my query with a look of confusion. Instead, I act it out, gesturing to the cart, pointing to the platform as he thumps up another step. This time he understands and nods, gratefully. I hoist the cart in the air, so it clears the height of the step. It's heavy, so I move quickly. The old man follows behind, pausing at each step, and using the railing as a guide.

When I get to the top, two girls from my school are waiting on the platform. Not exactly *mean* girls, but not nice ones, either. Both wear trending seventies bangs, jeans, and crocheted tops. One of them drinks something frothy from Starbucks. They look at me; they look at the shopping cart. My eyes follow their gaze. For the first time, I study the contents inside it. Tied off bags from the Dollar Store, cat litter, oh my God — incontinence pads.

I stare up at the LED next train indicator screen. It flashes, 1 MINUTE. My train. The old man is only two-thirds of the way up the stairs. The girls laugh. And I can't blame them. I look like a tool. The old man has stopped to blow his nose. *Fuck*. If they could at least see that I'm doing a charitable deed they might stop. Or move on, laugh, and get over it, but a warm wind blows and the green-and-white north line train pulls up to the platform. *Come on*, I urge, smiling down at the man. *Almost there.*

The doors open. A handful of people get off and scatter like spilled marbles. The girls get on. The blond one was in my math class last semester. I think she owns a horse. Or four. They laugh larger now, stumbling over each other to sit in a pair of front-facing seats. Below, the old man has stopped again to catch his breath. *For fuck's sake.* A person arriving from the other staircase runs and makes it inside a car just before the doors close.

I watch with my cart as the train slowly mobilizes and glides forward. The next train won't come for another twenty minutes. The cars tick by, swallowing the big-mouthed, shiny-haired girls. I hear the man cresting the top step behind me, breathing heavily and mumbling incoherently. *Finally*. But just as I'm about to turn around, a familiar face stares out at me from the last car. The guy from the alleyway, sporting the same dingy clothes he had on yesterday but paired with a film-worthy black eye.

CHAPTER 6

The old man is traveling in the opposite direction. When his train arrives, I help him on, and call my mom.

Can you come pick me up?

Where are you?

7th Ave station.

Yep. I'll be there in fifteen minutes. Just helping your dad to the bathroom.

I think of the man with the incontinence pads. Maybe a bit embarrassing for him, but at least he was probably in his eighties. My dad is forty-four. It's weird to think he needs help to go to the bathroom. How does a man go from having a personal trainer to a speech therapist in less than a year?

I take the stairs to the parking lot and wait for my mom. She's later than fifteen minutes. When she finally arrives, she jumps the curb in the van. Her hair is unwashed. There are flowers on the front seat.

"What are these?" I ask.

"They were delivered just as I was leaving. They're for you."

Hot pink roses, orange gerbera daisies, pale green carnations, and bear grass. This has Tall Dad all over it. I read the card. "*True love stories never have endings,*" *Oz*. I blush. Ozzy's always been a romantic, but theater's turning him into a cliché. Not that I'm complaining. Better daisies than a dick pic.

"They're beautiful," Mom says.

I rest the flowers on my lap. The van feels huge without Dad in the back, like we should be hauling cargo.

"You look tired," I say.

Mom smiles weakly. I can tell now she's been crying. She places a hand on my knee. "Today was not a good day."

This is the ongoing theme in our house as we navigate Dad's disease. Days fall into two distinct categories: good or bad. It's overly simplistic, but it's accurate. Sometimes I feel like I'm losing both my parents. They were high school sweethearts. I know they've had some tough times over the years, the "d" word being tossed around the summer between grades five and six and all of grade eight, but they always seem to work it out. They always come back to each other.

I check my phone to see if Ozzy's called. There's a text saying he has rehearsal until two, and that he's going out with a few of the guys from the play afterwards. I didn't think there were any more boys than him and the one who plays Romeo. I hope he remembers his lines.

When we pull up to the house, my brother passes by the front window with the broom in his hand. I'm surprised he even knows how to use it. My mom seems to think the same thing.

"Is he sweeping?" she asks, dumfounded. "Since when does your brother sweep?"

Next door, our neighbor, Beryl, pokes around a pot of herbs on her front porch. Our surrogate grandmother, Ike's best friend. He helps her do the things Dad used to do, but no longer can. She waves.

Mom grabs her purse and gets out of the van. She forgets to lock the doors, so I do it instead. I notice her shirt is inside out. I race up the ramp to catch up as she pushes through the front door. My brother is stooped on the floor in an awkward squat, the broom in one hand, dustpan in the other. He is surrounded by a minefield of glass and doing a terrible job cleaning it up. My dad sits in the midst of it, his hand dangling over the armrest of his wheelchair.

"Let me do it," I say, nudging my brother aside.

"It was my fault," Ike says. "I startled him when I was coming out of the kitchen."

Mom bends to pick up the larger shards and takes them to the garbage. She doesn't bother to stuff them in a box or wrap them in paper. I can't even look at my dad. The shame in his eyes knocks me out, but I'm sure ignoring him hurts more. I pat him on the knee and dump the contents of the dustpan into the garbage. When a path is cleared, Dad maneuvers his chair toward the window and parks, his back to us. Mom, Ike, and I stand shoulder to shoulder, cleaning implements in hand, a motley crew of housekeepers.

The air is heavy like there's a cloud in our living room, bursting at the seams. My counselor only recently told me that the heaviness I described week after week in her little office by the chemistry lab was grief. *But isn't grief for after?* I'd asked and she'd replied that grief didn't have a before or after. That grief didn't follow a clock or a timeline or a twelve-step program. Grief, she'd said, came and went as it pleased.

My mom pours a glass of wine. I kiss her on the cheek and head down the hall toward my room. Ike leans against the wall, hands over his head, the way he looks when he gets thrown out of a basketball game. I can't think of anything comforting to say.

I layer my pillows against my headboard, grab my laptop from my desk, and sit cross-legged on my bed. I google Axel Barrett. His wiki page, Twitter feed, and Instagram pop up. Dozens of sports sites. I click on a UFC stats page and view his record: thirty-five wins, ten losses, and one no-contest. I scroll through his fight history: TKO, unanimous decision, submission by rear naked choke, split decision, submission by guillotine, TKO, TKO, TKO. *Geez, no wonder he goes by "The Fist."* His last fight was four years ago in Sacramento.

I click on a link to his first professional fight. He looks a bit like Leo with cornrows, taller on camera than at the gym. His opponent is a Russian striker with dark circles under his eyes, as though he hasn't slept since the end of the Cold War. Axel tags the guy with a spinning back fist, shot to the body, and a deafening right hook just behind the ear. Some of the shots make me wince.

I watch the highlights from six more fights. So many level changes and takedowns. A wrestler. I find his profile. Oklahoma State, four-time national champion in Greco-Roman, three-time all-American, and two-time NCAA Division I runner-up.

My phone buzzes beside me, inching its way off the stuffed polar bear Ozzy gave me for our one-year anniversary. The bear's lips are a felted pink heart. Pia asks what I'm doing. I send her a pic of my laptop screen.

You're watching fights??
Axel.
How come you're not out with Oz?
He had rehearsal.

There is a delay in our conversation. I take a sip of water from the cup on my bedside table. Ike must have put it there after I went to bed drunk last night. A sick dad has made better caregivers of all of us.

Pia sends a screenshot from someone's Instagram. Theater kids, crowded in one of their basements. The play's Romeo stuffs popcorn in some girl's face, jokingly, theatrically. I roll my eyes. There are two other girls and one of Ozzy's friends leaning into a coffee table, and just behind them Ozzy. And Juliet. Ozzy straddles a backward-facing chair. Juliet stands behind him but crouched so that her pointy chin is nestled on the top of his head. Her arm is draped around his neck, bunching up the black Adidas hoodie I got him for Christmas. #romeoandjuliet #theafterrehearsal *Hashtag, WTF?*

Pia doesn't follow up with a comment.

He did say he was going out after, I type.

With her?

Well, she's in the play. *Whatever. She's a loser.* I stare at the image. *Who wears a faux fur coat in April?* I pause, remembering Pia probably would.

Ugh, my mom's calling me, Pia types. She adds a heart afterward. A friendship heart? A pity one? I toss my phone. The polar bear tumbles off the bed. I don't pick it up. *Why would he let her be all over him like that?*

I watch all of Axel's fights, more than a decade's worth. His last win is by flying knee. I have the wrestling, the striking seems easy enough to learn, but I don't have any jiu jitsu. No arm bars, no kimuras, no americanas, no chokes. I search "best MMA submissions" and watch those videos too. I hang off my bed and swipe the polar bear from the floor and follow the instructions on rear-naked chokes. I slide my arm across the bear's plush neck and under its chin before I realize it doesn't have a chin, just one long stupid continuous throat. I throw it across my room.

Before I know it, it's ten o'clock. I haven't eaten dinner. I haven't touched my physics homework, and *The Invisible Man* lies unread on my desk. *Where even is my family?*

Ike's door is closed. I peek inside my parents' bedroom and note the unmistakable great lump of my father sawing it off in the middle of the bed. His breathing is nightmarish. I close the door and pad down the hall to the living room. Mom is asleep on the couch, mouth open, shirt rumpled, one foot on the floor, the other stretched across the backrest like a middle-aged frat boy.

"Mom." I gently prod her shoulder. "Go to bed."

Her eyes pop open with the sort of panicked expression people have when they wake up on an airplane.

"Go to bed," I repeat stroking her arm.

She sits up and massages her forehead. "What time is it?"

"Just after ten."

"Did you get your homework done?"

No amount of fatigue can stop my mother from micromanaging.

"I'm doing it now."

She yawns, eases herself up, and turns to look in the dining room. "You didn't eat your dinner."

A solo plate of spaghetti sits on the table. No utensils. Not even a paper napkin. It looks like a prison meal.

"No one called me," I reply.

"I'll heat it up for you."

"You go to bed," I say, clearing her empty wine glass from the coffee table. "I got it." I kind of want to tell her about Ozzy and Juliet. Ask her what she thinks. He seemed so happy in the picture.

"Don't stay up too late."

"I won't."

I watch her go.

I microwave my dinner and eat alone at the table. The noodles are overcooked. I'm about to scrape what I can't eat into the compost when my brother appears in the kitchen doorway.

"I'll eat it," he says.

"It's just a few mushrooms."

He gestures for me to hand it over. I pass him the plate and he plucks the mushrooms off with his fingers. His hair stands on end. The gold chain he's worn since third grade hangs lopsided, the cross caught up in a tangle of his chest hair. I have an idea.

"Help me move the coffee table."

"What for?"

"I need you to do something for me."

"Do I get anything for it?"

"Just my sisterly love and affection, dumbass. Grab that side."

We pull the coffee table into the hallway. I push back the couch. Ike picks up a piece of missed glass from earlier. I shove the rug into the open space. It's covered in crumbs that were once hidden by the table. I brush the carpet with my hand and toss the pile of fuzz and dirt into the fireplace.

"Okay, sit down." I point to the middle of the carpet.

Ike reluctantly complies. I sit behind him, wrapping my feet around his body so my heels dig into his torso.

"What are you doing?" he asks, a hint of scandal in his tone.

"A rear-naked choke."

"What for?"

"Because I want to learn how to do one."

He starts to argue, but before anything lucid comes out, I slip my forearm under his chin and squeeze. I think of Juliet's stupid flimsy arm around Ozzy's neck, her toothy smile and mermaid hair. I lean back and crank so hard on my brother's head that my muscles feel like they might combust. Ike makes a terrible choking sound, tries to pull my arm away, squirms, and then frantically taps.

"Fuck, Row," he says, scrambling to his knees. "The fuck did you do that for?"

"Geez, chill," I say. "I just wanted to see if I could get it."

"Well, you did get it. And I think you broke my neck in the process." He rolls his head in a fragmented circle.

"Sorry."

He points to my ankle. "You're bleeding."

A trickle of blood drips to the floor. Ike grabs my foot and lifts it into the light. He flicks away a piece of glass and dabs the blood with a dirty napkin that seems to have materialized out of nowhere.

"You didn't feel that?" he asks, dropping my foot.

No. I felt nothing but pure joy. You squeeze someone hard enough, you can choke out your opponent *and* your feelings.

CHAPTER 7

I sleep through my alarm. In a bit of a role reversal, it's Ike who gets me up by throwing the stuffed polar bear at my face. I can't look at it. I don't even want to see Ozzy right now. I'm desperate to see Ozzy right now.

"It's late," Ike says from my doorway, toothpaste and spit flinging off his electric toothbrush.

"Ask Mom if we can take the car to school."

He leaves, and I throw back my comforter, grab a towel, and take a shower. By the time I'm dressed, Dad's speech therapist is working with him at the dining room table. At this point, he's more like a *swallow* therapist since that's all there's left to help him with. Devices do everything else. Mom slices a bagel in the kitchen. She's wearing a suit.

"Why was the coffee table in the hallway?" She points to the toaster. "I put a bagel in for you."

I don't want a bagel. I never eat when I first get up. She knows this. "Sorry," I reply. "I found more glass on the floor. I was trying to clean it up."

She checks her makeup on a square fridge mirror. "I have to show some houses today," she says. "You can take the car." My mom is a real estate agent and has this dream that one day Ike or

I will pair up with her to become a team, our pictures plastered on billboards and benches with some lame slogan. No offense to her, but I can't think of anything worse, and Ike would be more interested selling hotdogs than houses. He doesn't even know what a mortgage is.

I butter the bagel I didn't want and wrap it in paper towel. I blow a kiss to my dad in the dining room. He acknowledges with a blink. His speech therapist looks like The Rock. He waves.

Ike and I climb into the Civic. He watches memes in the passenger seat, laughing and whooping alternately. "Check it out," he says when we stop at a red light. In the video, a man dressed as a pigeon jumps off a roof onto a trampoline.

"That's not even funny."

"Then check this out."

The light turns green and I push his hand away. When we pull into the school parking lot, Ike tries again.

"You'll like this one," he urges, shoving his phone in my face.

I take off my seat belt. He presses play. Two guys beat the shit out of each other in a makeshift ring. One takes a glancing blow to the back of the head and crumples to the ground.

"Did you see his knees?" Ike's eyes shine. "Go back and watch it again."

"We're gonna be late."

Ike takes his phone and pauses the video. "Look at dude's legs!"

"What is that?"

"I don't know. Like a fight club or something."

Half the recording is sideways. The whole operation, if you can call it that, looks illegal. And dirty. Like it was filmed in some Detroit basement. I wouldn't be surprised if the next matchup was a cockfight.

Ike shrugs. "I have a game after. I don't need a ride." His massive basketball sneakers stick out from his backpack.

"K, see ya." I'm not halfway across the parking lot when I spot Ozzy locking his bike to the bike rack. His dads must have had to be on the job site early this morning; he never bikes to school. I have to get it over with. Find out what the fuck was up with the cozy picture, the joy in his face. I make a beeline for him but get caught up in a parade of frazzled parents doing drop-offs. When I finally reach him, Juliet's there, hands hennaed and hair in a messy bun. They are fully engaged in a conversation, like long-lost friends. Or lovers. I wait for Ozzy to see me before I take off, changing direction and losing myself in the mosh pit of students migrating through the school's main doors.

He shouts my name. "Row!"

I turn back once, to see him trying to navigate his way through the crowd, his stupid blue helmet like a beacon. I'm faster than him. There's a reason he's no longer playing hockey. He didn't choose drama club over triple A. He got cut.

Inside, I take a quick left down the math wing. He knows I have social studies first period and won't expect me to go this way. I'll take the south stairs and double back, skip my locker.

The bell rings.

"Row!"

This time it's Pia. She sidles up beside me out of breath. "What's up?"

I know that if I open my mouth, it'll trigger tears, so I don't. Instead, I bite my lip and just shake my head at her.

"Did you and Oz get in a fight?" Her eyes are big and concerned. Teachers-talking-about-mental-health eyes.

I blow out a breath, willing myself not to cry, the way I do when I've lost a match I should've won.

"I went to go talk to him, but she was there."

She takes my arm, ushering me into the classroom, where we both sit in the back. A dilapidated map of the Silk Road hangs on a corkboard behind us. The intro slide of unit four, *Globalization*, flashes on the SMART Board. Our hipster teacher, Mr. Williams, stands barefoot up front. He was probably meditating before we came in. It's weird to think he also coaches the football team.

"If it helps" — Pia takes a pen from her backpack — "I did some digging. Juliet has a boyfriend. He goes to the sports school."

It helps. A little. The guy I tried to hit at the party walks into the classroom. He mouths something I can't hear and takes a seat a few rows up. I blast him the finger when his back is turned. Mr. Williams closes his eyes and makes prayer hands as if he's bringing the class and the whole universe into balance.

I glance at my phone hidden on my lap and shielded by my desk. A whole slew of texts from Ozzy. *Why'd you walk away when I called you? What's wrong? Is it because of Juliet?*

I show Pia the last text and whisper, "He has to ask?"

Mr. Williams looks in our direction. "Today we're going to explore multiple perspectives on globalization, including the impact it has on identity, land, and culture."

Namaste, I think. Mr. Williams is the poster child for globalization. *Why not teach it in Sanskrit?*

"Perspective," Pia echoes. "Maybe nothing happened."

But he looked happy with her. Happier than he looks with me. I don't text him back, focusing instead on the lesson, scrawling notes. They have to be legible for Pia to borrow.

We split up after social studies and agree to meet at lunch. I struggle through my next class, physics, not because I don't get it — it's probably my best subject — but because I'm behind. If I hadn't spent all night googling omoplatas I'd be fine. When the bell rings for lunch, I take the spiral stairs from the second floor art room to avoid any chance of seeing Ozzy. He'll be waiting at my locker.

But I'm wrong. When I round the final curve of the paint-splattered staircase, Ozzy's standing at the bottom with his arms crossed. It's almost comical. He looks more like a mad parent than a pissed-off boyfriend.

"Where's your little sidekick?" I ask. "Sorry, *castmate*."

"Castmate," he repeats. "Exactly. You're jealous because of some girl I'm in a play with? Come on, Row. You're the one who's rolling around with guys six nights a week. If anything, I should be the one who's jealous."

The art teacher, Ms. Gupta, tears sheets of brown paper off a wall-mounted roll.

"Right, cause there's nothing more threatening than your girlfriend getting thrown down and dragged across the mat."

Ms. Gupta holds up a Tupperware container and reminds us that the bell went. She moves to the back of the art room, where a microwave sits between stacks of unused canvasses.

"Yeah, a guy on top of you literally pressing his body into you and pinning you to the floor."

"Oh, is that what constitutes romance to you, Oz? Have we been doing it wrong all this time? Because I can assure there's nothing romantic about getting some sweaty guy's junk in your face."

Ozzy sighs. He's the one who looks teary.

"At least when practice is over, I don't go to their houses and rest my little chin on their heads."

"What does that mean?"

"I saw the picture of your little post-rehearsal get-together. If she's 'just a castmate,'" I say, making air quotes, "then why was she wrapped around you like some Shakespeare version of a puck bunny?"

"Wow," he replies.

"Yeah, wow."

He reaches for my hand. I bat it away and storm by him.

"Come on, Row." He follows behind.

I hyperventilate as I charge down the hall toward my locker.

"She's just a friend. She has a boyfriend."

I stop and turn. "At least someone does." Tears burn behind my eyes, but I refuse to cry.

"I love you."

"Well, you have a funny way of showing it."

People pretend not to pay attention, but all eyes are fixed on us. Nothing satisfies more than relationship drama playing out in real time. It's the perfect lunchtime entertainment.

"Be careful, bro," Mitchell warns, slamming his locker. "She might haul off and pop you."

"Fuck off," Ozzy and I reply in unison. It's the first thing we've agreed on in weeks. We both fall silent, our eyes locking in a sad marriage. We are both hurting. He takes my hand and pulls me toward him. It feels a bit aggressive, but in the moment, it's exactly what I need. When I'm constantly the one fighting, sometimes I need to feel like someone is fighting for *me*.

CHAPTER 8

At the 7-Eleven across the street from the school, Ozzy buys me a bubblegum Slurpee in a cup the size of a beach bucket. Coach would kill me if he saw me *poisoning my body with that crap* but I sip it all the way down to the ice at the bottom. I have dry-land training on my own tonight — I'll just run an extra kilometer. Or five.

Pia eats a bag of toasted chickpeas in the parking lot. She eyes my drink.

"Don't judge me," I say, tossing the empty cup in the garbage.

Ozzy leans in and kisses me on the cheek.

"Good to see everything's back to normal," Pia chuckles.

"For now," I mutter.

We eat lunch outside, the three of us together until Pia sees a friend and chases after him.

"We should blow off the afternoon," Ozzy says. "Go see a movie or something."

"Don't you have rehearsal after school?"

He picks through his quesadilla and sighs. "Yeah."

"What about third period then? What do you have? Gym? Just tell Mr. Chang you need a study block."

"What about you?"

"I have LA. I already didn't do the reading for it. I'll just say I need to see the counselor."

Ozzy checks his phone. "Meet you back here in ten?"

I go to my locker and grab my stuff. A lunch container from last week falls from the top shelf. I shove it back inside and head toward the main doors. I don't get ten feet when Ms. Foy comes out of the counseling office.

"Hi Rowan," she says.

Go away. I mean, I love her, but I wish she didn't feel the need to check in on me every five minutes. She waves me into the counseling waiting room, which is wallpapered with inspirational quotes and mental health propaganda. Unlike the office chairs, which are metal and uncomfortable, the counseling chairs are big and overstuffed to give the illusion you're sitting in a hug. There are Kleenex boxes on every surface, blinds on all the windows, emergency phone numbers, plants, and stress balls. If anything, it seems designed to uphold the stigmas around mental health rather than to break them. Every second poster asks if you're having suicidal thoughts.

A grade twelve girl sits in one of the chairs, playing on her phone. Pia knows her from field hockey. She tried to kill herself in March. The scars are still visible on her wrists.

The girl doesn't look up when Ms. Foy leads me through the waiting room to her office. *Do I actually have a counseling appointment right now that I forgot? What day is it?*

"Have a seat," Ms. Foy gestures.

"Is this going to take long?"

"It shouldn't." She smiles, rolling forward in her high-backed desk chair. "But I'm always here if you need me."

"I'm okay." *Why am I here?* I remember in grade eight Neville Lewis was taken out of class by the counselor to learn his mom got hit by a car. *What if something's happened to Dad?*

"I just wanted to go over your class selection for next year. If you're still considering a US college, I have a few suggestions."

Now? Ugh.

She places my class selection form in front of me. It's marked up in Ms. Foy's signature green pen. She suggests switching my math and social studies and moving chemistry to second semester.

"You want your strongest classes in the first semester when you apply for early admission."

My phone chimes. We both pause.

"Do you need to get that?" she asks.

"It might be my dad." I know it's Ozzy.

Ms. Foy nods sympathetically and starts typing something on her keyboard.

Where r u?

I'm in the friggin counseling office, I text back.

?

Ms. Foy dragged me in.

Are you coming?

"Is everything okay?" Ms. Foy asks.

"Yep," I reply. "I just don't want to miss class. I have a big tournament in New York coming up and I'll be missing a lot of school. I don't want to get behind."

"Of course. Well then, if you're okay with these changes I'll get them switched in the system. And don't forget to fill out an absence form before the tournament. You're gonna love New York," she says wistfully.

I'm gonna love seeing my boyfriend if I can get the hell out of here. I sling my backpack over my shoulder. The bell rings. I dash out through the front doors. The schoolyard smells like weed and diesel from the neighboring bus terminal. Ozzy waits on a picnic bench, which is chained to the ground beside the football field. I fold into him. His hoodie smells like salsa and the vanilla dryer sheets Tall Dad loves.

"What was that all about?"

"US college stuff. Ms. Foy just moved around some of my classes."

When Ozzy still played hockey, we had a plan. We'd both get NCAA athletic scholarships. We'd aim for some Midwestern state in America's heartland, where both wrestling and hockey were prized. We'd try for the same school. Meet up between practices and dual meets and home games. Do our laundry together. Eat our way through all the wacky fast-food joints not available in Canada: *Shake Shack, Jack in the Box, In-N-Out Burger, Sonic Drive-In.*

"I have the car. We could drive somewhere?"

"We only have an hour before last period."

"Shit, is that your gym class?"

Mr. Chang opens the orange steel gym door and a stream of students files out in Southwest Memorial High School branded shirts and shorts. The logo would look good on a singlet. I wish we had a team. The students shield their eyes from the blazing afternoon sun. Some drag their feet.

"Crap. He thinks I'm in the library."

"Let's go to my car." We slip away from the picnic table and weave through the labyrinth of SUVs poorly parked in the student lot. Mr. Chang leads his class to the football field. We climb inside my family's dated hatchback and recline the seats. There's a burn mark on the upholstered ceiling from when Ike took the car to Punkfest last summer. The ceiling is low like you're sitting in a basement. My father's hair used to graze the top when he drove.

"She really is just a friend," Ozzy starts. "Juliet."

"I know who you're talking about. You don't have to keep saying her name."

"I think you'd like her, Row. She's been good to me, helping me learn my lines. I'm late to the acting game. I need people who can help me."

I see his point, but it still bothers me.

"This play's really important to me."

His face is sincere. I know what it's like to want something. I feel it every time I compete.

"That's good, Oz." I take his hand. "I'm happy she's helping you."

We stare at the roof in silence, his fingertips gently pressing into my bruised knuckles. I close my eyes and remember when we used to drive out to the foothills, lie on the hood of his car, and watch the stars. How alive I felt in the quiet darkness, the city at our backs.

"How's your dad?" Ozzy asks.

"Not well," I say without hesitation. "Every day he seems worse."

"I'm sorry, Row."

"And I can't do anything about it. That's the hardest part."

A dog barks. There's a green space behind the rec center across the street, but the bark sounds closer than that. In the rearview mirror, a football bounces down the embankment from the field. Two guys race to retrieve the ball, jostling each other on their way back up. A lady walks her poodle near the 7-Eleven. She stops so it can sniff a garbage can, and then she tugs the dog away.

"Did you hear barking?"

Ozzy sits up and looks out the window. The back of his hair curls over his shirt. It hasn't been this long since quarantine. Before Short Dad finally sheared it into a pandemic mullet.

"You need a haircut," I say.

He runs his fingers through the offending shag. "I'm growing it out."

Since when? "How come?"

"I want it long."

I try to picture Ozzy with long hair. More barking. I sit up fully and scan the schoolyard. A dog limps around the periphery of the football field, passing behind the uprights.

"Do you see that dog?" I ask.

"The mutt?"

"Does it have a black patch on the left side of its body?"

In contacts, Ozzy's eyesight is better than twenty-twenty. He wrenches himself around in his seat to get a better view. "Brownish-black," he says. "Doesn't have a collar."

"I think it's the dog from the alley."

"The one the guy threw the brick at?"

I sit up straight. "Looks exactly like it."

Ozzy winces. "It looks diseased."

I place my hand on the door handle. "I have to go see."

"What if it bites you?"

I'm out the door before he can ask any more questions. I walk a few steps and crouch down. "Come here," I call, patting my thigh.

The dog's ears prick up.

"Come," I say again.

The dog nudges a wrapper on the ground. I take a cautious step toward it.

Ozzy stoops down beside me, his backpack between his legs. "I think you should leave it," he says.

"Do you still have the falafel wrap?"

"Why?"

"I need it."

"That's my after-school snack. For rehearsal."

"What are you, five?"

He frowns and unzips the front pocket of his bag. I can tell Tall Dad made the falafel because it's wrapped in sustainable beeswax instead of plastic.

"I have to get back inside before Mr. Chang does." He kisses me, swipes his bag from the pavement, and heads to a side door away from the football field.

The dog licks its paw. I take a bite of the wrap and then offer it to the dog.

"Come get some falafel," I say, backing toward the car. The dog follows. I guide it around to the passenger side and place the wrap on the seat. It struggles to climb up. It smells like garbage. I boost it into the car. The black spot on its side leaves an oily residue on my fingers. I wipe my hands on my jeans and shut the door.

What am I doing?

I settle back into the driver's seat and google nearby veterinarians, since Larry goes to a cat specialist in the suburbs and Pia's mom's clinic is on the outskirts of the city. *Cedar View Animal Clinic, 4.1 km.* Perfect. I put on my seat belt and glance over at the dog. It sits at attention, eager and proud like we're about to embark on the adventure of a lifetime. Its body fills the depression Ozzy's left behind.

I'm heading in the direction of Cedar View when a call comes in over the Bluetooth. Mom. She usually texts when she knows I'm in class. My heart rate quickens.

"Mom?"

"Rowan, I need you to go the house right now."

"Is everything okay?"

"I have to write up an offer for a client. I just need you to let Dad's physical therapist in. Beryl was supposed to do it, but she's still at the dentist."

Beryl's lived on our street since the time when her house was the only house on it.

"Sorry to pull you out of class," Mom says. "I've just got to get this offer in, and your dad can't answer the door."

"Yep."

The call disconnects and I look over at the dog. I snap a pic of it. I swear it's smiling. It smells like a Sunday morning subway station. It needs a bath, and a grooming, and a liter of mouthwash. I roll my window down for fresh air but inhale the exhaust from a pickup truck covered in oil and gas decals.

Beryl is still not back from the dentist when I pull into our driveway. Her ancient Pontiac is not perfectly parked in front of the lattice beneath her deck. Dad helped install the lattice when she had the deck refurbished a few years ago. It needs a new paint job.

Based on the time, I'm assuming the next member of Dad's "care team" isn't due to arrive for another ten minutes. I can't leave the dog in the front seat that long. The car would be condemned. I'll put the dog in the shed.

I grab the shed key from its hiding spot inside one of the raised garden beds. The padlock is rusty, but the lock gives, and the door pops open with ease. The lawn mower starts to roll backward because Ike never bothers to put anything away properly. I kick through grass clippings and wheel the lawn mower into the corner, parking it beneath the bikes mounted to the ceiling. Mine, Dad's.

The shed is a memory box. It smells of road trips and weekends as a kid. Of when Saturdays were for exploring, and not for tournaments or therapeutic swims. I think of all the times Dad and I would come in here, survey our cache of equipment, and then hit the road with a trunkful of possibility. A live-action choose-your-own-adventure.

My dad's hiking poles are crisscrossed on the floor. I pick them up and lean them against the wall beside my own. I clear the debris from the ground and spread a piece of tarp over the weathered planks. Ike's old Spiderman comforter is stuffed into a shelf. I haul it down, form it into a dog bed, and arrange it on the tarp.

I coax the dog into the shed with the promise of more falafel.

"Stay here," I say, stroking its dirty head. "I'll be back in a bit."

I close the door but it pops back open before I even get to the wheelchair ramp. I go back and ram it shut with my shoulder. This time it holds. Inside, my dad watches a documentary on Tsingy de Bemaraha National Park — a UNESCO world heritage site in Madagascar. The park is covered in razor-sharp limestone rocks and cliffs. The landscape looks like something out of a dystopian novel. It's a place I know he wanted to visit.

"Hey, Dad."

He smiles, lifts his hand an inch from the armrest of his wheelchair. This action now constitutes a wave. As his muscles weaken, my attention to detail strengthens. Even his most finite movements — a twitch, a blink — can mean something. *I love yous* are now transmitted in flutters.

I scrub the dog from my hands with lemony soap and search for a bowl Mom won't miss, to use as a water dish. In the back of the corner cabinet, I find a chipped bowl, "popcorn" embossed on the rim in red and yellow big-top letters. I remember having a complete set in our old house. Ike probably broke them all. No one eats popcorn anymore.

I fill the bowl with cool water and take it out the back door so Dad can't see what I'm doing. When I open the shed, the dog greets me hopefully, tail wagging, eyes pleading. It drinks sloppily, the way Pia does mid-match, water pouring down the front of her singlet and all over Coach's value-buy Brooks sneakers.

"You were thirsty." I sound like a playground mom. "Wait five more minutes."

I push the door closed as Dad's physical therapist pulls up to the curb. He also looks like The Rock — shoulders wide as a linebacker's and a helper's face, kind and sympathetic. I lead him up the front steps. He takes off his shoes in the entryway.

"Tyler's here."

Dad manipulates his chair, spinning to face his therapist. He likes Tyler. We all do. He calls my dad "big man" and "boss." He never just calls him Scott.

"Boss," Tyler says. "You're looking fitter today. What did I tell you about over-training?" He winks and my dad's face brightens. Once they are settled into their routine, I text Ike.

Bring home some dog food after practice.

Why would I do that?

Because I asked you to.

Since when do you eat dog food?

I'll tell Mom you're vaping again.

Wet or dry?

Dry.

I pack clothes for the gym and fill a water bottle.

"My mom will be home soon," I tell Tyler as I braid my hair in the front hall mirror.

"All good," Tyler replies. "She let me know she'd be late."

I dump my gear in the back seat of the Civic. Pew. Maybe Ozzy was right and the dog does have a disease. I head down the driveway toward the shed. The door hangs open. What the heck?

The dog is not inside. I move a few sleds in case it managed to wedge itself behind one, but it's not there. It's not behind the old blow-up backyard pool, either. *Why do we still have that?*

I stand in the doorframe, looking out into the yard and down the driveway. How do you call for a dog when it doesn't have a name? I stare at the nearly empty water bowl that's been pushed to the edge of the tarp.

"Popcorn!" I call. "Come here, Popcorn."

Next door, Beryl eases into her driveway the way you'd expect from a woman who drove a tank in World War II. She gets out of the car in phases. One leg, then the other. Her glasses resemble swim goggles. She raises her hand when she sees me.

"Popcorn?" I whisper, looking helplessly into the street. My shoulders fall, acknowledging the ridiculousness of calling a dog by a name it doesn't know; a stupid name at that.

"Whatcha doing, honey?" Beryl asks. She comes up to my chest, body frail and hunched on the top, solid on the bottom. A trace of her British accent is still detectable when she speaks, like the contrail of a passing 747.

"Looking for something," I reply.

She hauls out a pack of cigarettes. "You want one?" A flake of tobacco flitters to the pavement.

"No, thanks, Ms. Colvin. I don't smoke."

She shrugs. "Your brother does."

Of course he does.

"You need help with anything?" I ask, as she lumbers back to her car, pantyhose thick as ski pants suctioned to her legs.

"Nope. No groceries today. Just had my teeth cleaned. Don't know what the point of that is. Nobody's gonna be dating me for my teeth at this age."

I smile. Then I remember Popcorn. "Have a good day."

She waves again, more of a shrugging off the notion of a good day than a goodbye. I take one more look around the yard and down both sides of the streets for the dog. Vanished. Tears sting my sinuses. I sniff to keep the tears there and sink into the car.

CHAPTER 9

I skip the rec center across from the school and head to the club. I'm not in the mood to compete with the leathery triathletes and the sexy Avas for the good spin bikes. I'll use Coach's behemoth treadmill and the squat rack instead. I recognize Axel's Audi when I pull into the strip mall parking lot.

A new vinyl banner hangs on the wall behind the front desk: *POTENTIA MMA*. Latin doesn't sound very threatening. Axel is in the center of the mat, tied up with another fighter. Both are upside down, torsos tangled, legs flailing. I slip into the change-room unnoticed.

When I come back out, Axel is breathing heavily on his knees, his opponent flat on his back, shielding his eyes from the fluorescent lights overhead. Both are barefoot.

"Rowan," Axel waves me over. "I need you for a second."

I hesitate, unconvinced there's any reasonable need of his I can fulfill. I don't know their kind of grappling.

"It'll just take a minute," he adds.

I tuck in my shirt and tighten my braid.

Quietly, Axel says, "I'm taking front head position on you."

I nod, ditch my headphones, and drop to the mat. Axel traps my head and arm.

"Caspian, watch. Look at my left arm and the position of my shoulder."

Axel squeezes my head and arm and rolls me into a choke. It's similar to a wrestling Gabori roll. I feel like a shelled animal that's gotten stuck on its back. Axel's forearm is like rebar against my throat. He releases and my body goes limp for a second before I scramble to sit up. Heat rushes to my cheeks.

"Thanks, Rowan. Caspian, did you get that?"

Caspian is not paying attention to Axel. Instead, he stares at me with the dreamy look usually reserved for suitors in old-timey romance films set in state fairs. I half expect him to pull a bouquet of flowers from his rash guard. I half expect him to propose.

I clear my throat and look away, embarrassed, intrigued.

Axel snaps his fingers. "Cas, dude, pay attention."

Caspian adopts a serious expression. Axel tries to keep a straight face, but he turns away, laughing.

"Yes," he says. "She's strong. And a very good wrestler. Caspian, Rowan, Rowan, Caspian. I probably should have introduced you first."

Caspian has bed head and hair the color of an oatmeal muffin. Just sitting, I can tell he's at least six feet, probably more. He has a single dimple, deep as a ditch, on the left side of his face, cauli-ears, and green eyes, unlike Ozzy's chocolate brown ones. A scar gives the illusion his left eyebrow has been stitched into place.

"Caspian's one of my top prospects," Axel says. "He has his first professional fight in June." He sighs. "If he can pay attention long enough to get there."

"I was paying attention," Caspian argues. "I was just going through the move in my head."

"Which move?" Axel asks. "Because it looked like the one where you ask her to dance. Now focus."

Oh my God, Axel sounds like Coach.

"Rowan, do you have time for one more? With Cas? I want you to put him in the head-and-arm so he can feel how tight it needs to be before the roll. You've done something similar like this in wrestling, yes?"

I nod. Caspian awkwardly lines up across from me. I wrap my arms around his head and neck. He smells like Leo, like Old Spice deodorant and hill sprints, with a hint of Pop-Tarts.

Axel makes an adjustment to the setup and then calls the move. We end up doing it half a dozen more times, switching between offense and defense. I learn a new escape technique I can use in wrestling. Caspian regains his concentration and barely cracks a smile for the rest of the drill.

Axel gets a call and excuses himself.

"Want to keep going?" I ask Caspian.

"You know wristlock from side control?"

I reply, "Not really."

"Go on your back."

I lie down and he mounts me from the side, his legs perpendicular to mine. He's heavier than Ozzy. He takes an underhook. I defend by trying to snake my arm under his, but he pinches my wrist between his shoulder and chest, trapping it — bent — under his armpit. Breathe. I study his face. There's another scar resembling staple marks on his hairline, and remnants of a bruise along his jawline. He looks like he's already fought his first professional fight and lost.

A drop of his sweat lands on my cheek. He makes an adjustment with his body, slides his other arm across, and cranks on my wrist. His ribs press into mine like he's trying to fuse them together. My hand might snap clear from my arm.

Tap.

"Switch?"

I sit up and move on top of him. His hip bone digs into my flesh. I feel his breath in my ear. He guides me through the technique, all business until he winces.

"Did I get it?"

He responds by tapping.

Outside, Coach pulls up in his Jetta. I peel myself off the mat, snatch my headphones, and jump on the treadmill. No time for programs. I push "quick start" and run. The motor groans as the speed and incline increase. I feel exhausted and high. There's something intoxicating about establishing control and making someone tap. Power. *Potentia*.

Axel rejoins Caspian. They roll, and stop only when Coach steps on the mat to chat. A few minutes later, Coach goes back out to his car and hauls in a case of cleaner. He puts the jugs in the storage room and then comes to the treadmill, track pants swishing and a smile on his face. He loves hard work.

"Six minutes and thirty-two seconds," he grumbles. "That it? Only one k? My dog can go faster than that and she has three legs."

Popcorn. I pick up my pace. "I'm doing sprints," I lie. "This is my fourth set."

"Hitting up some squats next?"

"That's the plan."

He slaps the treadmill, which is as close to a compliment as Coach gets. I dial up the speed, sprint hard for a minute and then hop off, straddling the footboards to recover. I repeat the sequence until I taste blood. I can barely breathe. This is how my dad feels just sitting in his wheelchair. Breathless from watching the sunrise, the sunset. Breathless from doing nothing.

I climb off the treadmill and stagger toward the fountain where Caspian is bent over, hands shaking and water spilling from his chin down his front. I wonder how he manages to train during school hours. He must go to the Elite Sports Academy with Juliet's supposed boyfriend. On his calf is a bruise the size of a softball.

"Do you go to the sports school?" I wipe sweat from my face with my shirt.

"No." He fills his water bottle without offering any more information.

Awkward. I flick a hairball from my leggings. "How long have you been training MMA?"

"Since birth." He screws the lid back on his water bottle and raises his eyebrows.

The hell does that mean? Though he has enough scars to make it believable. Maybe he grew up in a prison.

The bell above the front door chimes and we both look over. UPS. Coach signs for a package.

"Hey, Rowena," Coach yells. "That barbell isn't gonna squat itself."

"Got it," I holler.

"Is that your real name?"

"No," I reply, embarrassed. "He just calls me that."

Caspian smirks and retreats to the heavy bags without saying another word.

I head to the ancient squat rack on the other side of the gym and load the bar with plates. Coach watches. I should have just gone to the rec center. I adjust the neck pad and lift the bar to the back of my upper spine. I barely get through ten reps. I can almost taste the hard lemonade from Saturday night.

When Coach is distracted, I remove some of the plates and finish my remaining five sets in peace. It feels good to finish my workout early, even though I'll have a lot of work to catch up on from my missed fourth period.

Caspian comes out of the guys' changeroom wearing a red hoodie and faded gray jogging pants. He pulls a black mesh hat down low on his forehead and heads out the back door. I tidy up the weights and collect my stuff.

Coach and Axel install another chin-up bar, the club's fifth, as if we need another. People aren't exactly lining up to use them. I wave and head out the front door to my car. I sit for a few minutes, trying to muster the energy to turn the key in the ignition. I check my phone. Ozzy is texting. My heart jumps a little.

How did you make out with the dog?

Long story, I type. *It escaped.* I add a sad face.

That sucks. Are you at the gym?

Just finished.

We r just about to start act two.

K, call me after.

He types a heart.

I hang up and bend my wrist back and forth a few times. One wristlock. *Ouch.* I start the car and pull into traffic with my window down. The breeze cools my sweat-drenched hair. Traffic is heavy. I voice text Mom at a red light and ask her what's for dinner. She calls.

"Did the offer go through?" I ask.

"We just sent a counter," she replies. "I think they'll accept it.

As for dinner, can you pick up a chicken and a salad at Safeway? I'm just making your dad some soup but there's not enough for all of us."

"Sure." I hate soup. I hate that my mom will feed it to my dad, that he has to be spoon-fed. It's so insulting. Next, he'll be wearing a bib. I can't even. I make a terrible lane change across three lanes of traffic to reach the Safeway and end the call.

The grocery store parking lot is jammed with the after-work crowd. Irritated parents wrangling their kids into submission with bribes and threats. Women in heels move with aggression. Caspian, in his red hoodie and mesh hat, loiters out front. I think about going in the far doors to avoid him, but it's too much effort. I can barely put one foot in front of the other.

He talks animatedly with someone invisible behind a brick pillar. I stop to let a car go, and then cross. When the other guy comes into view, I recognize him immediately. The mark I left on his face is still visible, only a little more yellow.

I'm too close to the door to back away now. We make eye contact. Fuck. His gaze follows me into the store. I grab a rotisserie chicken and a pre-made Caesar salad. My mom used to sneer at people who bought this shit for dinner. Some of the romaine is already brown. I do the self-serve checkout. Alley Boy comes in as I'm paying. I wait until he nears the bananas and duck out the door. Caspian stands in my way.

"Rowena!"

"It's Rowan," I say shouldering my way past him, the chicken swaying recklessly.

"Hold up." Caspian reaches for my arm. I knock it away. "How do you know Degan?"

"Is that his name?"

"You don't know him?"

"I know he threw a brick at a dog. God knows what else he did to it."

"Wait a minute." A smile forms in the corner of his mouth. "You're the one who did that to his face? In the alleyway?"

I cross my arms.

"Shit, you nearly shattered his eye socket." He covers his mouth in awe.

"He nearly shattered the dog's." *Popcorn.*

His smile disappears and he places his hands on my shoulders. "Listen, Degan is bad news."

"And what does that make you, if you're friends with him?"

"I never said I was friends with him."

Caspian releases his grip. A man coming out of the store scolds us for blocking the exit. For a second, I think I see Tall Dad squeezing an avocado in the background.

"Listen, Degan means well, but he's got issues. Been hit in the head too many times, if you know what I mean."

"Yeah, I got that when the brick whizzed by my skull."

He steps back, sizing me up as though it's the first time we've met.

"Yeah," he replies. "I'll see you tomorrow."

I blow by him to the parking lot, only to forget where the hell I parked. I don't look as tough when I'm blasting the remote key in all directions. By the time I find the car, Caspian is gone. No sign of Alley Boy. My adrenaline races and I squeal out of the parking lot. *Calm down.*

I pull onto the main road and think of Coach's cues during a tough match. *In through the nose and out through the mouth.* Isn't this every breathing instruction from every coach ever? By the time I get home, I just want to crash. I imagine this is how Mom feels when she says her nerves are shot.

I swing the bag of groceries onto the counter.

"Geez, Row," Mom says, rushing over. "I hope there's nothing breakable in there." She removes the plastic dome on the chicken and transfers the bird with her bare hands onto a plate. "Grab me the scissors," she says, gesturing to the junk drawer.

I hand her a pair, and she savagely cuts the rope binding the chicken's legs. "I'm starving," she says, licking grease from her fingers.

No kidding. I grab a mixing bowl and dump the bagged salad inside, sever the dressing pouch, and squeeze it in.

Mom tosses me the tongs. "How was training?"

"My legs hurt," I reply.

"Squats?"

"And sprints."

"That'll do it." She turns up her nose. "This chicken isn't very hot."

I make myself a plate and curl up on the couch in the living room. Dad is watching *Shark Week*. A diver is lowered into a cage off the tip of South Africa. A crewmember chums the water with fish. Great whites, with their vacant black eyes, circle. Their teeth always look infected, jaws open, as if their entire disposition is linked to the fact they need a root canal.

"Who would voluntarily get into a cage with those?" A crouton falls into the seam of the couch. I dig it out and analyze my dad for a response. His shoulders twitch: a shrug.

"Exactly," I reply. "Crazy people. Would you ever do that? If you still could?" There's no sense pretending it's a possibility. We're beyond the *you never know, they could find a cure* stage.

Mom jumps into the conversation, sinking onto the other side of the couch, her face glistening with chicken fat. "No way." She laughs. "Did I ever tell you about the time we went snorkeling on our honeymoon?"

Dad does something akin to an eye roll.

"A mile offshore your dad saw a dolphin and screamed bloody murder, ha!"

"I'm sure he didn't *scream*."

"Didn't scream? He was so loud, the guide triggered the shark alarm. I've never seen a beach clear so fast."

I look at my dad for confirmation while Mom loses it on the other side of the couch. The cushions shake.

"It's not *that* funny," I argue.

But she is bent over, hand to her face, unable to speak, her whole body convulsing. A piece of chicken slides off her plate to the floor.

My dad smiles.

"The hell's so funny?" Ike stands in the doorway, kicking off his basketball shoes. He smells like he brought the whole court home with him. "Is there chicken for me? Please tell me there's food."

I gesture to the kitchen.

"Oh, thank God," he says.

Whoever dropped him off makes a shoddy U-turn and rips down the street. If Beryl were outside she'd throw something at the car.

Ike comes out of the kitchen with just the chicken on his plate. No salad, no fork, no napkin. He sits on the rocking chair and uses the footstool as a table.

"Did you even wash your hands?" Mom asks.

"I washed them at school." He talks with his mouth full, a flap of chicken skin hanging from his lip like a second tongue. "Who's watching *Shark Week*?"

"Dad."

Ike tears off a wing. "Dad'd never do that," he says, nodding toward the TV.

The great white on camera is identified as a fourteen-foot female named Helen. She charges at the cage with jolting speed.

"Crazy bitch," Ike says.

"Don't use that language," Mom cautions. "I sold a house today."

"I had four three-pointers," Ike says.

"And how many fouls?" I ask.

He spits a bit of gristle onto his plate. "Five."

My dad types, *I binge-watched season six of Alone.*

"Without me?" I put my plate on the coffee table. *I learned how to break someone's wrist.* Another shark has joined Helen, a juvenile named Luis. The water is murky green. A fish head floats by the screen. Luis goes after it, while Helen continues to pummel the metal box.

The diver hovers, sunlight glinting off his silver scuba tank. The top of the cage has a chain-link pattern similar to that of an MMA octagon and I imagine, for a moment, what it would be like to fight in one. *Would I be the diver or the shark?*

"Well, this is boring as shit," Ike announces. "Once you've seen one *Shark Week*, you've seen them all." He belches and, surprisingly, collects the empty plates littered around the room. Mom follows him to the kitchen.

The cage is slowly winched to the surface. The diver inside gives a thumbs-up. Dad turns his chair to face me.

I ask, "You want to watch some of my old fights?"

His eyes brighten. I connect my phone to the TV and scroll through my videos. I click on last year's Nationals and press play. I drag the footstool and sidle up beside his chair. He winces when my opponent gets a takedown.

"I know," I sigh. "My hips weren't back."

We replay my semi-final bout. His posture changes when my arm is raised at the end. My final match has us both on edge. We watch side by side, heads tilted, shoulders tensed. With thirty seconds to go, I'm ahead by four. My opponent scores a two-point takedown. I make a mistake trying to escape, and nearly get pinned. In the final seconds, I reverse the position and pin her instead. If it were an MMA fight, I could have just knocked her out.

Light fills my father's face.

"It was a good one, wasn't it?" I kiss him on the cheek. "I'm going to do some homework."

"Here's your dog food." Ike carries a bag on his shoulder and dumps it down on the couch. The food bounces off a pillow and lands upside down on the floor.

I glare at him.

"Did you just say dog food?" Mom calls over the hiss of the dishwasher.

I look at my dad. His expression is puzzled, and I motion for him not to say anything. He makes the equivalent of a facepalm with his eyelids.

"It's for a school project," I sputter.

"What kind of school project requires you to have a bag of dog food?"

I ignore Mom and haul the bag to my room.

CHAPTER 10

The next day during first period, Pia texts me a selfie from the X-ray clinic changeroom. Her hospital gown is pale green with a dot matrix pattern. She's knotted it at her hip and tugged the neckline down to show off her shoulder. Only Pia could style a hospital gown. #hospitalgown will be trending by lunch. Since breaking her arm, she's grown out her nails. They're perfectly manicured and polished a burnt orange. My nails look like shit. So short you can only see the frayed cuticles and the knobby tips of my fingers.

I slide my phone under my notebook and shift my focus to the Red Cross instructor who's standing in the middle of the room. He's a small man like Axel, with serious eyes and a pronounced cowlick.

A CPR dummy with a blue chest sits at my feet, his mouth open like he's waiting for someone to shove a cake pop inside it. Other students have newer, female dummies, with boobs. My partner is some dude I don't know. He practices tilting the plastic head and lifting its chin.

Mr. Chang wanders around the room, observing. He knows I already did CPR last year and pays minimal attention when it's my turn to do compressions. The bell rings before we get to the First Aid portion of the certification.

I text Ozzy, *What do you want to do for lunch?*
I got a costume fitting.
I remember going with him to buy new skates last year. A job normally reserved for Short Dad, but Short Dad had been stuck at city hall sorting out work permits, and Tall Dad had to do the honors. He'd acted like Oz was getting fitted for prosthetic legs. *Are you sure they fit? Can you feel your toes? Why are they so hard?*

On my way to LA, I pass the digital news board run by the journalism class. Promos for *Romeo and Juliet* cycle through the school news segments. Characters from the play talk about show dates and ticket prices in their best Shakespearean accents. Ozzy sounds like a gang member crossed with Prince Charles. No wonder he needs help. Juliet is a born star.

I can pick you up from practice tonight. We can get Blizzards or whatever if you're cutting weight.

K, I reply. *I'm done at 7.*

The thought of a date makes my lunch salad more tolerable. Coach told us to come early tonight for weigh-ins. I shouldn't have had the Slurpee. By fourth period, I'm starving. I eat half an energy bar on the way to practice. Pia texts as I'm transferring from the CTrain to the bus.

I get my cast off in two weeks.
Does that mean you're good for NY???
Depends, she replies. *Physio and shit.*

I show my transit pass to the driver and take a swivel seat in the middle of the bus. Coach isn't bad to travel with, but I can't imagine going to New York without Pia. Before last year's tournament was canceled, she had every detail of the trip — outside of wrestling — meticulously planned. Without her, Coach and

I will end up eating mediocre cheesecake on a street corner in matching souvenir NYPD hats.

I weigh in in my singlet. Exactly 62 kilos. *So much for a post-practice Blizzard.* One scoop and I won't make weight tomorrow — when it counts. Coach records my weight in his blue hardcover notebook and shrugs. Leo climbs on the scale after me as I head to the changeroom to swap my singlet for regular training gear.

During warm-up, Coach goes over the upcoming local tournament. Girls compete Friday night. I hate Friday tournaments. Even though getting up is hard, I feel stronger in the morning. He says he needs volunteers to help out on both days, and just like that, my entire weekend's planned.

We spend the first hour and a half going over leg attacks. Coach is in a pissy mood and doles out push-ups like Halloween candy. I avoid all but one set. Just before we start live wrestling, Axel arrives, followed by a parade of fighters. Some look like they've never made a fist before, others resemble meth addicts. I glance at the clock. Our practices must overlap.

"Leo, stick with Rowan," Coach says when we're cued to switch partners. I shoot in a low single and get a quick takedown. I lose a chunk of hair when Leo pushes down on my head.

"What the hell was that?" Coach yells.

Leo mumbles, "Damn it," as Coach storms over, his face red as a fire alarm.

"If you're not going to defend your legs, you might as well take up polka dancing instead. Now, anticipate her shot, and respond like a wrestler."

"Yes, Coach."

Leo and I square up. He flicks his hair incessantly, the way he does when he's frustrated.

Coach leans against the wall beneath a chin-up bar. He looks like he might have a heart attack. He sets his timer. "Go."

I alternate fakes with snap downs before I shoot in for a single leg. Leo sprawls hard this time, his weight a tractor tire on my upper back.

"Better," Coach yells at Leo. "Rowan, don't hesitate. You did a fake and then you paused for a second. Don't do that."

I get the next shot and take Leo's back. Coach doesn't see. He's on the opposite side of the mat with a group of younger boys working on gut wrenches. Axel, however, does. He nods approvingly in my direction.

We take a quick water break before it's my turn to defend. Leo drives in for an explosive low single but misses.

"Fuck." He slams the mat with his fist.

Coach tells him to do chin-ups. He doesn't approve of swearing when there are younger kids at practice. He takes Leo's place and shoots a single leg. I push down on his wiry old man hair and circle.

"That's good leg defense," he says, out of breath. "Let's take that to New York."

He stands and adjusts his wrestling club jacket. "Last one," he says.

Leo returns and shoots. I sprawl on his head, pushing my pelvis into him, but he continues to drive forward until we're clear off the mat. Caspian jumps out of the way. I avoid eye contact with him as Leo yanks me up from the ground with such force I get air. We start to jog.

Coach waxes on about effort and commitment the whole

time we cool down. When he gets like this, Pia and I usually joke that he must be on his period. The thought makes me smile as I switch from a jog to a slow side-to-side shuffle.

"Some of you weighed in like you slept in a food truck last night. Even some of you younger boys. You eat shit, you wrestle like shit. Now get out of here and fix yourself a stir-fry."

We clear the mat and Axel's group moves in.

"Rowan," Axel calls. "Can I borrow you?"

Coach nods his approval. *Was this pre-arranged?* I look at the clock and then out at the parking lot. 7:03. Ozzy should be here any minute. I smell like a barn. I wanted to at least rinse off before we went out.

"Sure."

"Caspian, come here," Axel says.

Caspian joins me in the center of the mat. He wears a white rash guard and black spats with BJJ shorts on top. The rest of the fighters crowd around in a semicircle.

"Same thing you were just doing in practice," Axel quietly instructs. "Caspian will go in for the single leg; Rowan, you defend." He turns to the group as we start hand-fighting. "Now, watch what she does when Caspian shoots in for the single leg. See how she pushes down on his head and breaks the grip? You gotta keep your hips low and heavy, crush his head. See? He's got nothing."

Is that Ozzy? I squint in search of the tired beige Corolla that used to belong to Tall Dad. *Is that him?*

Axel leans in. "Now, let's switch. Caspian, you defend." He steps back and motions for us to drill.

Caspian puts his hand on the back of my neck. I push him away, fake a shot. He reacts. I go high, then level change when he's not expecting it and shoot a perfect single leg.

Axel addresses the group. "You see how fast that was? Remember, this is MMA." He pounds his fist into his hand. "If you don't commit to the shot, you're gonna get kneed in the face, and trust me that doesn't feel very good." He points to one of the scars on his forehead.

"I wasn't really defending," Caspian mumbles.

"Yeah, well I wasn't really trying," I reply.

Ozzy pulls into a spot just right of the chin-up bars. I try to wave and tell him I'll be out in a few minutes. But he doesn't see.

"Do you have to go?" Axel asks.

I hesitate.

"Just a few more? As you could tell by that last drill, Cas isn't so good at defending his legs."

Caspian scoffs.

"His first pro fight is against a wrestler."

Ozzy comes in the main door wearing his glasses instead of his contacts. He looks hot in a geeky-artsy way. He wipes his feet in the entry.

"You here for MMA?" Axel calls to him.

Oh my God, no. A rush of heat flushes my cheeks.

"I'm here for her." Ozzy points to me. Everyone stares.

Caspian's expression changes. "Is that your boyfriend?"

I ignore him.

Axel makes an offer. "Give me five more minutes, ten max, and I'll come in early tomorrow and do some striking with you, one-on-one."

I eye the heavy bags.

"That's if you're interested."

I give Ozzy the signal for five more minutes. He acknowledges. "Deal," I reply.

Without even giving me time to get into a proper wrestling stance, Caspian barrels into me. He's fast, but his technique is sloppy and I end up on top. Full mount. He yanks my arm and goes to wrap a leg around my neck. Axel stops him.

"Dude, no submissions. We're just doing takedowns."

Caspian releases and we both scramble to our feet. This time I shoot in on him. He's slow to react, but muscles his way out of the position, and back to standing.

Ozzy watches intently from a side bench, chin in hand. On the last rep, Caspian ends up on top of me, arms wrapped around my head so I can feel the squeeze of his bicep at the base of my skull. My mouth is pressed into his neck. *Is he wearing cologne?*

I taste the scent of a holiday gift pack.

Axel claps his hands. "Okay, grab some water," he shouts, "and everyone say thank you to Rowan for helping us out on leg attacks and single-leg defense."

Everyone mumbles, "Thank you Rowan," except for Caspian who yells, "Thank you, Rowena." *Oh, fuck off.* I grab my water, drink until my stomach bloats, and go to Ozzy.

"Did he just call you Rowena?"

I shake off the question.

"Who is that guy?"

"Just some fighter."

"Since when are you doing MMA?"

"I'm not," I say. "Axel just asked me to demo a few moves."

"Who's Axel?"

"If you'd been around last week, you'd know he's a former UFC champ. Coach is renting him out space." I gesture to the group. "They train here now."

"Those moves didn't look like wrestling moves."

"I'm taking a shower."

Oz puts his hands in his pocket and leans back against the concrete wall.

And that picture didn't look like you and Juliet were just rehearsing your lines.

"I'll be quick."

He grabs my hand and pulls me in for a kiss. Awkward. He never does this in public. *Is anyone watching?*

I hurry to the changeroom and take a shower. I towel off, wrap my hair in a loose bun, and put on my school clothes. Skinny jeans are the worst after practice.

When I come back out, Ozzy paces the lobby. He stops and stares at a picture from last year's Nationals. Me and Coach standing in front of the Wrestling Canada banner, me with a medal on my neck and my hair a disaster because I had to get Ike to braid it, instead of Pia.

Next to it is a picture of Caspian, one of several I haven't had the chance to look at since Axel added his own propaganda to the brag wall. Based on the signage in the background, it was taken at a jiu jitsu tournament. A gold belt is draped over Caspian's shoulder. He is shirtless and scarred, and sporting a ridiculous six-pack. His abs almost look photoshopped. Axel stands beside him in a fighter's stance.

Ozzy grabs my hand. "That guy's a douche."

I sink into the passenger seat of Ozzy's impeccably clean car. Tall Dad's shampooed the upholstery again. Ozzy is quiet.

"What?" I say.

"Nothing it's just … I thought you had an important tournament coming up in New York."

"I do."

"So it seems weird you're taking part in an MMA class."

"I told you: I was just demoing a move." I put on my seat belt. "You know wrestling's a big component of MMA, right?"

He shrugs.

"Well, it is. That's Axel's background. He's an NCAA two-time All-American."

I can tell Ozzy's still irritated. I'm ashamed to admit I enjoy that he's a bit jealous. I was beginning to wonder if he still cared. I change the subject.

"How'd your fitting go?"

He brightens. "I get to wear this sick green velvet vest."

"Since when do you get excited about medieval fashion?" I laugh.

"Row, this is my first *big* production. Trying the costume on today made it real. I love being on stage."

"You sound like Short Dad when he gets a new tool."

"Kind of," he agrees. "Actually, a lot. And it's so much different than hockey. If I missed a shot or had a shitty game, I always felt like I was letting the whole team down. In theater it's the opposite. Everyone's there to build you up."

"K, I'm starving. Let's drive."

"Do you want to just go back to my house? My dads aren't home. They're at some private sale trying to buy up a load of barn boards."

"Yeah, let's do that."

We lock eyes and he runs his hand up my thigh. I don't remember the last time we were *alone* alone. He puts the car in reverse and cranks the steering wheel. Before he switches gears, I notice Caspian in the window, sparring with Axel. He throws an incredible spinning back fist that Axel narrowly blocks.

Ozzy continues to drive with one hand on the wheel, the other on my leg. We barely make it up the driveway before he starts kissing me. Inside, he does a quick check to make sure no dads are down in the workshop or having a drink on the back deck. When it's clear we're alone, we slip into the bedroom. He pushes me into the wall. I wrap a leg around him, and we tumble sideways onto his twin bed. His glasses fall to the floor.

Somewhere in his room a watch ticks. The headboard creaks when he reaches into the drawer of his bedside table. His plaid sheets, smelling of an all-nighter, stretch under my back. His pet goldfish swims back and forth, back and forth, slow and then faster, until an eruption of bubbles races to the surface.

I exhale. Ozzy is heavy on my chest, as Caspian was not an hour ago. Ozzy rolls off me and we stare breathless at the ceiling. He takes my hand. The light flickers.

* * *

Ozzy tosses me a pair of his jogging pants. It's too late for skinny jeans. He cleans up in the bathroom and throws on the clothes he was wearing earlier. I scoop my bra up from the floor. The metal clasp snags on the carpet, and I have to fight to free it.

"Okay, now I'm starving. My dads didn't take anything out for dinner."

I pull my shirt over my head. "What do you feel like?"

"Greek?"

"Sure. There's a new place near Pia's. We can get takeout and go to the park beside the velodrome."

He gets a text, looks at his phone, but doesn't respond. "I'm down with Greek."

Outside, the air is uncharacteristically humid, and Ozzy's hair immediately starts to frizz. He backs down the driveway. I connect my phone to his Bluetooth and play a pandemic playlist we made together last year. I keep the volume low.

"So, what are some of your lines in the play?"

"My lines?" He smiles. "Oh gosh, okay. It's kind of hard to do them without the other actors."

"Who cares about the other actors? Just give me a few lines. Like maybe your favorite lines from the play."

"Okay." Ozzy clears his throat. "Alas, that love, so gentle in his view, should be so tyrannous and rough in proof."

I giggle.

"Did it sound good?"

Better than he sounded in the show's promo that was playing on the school's digital news board. "It was!" I smile. "What kind of accent is that?"

"I don't know." He frowns. "A Shakespeare one?"

"Weren't Romeo and Juliet Italian?"

"Yeah, but ..." His voice trails off.

"It was good, Oz."

He smiles as we pull into the parking lot of the Greek joint. We both order souvlaki and walk over to the velodrome. Ozzy brushes debris from a vacant bench and we tear into our meals. I get tzatziki in my hair. Halfway through my chicken skewer, I freeze.

"What?" Ozzy says.

A kid races by on in-line skates.

"It's him," I reply, cautiously rising from the bench.

"Who?" he asks, alarmed.

"Popcorn."

The dog sniffs a picnic table fifty yards away. Ozzy finishes his pita by tearing it into small strips and then folding them into his mouth.

"Who's Popcorn?

"The dog from the alleyway," I say. "Same one that came to school."

"His name's Popcorn?" Ozzy cleans up our mess, stuffing everything into a fast-food bag.

"Or hers. I'm going to lure it over with my skewer." I edge my way down the bike path and then cut into the green space where the picnic tables are scattered like forgotten toys.

"What are you going to do if you catch it? Tall Dad just cleaned my car. He'll kill me if I put that in it."

"Then I'll walk."

"You don't have a leash."

A family riding bikes in descending sizes crosses in front me. All of them wear yellow helmets.

"Here, Popcorn."

Ozzy tosses our trash into a weathered metal garbage can, the kind you see homeless people setting fires inside, to keep warm. "I don't think that's the same dog."

I spin around. "I'm sure it is."

"The other one limped."

"It's the exact same color."

A stick whizzes by and lands with a light thud at the foot of the picnic table. The dog pounces, secures the stick in its teeth, and wags its bedraggled tail. I halt, chicken skewer dangling from my left hand, and watch as the dog prances back to its owner, a balding man in cargo pants.

"Maybe that's CornPop," Ozzy offers, smiling.

"Not funny," I say. "K, it sort of is."

He pulls me into him and then spins me in the direction of his car, which is parked back across the street.

"I'm sorry, Row. I know you want that dog. Not a hundred percent sure *why*, but …"

"Because I can save it."

We walk in silence, the sun sinking into the neighborhood and casting a pinkish glow across the rooftops. A breeze rustles the leaves. I shiver. Ozzy puts his arm around me, burrowing his face into my neck, and for the moment, everything feels right. The subtle chafe of his stubble below my ear, the warmth of his breath, and the squeeze of his arm around my body.

"I love you," I blurt.

He tucks a section of hair behind my ear. Of course it's the tzatziki piece.

Ozzy laughs. "Love you too."

When we get to the street's edge, he says, "First one to the car gets the leftover skewer," and then he takes off, sprinting across two lanes of traffic, the grassy median, and another two lanes. I take an alternate route. I should lose, but a truck and a kid on a scooter waylay him.

Victoriously, I scramble onto the hood of his car. "I win."

Out of breath, he unlocks the doors and we both collapse into our seats. I feed Ozzy the chicken as he drives, the pandemic playlist and late April air serenading us through the suburbs. When he turns onto my street, I drop the skewer. My heart plunges, and I have to brace myself against the window and the dashboard.

Ozzy slows. I see him gulp. An ambulance is parked in front of my house, red lights clashing with the pink sky. The front door opens and paramedics spill out, my dad — buried in blankets and an oxygen mask — between them. They wheel him down the ramp, my mom on their heels, holding her chest. I can't move my legs.

Ozzy parks half on the lawn and comes around to the passenger side to help me out as Dad is loaded into the back of the ambulance. Metal clanks and the white lights blind. Even from ten feet away I can see Mom's hand tremble as she brings it to her face.

"What happened?" I stammer.

"He choked on a strawberry."

"On a strawberry?" The strawberries I know are the happy ones that dance across little kid pajamas and scratch-n-sniff cards.

"Ike made a smoothie."

Oh my God, Ike. I told him to always use the LIQUEFY setting. The GRIND one leaves chunks.

"Is he going to be okay?"

The female paramedic climbs out of the back. "He's stable," she says with a cautious but kind smile. "Your dad's a strong man."

A strong man? He choked on a fucking strawberry. He's not strong. He's weak because that fucking asshole ALS is killing him. I cry into my hands, but what I want to do is scream. I want to kick the tires, punch the nauseating lights. Ozzy wraps his arms around me, constricting and tight, as Mom climbs into the ambulance.

"Stay with your brother," she says, wiping her eyes. "I'll call when I have an update."

I whisper, "Okay," my face wet with snot and tears.

"I can stay," Ozzy says.

The ambulance pulls away. Neighbors on porches slip back inside their homes, arms folded and faces down.

I shake my head. "I've got to be with Ike."

Ozzy uses the sleeve of his hoodie to wipe my face. "Are you sure, Row? I can stay as long as you need."

I nod. He gets my stuff out of his car and guides me to the front door. I hug him goodbye and go to Ike, who is slumped in the hall, his back against the wall, and his legs splayed. He sobs. I fold in beside him and place my hand on his shaking leg.

"I killed him," he wails.

"You didn't kill him, Ike."

"His face turned blue." He spits.

"Yeah, that happens when someone chokes. But he's okay now."

He cries loud and messy. "I just wanted to make him a smoothie." He elbows the wall behind him and then winces in pain, cradling his arm. "There's nothing I can do. Mom reads to him, you play your matches for him … I thought at least I could make him a smoothie." He looks at me. "And I almost fucking killed him because of it."

I don't ask him what setting he used on the blender. I put my arm around him so his head rests on my shoulder and whisper, "He's going to be okay."

The dishwasher beeps from the kitchen, letting the world know it's completed its cycle. I note the spilled smoothie, a pink cloud, settling into the carpet behind me. I slowly detach myself from my brother and grab some rags from the drawer to sop up the mess.

Ike stops crying and stares catatonically at the wall across from him. I wring the cloth out in the sink. Hints of blueberry stain my fingertips. I don't dare tell him I find another chunk of strawberry. *What the hell was he thinking?*

I violently scrub at the stain until a ghost of it remains, then fall back onto my knees. The tears start all over again. I cry in silence. Larry meows and jumps onto the dining room table. Neither of us tells him to get down.

I carry the soiled rags to the kitchen and dump them into the sink. Down the hall, the dryer chimes. All these domestic reminders that accidents, that death, can happen in the time it takes to wash a load of dishes or dry a pair of underwear.

"He's going to die," Ike says, his voice clear as a boys' choir.

I brace myself on the counter. "Yes," I reply quietly. "He is. But not tonight."

Ike sniffs. I tidy the kitchen. I can't even look at the blender. I throw a dish towel to cover it. There's a knock at the door. Ike and I lock eyes.

"Should we answer it?"

"Who is it?" he replies.

I tiptoe down the hall and peer through the peephole. Beryl stands hunched on the stoop, her goggle-glasses nesting on the top of her head. She wears a long coat and a Band-Aid on her cheek.

"It's Beryl."

"Ask her if she has any cigarettes," Ike says, dead serious.

"I'm not going to do it."

Ike peels himself up off the floor, brushes past me, and opens the door.

Beryl charges in. "Now listen up," she says. "Choking is bad, but it ain't the end of the world and it ain't the end of your dad either. Come here." She gathers us into an awkward three-way hug. She's stronger than her soft, drooping arms suggest.

"I've seen a lot of people get whisked away in an ambulance." Beryl clears her throat and points at Ike. "Some as young as you. It's not easy, but you know what? Life never is." She pulls a bottle out from under her coat. We follow her to the kitchen, where she sets the bottle on the counter and begins rummaging through the cupboards for glasses.

"You got anything other than plastic?" she asks, rifling through a column of stacked Ikea cups.

Ike opens the dishwasher and lines up three juice glasses. They're still hot.

"Open this, will ya?" She holds the bottle up by the neck and hands it to me.

I unscrew the cap and pass it back. "What is it?" I ask, unable to discern the scent wafting from the bottle's lip.

"Is this what you used to give the soldiers?" Ike asks, wide-eyed and sentimental. "The ones that were dying?"

Beryl shakes her head. "This is what we gave the living." She pours a splash into each of the three small glasses. The liquid resembles vanilla extract. "It'll get you through anything." She shoots hers and slams the empty glass back on the countertop. Ike and I exchange glances.

"It's all natural," she assures. "You're not gonna lose a wrestling match over it."

Ike and I pick up our glasses. I sniff mine; he shoots his.

"Tastes like tea," he says.

I down mine. It does take like tea. Herbal and dirty.

"That'll help you sleep tonight," Beryl says. She pats my hand. "Everything's going to be all right."

She exits the kitchen and heads back toward the front door. Before she leaves, she pulls a crumpled pack of cigarettes from her pocket. I look at Ike and then back at Beryl.

"You can't keep giving him smokes, Beryl. It's not good for him. Ike? Come on."

"I don't give them to him," she says, flipping the lid.

Ike withdraws a cigarette.

"See?" she says. "He steals them."

"Last time," I warn.

Beryl shrugs. "You call if you need anything. And Ike, don't forget to pick up my eggs."

Ike sticks the cigarette behind his ear and walks Beryl home. I sit on the doorstep waiting for him to return. There's not a single star in the sky. I check my phone. Hearts from Ozzy. More hearts from Pia. Nothing yet from Mom. Ike traipses back up the wheelchair ramp, the wood creaking beneath his feet.

I stand, turn out the lights, and lock up. We both retreat to our rooms. I climb into bed and stare, unblinking, at the moon.

CHAPTER 11

I wake with a jolt and check my phone. My mother, with her full-sentence texts: *Your dad's doing well. They're going to keep him overnight and run a few tests to make sure there are no internal injuries or damage to his airways.*

The timestamp says 2:13 a.m. It's now just shy of seven.

Do you want me to come get you? I type. She'll need the van to get him home. I jump in the shower and accidentally lather my hair with shaving foam. My eyes burn. I skid on the wet tile and rush back to my room when I hear the phone ring.

"Mom? How is he?"

"He's okay," she says.

There's clatter in the background as if she's standing in an operating room or the hospital cafeteria.

"Sorry," she mumbles, "I was just paying for my coffee."

"Should I come get you?"

"They're going to keep him in for another night. One of the tests showed a bit of an anomaly." She slurps and swallows messily. "They want to be sure before they discharge him."

I do a shoddy job of drying myself off and throw on leggings and a hoodie.

"Stay home if you need to," Mom says.

"I have a unit test in physics. Plus, I'm going to miss a bunch of classes for New York. I'll come visit Dad after school. I'll just worry if I stay home."

"If you think you can manage school, then go for it. Your dad will be happy to see you this afternoon." She takes another noisy sip of coffee. "How's Ike? I've tried texting him, but I assume he's still asleep."

I put on socks and slide down the hall to Ike's room. I turn the doorknob. "Still asleep," I confirm. I don't tell her he has Dad's favorite pillow wrapped tight under his arm. "He's pretty messed up."

"He can't blame himself. It wasn't his fault."

"I know," I say quietly, even though I cannot stop picturing the chunk of strawberry I found on the carpet. "Does this mean Dad needs a feeding tube now?"

My mom sighs. "We're discussing that."

"I love you."

"Love you too, and Row? If school's too much, come home. You don't have to win this. It's not a wrestling match."

I text Pia and ask for a ride. I make a sandwich for Ike, ham, mustard, and a leaning tower of pickles. I leave it in a container in the fridge. He'll be too lost to look after himself when he wakes up. I don't want to imagine what it will be like when the ambulance trip is one-way.

I look like shit and, in an attempt to cover the bags under my eyes, I put on too much makeup. Black eyeliner, thick as a Sharpie, mascara, and ten pounds of concealer. I overfill one of my brows.

Pia texts from the driveway. I madly search for my calculator and shove my books and training gear into my backpack. I don't bother to properly put on my sneakers. I step on the backs and have to scuff down the ramp. If ALS doesn't take him first, my dad will die from watching me *ruin my sneakers*. He hates this habit.

"Wow, your eyes," Pia says when I sink into the car.

"Are they bad?" I knew I went overboard.

"No, you look amazing."

But she's the one that looks amazing. She's reconstructed the pink dress I was supposed to wear to the party and paired it with tidy platform sneakers. She can't do much with her hair with one arm, so she leaves it down and wavy. It shines like a magazine page.

Her tone changes. "Oz said they took your dad by ambulance?"

I tell her the story, texting Ozzy at the same time, with an update.

"But he's going to be okay?" She turns out of my neighborhood.

"I'm going to visit him after school."

Pia knows when I don't want to talk anymore and puts on a terrible song from the nineties that Coach plays and we love to hate. I mouth the words out the window. A pair of Canada geese waddle down the sidewalk in front of the bank as if they've just applied for a mortgage. I smile.

She gestures to the cupholder. "That one's yours," she says pointing to a Starbucks. "I already drank mine. And it's just the way you like it except I added whipped cream. I figured you could use a few comfort calories."

I don't realize how much I need caffeine until I suck back the first creamy gulp. Perfect.

"There's a cookie too," she says. "I knew you wouldn't eat this morning."

The cookie is oatmeal and heart-shaped. I think of what I weighed in at yesterday. Whipped cream is one thing; whipped cream and cookies are another.

"I'll split it with you," Pia offers, noticing my hesitation. She breaks the cookie in half on her lap and hands me a piece. "Coach is going to kill me," she says. "I'm going to be two weight classes heavier by the time I get my cast off. I'm coming to practice tonight, just to use the treadmill."

She pulls into the student parking lot.

"Look, if you need some space or want to get away during class, just text and you can come sit in my car. And here." She roots through her bag. "Packed you this." She hands me a container of chopped vegetables. Carrots, snap peas, celery sticks, cherry tomatoes. No cucumbers. She knows I hate them.

"Thanks, Pia."

She places her hand on the door and takes a deep breath. "K, I need to go make Ahmed Amari love me."

"Isn't he not allowed to date?"

"Exactly, and technically neither am I. It will 'distract me from my schoolwork.'" She winks and we head into the school as the bell rings.

I suffer through first period. Mr. Williams makes us meditate before assigning a concept web on social globalization. I focus on physics instead: *what is the gravitational field strength of planet Earth at the International Space Station?*

I breeze through my physics unit test in period two, but as soon as I hand it in, I notice Ms. Foy lingering outside the door. My physics teacher motions for me to go. *Why? I don't need a counseling session right now. I need a distraction. I need multiple distractions.* I gather my stuff and exit the class.

"You didn't rush on my behalf, I hope," Ms. Foy says.

"I was finished."

"Good. Walk and talk?"

Oh my God. Who sent her? Did Dad have some sort of relapse? My heart races and I scramble to find my phone. Mom's sent a pic of her and my dad. He's hooked up to IV. There's color in his face. I exhale.

"Your mom called," Ms. Foy says. "She thought I should check in on you after what happened last night." She leads me to her office. A sullen looking police officer occupies one of the chairs in the waiting room. I wonder if he's here as a member of law enforcement, or as a dad.

Ms. Foy closes the door behind her. "You know, seeing a loved one being taken away by ambulance can be a traumatic experience. It may take you some time to process your emotions around that."

"But he's okay," I reply.

"I know." Ms. Foy offers her signature sympathy smile. "Just be gentle with yourself, Rowan. It's okay to take a day off here and there. You don't always have to be working."

"What if working is how I cope? Is that wrong?"

"Not at all," she says, extending her hand.

I'm getting triggered. I don't want her to touch me. Why does everyone think there's something wrong with how I choose to handle things? *Be GENTLE with myself? What the hell does that even mean? That's Ike, not me.* I take a deep breath.

"Thanks, Ms. Foy. But I'm feeling pretty stable right now. I don't need to take time off. If that changes, I'll let you know."

"Your mom was concerned you might not have brought lunch. If that's the case, feel free to see Mr. Gerard. He'll hook you up."

He'll "hook me up?" Fuuuucccckkkk.

"Pia already 'hooked me up,'" I say, knocking the container in my backpack.

"Great," she replies. "Okay, then if you're feeling good, then I guess we catch up later. And I got those classes changed," she adds. "You're all set for grade twelve."

"Thanks."

I can't get out of her office fast enough. Ozzy and I have a quiet lunch on the edge of the football field. He tells me I look pretty in my garish makeup. I half-sleep through my afternoon classes. As soon as the bell rings, I skip my locker and head straight for the train. The hospital requires a transfer to the north line at the downtown junction. I text my mom when I arrive.

Seventh floor, she instructs. *Meet you at the elevators.*

I press the arrow UP button and file into the elevator with half a dozen orderlies and a man with a foil balloon tied to his wheelchair. I'm the last to get off. Mom is there when the doors jerk open. She looks ten years older than she did yesterday. She hugs me.

"They're just adjusting his meds," she says. "We'll go in in a minute."

She leads me to a family waiting area with blue vinyl chairs and fake jungle plants. The carpet looks like something you'd find in a Vegas hotel. There's a snack bar with dry muffins and ice water.

"Help yourself," she says.

I fill my water bottle and stare through the open door down the hallway.

"What's that?" I ask

Mom leans forward in her chair. She smiles. "That's Bitzy."

"Bitzy?"

"She's a therapy dog. There are two on this floor. You should see the other one. It's an ornery old dachshund named Stu."

Bitzy's a golden retriever. She and her trainer wear matching maroon vests the color of the hospital's logo.

"Can I see her?"

"It looks like she's about to go on her rounds, but you can ask."

I speed walk down the hallway with the urgency I once used to stalk Buzz Lightyear all over Disneyland. I think Dad finally had to pay someone to get me an autograph and a picture with him.

"Can I pet her?" I blurt just as the trainer's about to press the oversized square button to gain entrance to whatever unit they were scheduled to visit.

The trainer turns around. She looks mildly startled as if she's not able to reconcile my childish plea with my party makeup.

"Sure," she says. Her smile is warm. "Sit, Bitzy."

Bitzy obeys. I let her sniff my hand. She nuzzles my face. Her brown eyes remind me of Ozzy's. The trainer is patient and doesn't pull away when I know I've probably abused my time limit. There are actual patients they've come to visit. I thank her as they slip behind the double doors.

I watch from the narrow window. They stop at a stretcher parked in the hallway. A man, no older than my dad, lies partially reclined, his eyes fixed on the stucco-style ceiling tiles above him. When I assume he's sensed Bitzy's presence, he drops a crippled hand through the metal bars of his bed prison. Bitzy licks his hand and then pokes her nose through the stretcher's safety railings. I stare at the man's face. It fills with light.

"Excuse me," a nurse barks gruffly behind me. Her body language is hard and her face sags. I move out of the way as she admits herself to the wing and catch a trace of Bitzy's blond tail as she disappears inside a room. The sign above the access button reads: PALLIATIVE CARE. I find my mom back in the waiting area, picking at a muffin.

"We can go see your dad now."

"What's palliative care?" I ask.

"It's where people receive end-of-life treatment," Mom says, clearing her throat.

"You mean where people go to die?"

"Yeah," she whispers.

She takes my hand and leads me down another corridor, away from the palliative care wing, to room seven-fifteen. My dad looks identical to the man in the hallway, his bed reclined at the same angle, bedding rumpled around his chest, except my dad has a ventilator.

"He can't breathe?" I ask. No one thought twice about ventilators until the pandemic caused worldwide shortages of them, and then when someone got put on one you knew there was a good chance they were going to die.

"He can breathe on his own," my mom assures. "The ventilator will just take some stress off his respiratory system."

"Hi, Dad." I bend to kiss his forehead. His eyes are closed but the twitch in his shoulder indicates he knows I'm here. "Killed my physics test today," I say knowing that next to wrestling, academic success is what my father lives for. "Hurry up and get out of here," I ramble on. "I have a tournament on Friday. It's just a local one, nothing too exciting, but I'll probably get at least two good matches. Maybe three. Coach said I'd probably double-bracket, depending on how many people register. I need you there."

He blinks. I don't let myself cry. I kiss him again. "You just made a promise," I say. I imagine he smiles. My mom fixes his blankets. She's become an expert at blanket fixing and pillow fluffing. Comfort is the new love language.

I study my dad's hands. They look off, the way hands do when inserted incorrectly into gloves. One finger dangling, two others jammed into a single finger slot. "Do the dogs ever visit this wing?" I ask.

"I don't know," my mom says. "It was late when we were admitted and assigned a room." She rests her head beside my dad's. "Are you training tonight?"

"Yeah." I check my phone. "I'll probably go in a bit early. Pia needs help," I lie.

"Don't overdo it."

"Can you braid my hair?"

My mom weaves my hair into matching French braids. I tie them off at the nape of my neck and remember the time Dad tried to braid my hair for a tournament and he basically just knotted sections together like he was building a tarp shelter with cordage. It took me a day to untangle.

I check the transit app on my phone. "I should leave now," I say. "Any later and I'll have to wait for the second bus to the gym." I hug both my parents and head down the hall toward the elevator. When the door opens, an overweight dachshund with a terrible groom lumbers out. I hope he's on his way to visit my dad.

CHAPTER 12

Axel's cleaning the mats when I get to the gym.

"Rowan," he says, "watch your step. Of all the things the UFC taught me, mopping isn't one of them. Look at this thing." He gestures. "It's like pushing around a welterweight."

I smile and then frown. There are literal puddles all over the mat. "That thing's ancient," I say. "There's a better mop in Coach's office. I'll grab it."

There's a note on Coach's desk. *ROWAN NO PRACTICE.* The *no practice* part is circled in exaggerated black pen. I find the mop in its usual spot and bring it to Axel.

"Is Coach here?" I ask.

"He was earlier. He picked up a bunch of scoreboards and timers. He was dropping them off somewhere and then coming back." He mops a pool of soapy water. "Much better. Why don't you go wrap up and we'll get some striking in?"

No practice. The hell does that mean? I fish through the crate of hand wraps, select a dingy red pair, and lock up my wrists. I sort through the bucket of gloves trying to find a match. They smell like Ozzy's hockey gear.

"No, no," Axel says. "Those ones there."

I follow the tip of the mop he uses as a pointer. A pair of rose gold gloves lies palms up on a plyo box. I'm almost embarrassed by the thrill that surges from my chest into my face. This is my Christmas morning.

"Don't get too excited. They're limited edition. I can't guarantee the boys won't be fighting you for them." He winks.

I peel back the Velcro and slide my left hand inside, opening and closing my fingers. I make a fist. Perfect. I tighten the wrist strap and put on the other. Axel wheels the bucket and mop to the storage room. "Run a few laps and get warm," he says.

I jog, swinging my arms. My shoulders and lats burned after the heavy bag workout the other day, and that only lasted ten minutes. I'm surprised when Axel straps a body protector around his waist. His coach mitts are white.

"You ready?" he asks.

I nod. He corrects my stance and demos a basic one-two, something I've done before.

"No pivot on the jab. That's your longest and fastest punch. Come straight to me."

I exhale sharply every time I throw.

"Your cross is good, just don't let your head lean past your front knee. Ten more times, let's go."

By five, Axel starts to move, and I have to adjust.

"Keep your stance, Rowan," he says, counting me down.

My heart's on fire. He lets me catch my breath and then adds a left hook to the body.

"Whoa, whoa, that's a wild punch," he says referring to my hook. "You gotta keep your range of motion contained. Tight and explosive. Like this." He demos the combo, but I watch his eyes. They are as intense as they were in the countless UFC clips and highlights I pored over. My dad's eyes when he was first diagnosed and was determined he would win against an opponent with a perfect record.

I correct my hook. We keep the combo but alternate between the body and the head. I take a break and he adds a right upper.

"Keep it compact," he says after I throw a loose uppercut. "You got to recover your stance quickly."

Every shot is exhausting. Every shot is exhilarating.

"How are you feeling?" he asks. "Ready to add some kicks?"

I pace the mat, trying to lower my heart rate.

"Get some water," Axel says.

He shadowboxes when I go to the fountain. I eye the wall clock. I've only been at it for twenty minutes. I'm going to die. Water drips down my chin. I wipe my face on my bicep. One more round and I'll have finished the equivalent of a title fight that went the distance. My muscles twitch.

When I return to center, Axel says, "I want to see a little more movement. Light on your toes."

He gets into his stance. I follow.

"Last round for the day. This time I want you to go for the knockout. It's about power. Okay?" He focuses in on me like the pre-bout weigh-in stare down. A challenge. "Okay?" he repeats.

"Got it."

We start sparring. I throw a few decent combos, but fuck up a roundhouse.

"We didn't get to that," he says, adjusting his body protector. "Stick to punches for now."

I square up and throw a one-two-three-two, jab, cross, hook, cross.

"Good," he says, "but keep the energy consistent throughout. No sense throwing that last cross if it's gonna be half-power. Go again."

My body starts to fatigue and with it, my brain. I switch my stance and throw a punch that's neither a jab nor a hook. It's somewhere in between. Purgatory. I drool.

"Focus, Rowan. Last round."

I throw a shoddy upper.

"Nope," he says. "Can't drop your guard like that. Come on, finish it."

I inhale and line up again in my proper stance. I can't even feel my feet inside my wrestling boots. Can't feel my identity. I feel void. A machine on an assembly line. Focus.

He whispers through gritted teeth and dark eyes. "Think of something unfair and Finish. This. Fight."

I ingest his words. They go down like some toxic elixir. Whatever that shit was Beryl gave us to drink after they took Dad in the ambulance. I throw a one-two.

"Come on," Axel urges.

I think of how only four summers ago my dad finished his first Ironman. Jab, cross, knee to the body. I remember the day his fancy new wheelchair showed up at the house. The eerie resemblance it shared to an electric chair. Hook. Upper. I remember only months ago when he lost his speech. The Tuesday morning he stopped speaking. Jab, cross, hook. And then I stop remembering. I am in the present.

"Let's go, Rowan. Finish this fight."

I raise my fists.

"What's going through your head?"

"My." Jab. "Dad's." Cross. "Going." Hook. "To." Upper. "Die."

I collapse to my knees and break. Emotions I didn't even know I had spill out of me and flood the mat. I can't control my volume. I start to crawl, looking for an escape. Axel's coach pads bounce off the floor in succession. He drops, and I feel his hand on my back. Everything seems out of place.

"What the hell's going on here?"

Coach.

I roll onto my back, sobbing, concealing my face with my gloves.

"Axel?" Coach says. "The hell's going on with my wrestler?"

I feel Coach hover over me, his presence heavy. He puts a hand on my knee and then finds some old-man strength to scoop me up off the floor and carry me off the mat like a baby. It's humiliating. It's compassionate. It's Coach.

He sets me down on a bench. I recover enough to make sure no one else is around. Caspian stands paralyzed at the front door. *For fuck's sake.* Coach rips open the Velcro securing my gloves to my wrists and yanks them off.

He yells across the room at Caspian, "Get her some water."

Caspian bolts into action, dumps his bag, snatches a bottle from the lobby fridge, and brings it over. I drink half. Coach pats me on the back.

"Take off those wraps and clean yourself up."

I ignore Caspian's gaze, even though it's sympathetic. When my legs feel strong enough to support my weight, I stand and drag myself to the changeroom. I lean over the gas-station porcelain sink and stare at my reflection in the mirror. All that extra makeup. My face is a horror show.

"Oh my God, what just happened?" Pia stands in the doorway, sneakers dangling from her unbroken arm. "Coach is freaking out out there."

"What's he saying?" I wipe my face with the shitty brown paper towel that shreds on contact.

"You're not supposed to practice today."

ROWAN NO PRACTICE. I sigh. "Since when?"

"Since your mom called."

"Why does she do that? I told her I wanted to train."

Pia digs a shirt out of her bag and runs it under the water. She wipes my face properly. "Your mom's just worried about you."

"If she's worried about me, she should know by now that this is how I choose to deal with things." I slide from the sink to the wall to the floor. Pia squats down across from me.

"Cut her some slack, hey?" She touches my knee with the affection of a kindergarten teacher. A best friend. "Maybe this is *her* way of coping. She can't save your dad, but she can try to save you."

She sounds like Ms. Foy. She sounds right.

"How are you so smart?"

She smiles. "My dad would say it came from him."

He would. We laugh.

Pia gestures toward the door. "Who is that guy out there anyway?"

"Caspian?"

"Hot guy. Dirty blond hair, nice abs, looks like he might've got hit by a train in a past life?"

"Yeah, Caspian. One of Axel's *prospects*."

"At least he's someone's prospect. Is he single?"

"No idea. I trained with him the other day."

She smacks me with her cast. "You never told me that!"

"We just drilled some single legs."

"Is he nice?"

"Enough. He's really strong."

Pia slips on her sneakers. I lean forward to tie them. "You gonna practice then?"

"If Coach'll let me."

She hauls me up off the floor and we go back inside. "He will."

* * *

Coach makes me phone my mom before he lets me train. She and Ike are eating dinner at a restaurant across the street from the hospital when I call. She gives in easily, apologizing for meddling.

"How's Ike?" I ask.

She turns the question on him. "Your sister wants to know how you're doing."

He takes the phone. "Dad wrote a story on his device." Ike's voice is optimistic. "He's actually quite funny."

"He was always funny," Mom says in the background.

"Thanks for the sandwich."

"You're welcome. Can you hand the phone back to Mom?" A muffled exchange. "Are you staying the night at the hospital?"

"No," Mom replies. "I have a possession tomorrow. Ike and I will go back for another visit after dinner, and then we'll head home."

"K. I'll see you after practice."

I tuck my phone into my bag and melt into the warm-up. I can barely circle my arms. From the sidelines Axel mouths, *Are you okay*? I give him a thumbs-up when I run by. It was probably not the smoothest way for him to learn about my father. In fact, I think it's the first time I said the words out loud. *My dad's going to die.*

We work inside leg trips for the first half of practice. I get taken down way more than normal, my reaction time doubled. I am torturously slow. Coach's face turns red but he doesn't say anything. Then, after only three rounds of live wrestling, he sends me home early. I don't argue. I can barely form a sentence, let alone a leg attack.

"Get some rest," he says. He looks like he might add something more, but he stops himself. He can't yell at me after what happened earlier.

Pia offers me a ride home, but I take the bus. There's something soothing about throwing on headphones, resting your head against the window, and watching the world go by on mute. Strangers hauling groceries, drivers making deliveries, mothers walking babies. No pressure to talk, total permission to be anonymous.

I walk the block to the bus stop, past the alleyway where I first met Popcorn. Empty. The 305 pulls up minutes later, and I sit in the back. I'm nearly lulled to sleep by the rhythmic sway and jerk of the bus as it struggles to keep pace with the fading traffic.

Mom and Ike are just pulling in the driveway when I turn onto our street. I help them bring in a few groceries. All of us look like we just got off a transcontinental flight. Faces sallow, hair disheveled, clothing rumpled.

"Did you get any dinner?" Mom asks. She sprawls on the living room couch, groceries at her feet.

"I'll just make noodles or something," I say.

"Why don't you have a nice relaxing bath?"

This is my mom projecting. *She* wants a nice relaxing bath, though I must admit the idea of floating in bubbles right now sounds appealing, and I have a stockpile of bath bombs disintegrating in my bedroom.

"Will you play with me?" Ike stands in the doorway, palming his basketball. "Please?"

Physical activity is the last thing I want to do right now, but he looks so pathetic.

"I'll play for fifteen minutes," I say, scrounging through the grocery bags for something quick. Pizza Pops, cheese buns, Double Stuf Oreos, frozen jalapeno poppers. "Mom, did you even go into the store?"

"Huh?"

I hold up a box of Cinnamon Toast Crunch. "Did you buy all this?"

"I sent Ike in with my card," she replies. "Is it that bad?"

"Let's just say he bought the food group that's usually crossed out with the giant red X."

Ike smiles and spins the ball on his finger.

"Sorry," she mumbles. "I'll do a proper shop tomorrow."

I pick at a cheese bun and follow Ike onto the driveway. We play an easy game of one-on-one. My shots are off, everything hitting the backboard at precisely the wrong angle. Ike's tongue hangs out every time he goes in for a layup. Something Dad used to do whenever he was concentrating on some finite task: assembling a barbecue or fixing a racket. Beryl watches us from her window.

We play until the sun starts to drip and the air cools. We lose the ball when I jump to block one of Ike's shots. The ball rolls across the street to the neighbor's. Ike leaves to fetch it and I head back inside. A bowl of cheap ramen is on the kitchen counter.

"Thanks, Mom," I shout.

I carry the bowl down the hall and draw a bath, setting the tray Ike made in shop class across the tub. I pick a bath bomb shaped like a rocket and drop it in the water. It fizzes Florida green. I sink into the tub, careful not to get my phone wet, and FaceTime Ozzy. He's in the middle of a math assignment. Short Dad tells him to get off the phone and finish his work. Shakespeare is making him fall behind.

So … Pia texts. Caspian was asking about you.

In what way? I type.

I heard him asking Axel if you were okay.

How thoughtful.

Then one of the other guys was like "who's Rowena?"

He called me Rowena?

Yeah, but that's not the important part. He replies "the hot wrestler."

The hot wrestler? lol maybe that can be my new insta handle.

I think it's cute. Not the name, but the fact that he said it and that he was worried about you.

Because I had a full-blown, celebrity-grade breakdown on the mat.

He probably also thinks lower back tattoos and cosplay girls are hot.

Anyway, I'm coming to watch tomorrow. So jealous I can't wrestle.

I send her a string of emojis, hang over the side of the tub, and slide my phone away from the splash zone. I draw in a breath and slip beneath the water. Tomorrow, I need to focus on wrestling. I'll spend all day running technique through my head. I won't be able to eat. I'll warm up alone and fantasize about winning in New York and being anything but anonymous. I exhale.

CHAPTER 13

I hate Friday tournaments. I don't intentionally skip break-fast, but I can't eat. Every time I bring food to my lips, I gag. A smoothie is a viable solution, but I still can't look at the blender after Dad's choking. The base remains covered in dish towels on the kitchen counter like a piece of censored artwork.

Mom leaves the house early to deal with a possession, no lon-ger looking like a jet-lagged tourist. She'll pick Dad up from the hospital on the way home. I take the car to school and nearly rear-end a Jeep.

"Chill on the gas," Ike says, head slamming against the backrest.

I can't. Adrenaline has me driving like a NASCAR rookie, fast and foolish. Fridays are early dismissal days at school, and I turn into an ADHD kid, fidgeting, squirming. Mr. Williams lets me pace the back of the classroom to expel some of my nervous energy. I skip physics and break and spend all of periods three and four mind mapping offense from the two-on-one. When my LA teacher asks me a question about *The Invisible Man* I blurt, "Front head pinch."

When the final bell rings, I hurry to my locker. Ozzy's left a note with a little gift bag. *Kick some ass*, it reads. Inside, I find a new pair of socks and a bag of gummy worms. I smile. It's not the first time he's given me socks before a tournament. It's ridiculous and romantic. This pair is blue and features cats in singlets. I have no idea where he finds them.

The tournament is at the university. Traffic is a shit show. I have to park in a seedy area off campus beside a dry cleaner and the kind of pub that probably regularly gets shut down by the health department. I cut through the science building and take the underground pedway to the rec center. Four mats are set up inside the indoor track. New York will have twenty. Runners with bodies designed for endurance circle the track.

Coach hunches over a scorekeeping table by Mat B. I hope he's not still mad at me. He's the one who suggested boxing as a suitable cross-training option. *Please don't be mad at me.* "Hey, Coach."

He looks up from the bout sheet he's studying.

"Rowan," he acknowledges. "You got some rest?"

I nod.

"Have you eaten?"

I hesitate.

"We've been through this. You can't be explosive on an empty stomach. Go eat something."

Rows of mobile stadium seats have been wheeled into place. I climb to the middle, flip down a maroon vinyl chair, and dig through my bag. I alternate sips of yellow Gatorade with Double Stuf Oreos and carrot sticks. I can't stomach the congealed boiled chicken thighs my mom has packed, but I gag down half of one and chase it with water.

I pull on my Beats, rose gold like the gloves Axel lent me, and pick a Spotify playlist. I check my phone. Mom wants to know when the actual competition starts. My parents don't have to come early now. When the other spectators see my dad holed up in his chair like a war vet, they make space. He gets a front-row seat wherever he goes.

Pia gets roped into timekeeping. I watch her get instruction from an official as wrestlers begin to pour in by the busload. I see one of my opponents. She's quiet. A thrower. Never smiles. Skin like a country road, pockmarked and rough. Focus. Snap down, front head pinch.

I reply to my mom and text Ozzy. *Do u know if you'll make it?*

Probably not, he replies. *We haven't even started Act 1. There was something wrong with the soundboard. Good luck.* He sends hearts and biceps and trophies.

Focus. Arm drag, rip-by, throw.

Wrestlers converge on the mats for warm-up. Braids and ponytails with split ends whip around. Teammates and training partners tie up and mock wrestle. Pia makes a sad face from the scorekeeping table, sorry she can't help. My stomach cartwheels.

I jog a few laps, trying to ignore the stiffness in my shoulders and lats. Striking aches. I work through a number of movement patterns as an official tapes the bout sheets to the wall. A crowd of wrestlers flock to it. Coach has trained me not to look. *You have to beat them all to win anyway, so who cares who you have to wrestle first?* I at least like to know how many are in my bracket. Pia knows this. She slips away from the table and returns to flash me the number five. Round-robin. I'll have four matches.

When I turn around, Coach is there. "You eat?"

"I did."

"You ready?"

"I am."

He thumps my upper back — his version of a hug — and gives my shoulders a quick rub with his meaty hands. "Work your fakes," he says. "I wanna see a nice wrestling stance, lots of fakes, and then explosive shots." He demos. "Don't be afraid to take a few risks. Match six on Mat A. Go win."

Leo, dressed in black, waves at me from outside the officials' room. Red and blue bands are secured to his wrists. He's refereeing on Mat C. I acknowledge him, and he gestures the setup for the shoulder throw we were working in practice.

The tournament organizer calls all wrestlers to the mat. He goes over the rules, the illegal moves, all of the usual sportsmanship stuff, and gives a five-minute warning. I put my headphones back on and pace the perimeter of Mat A. Just before the first match is called, I see my mom barreling through the far doors like she's trying to get my dad to the finish line. She's still in her work clothes but without the grace of this morning. She walks like her high heels are construction boots and nearly twists an ankle.

I draw the letter A with my finger and point to the red mat. She brushes a rogue hair from her face and wheels Dad over. Even if Dad could, both of them know not to approach. Focus.

"Rowan Harper from Team Takedown and Chelsea Freeman from Dynamos," the ref calls.

I strip off my hoodie, remove my headphones, and step onto the mat. Ike saunters in the gym with a cheeseburger. Coach parks himself on the edge of a metal chair in my corner. He communicates with hand signals. The ref does a quick skin and nail check on both my opponent and me before we shake hands. He blows the whistle.

Chelsea's black mouth guard bulges between her lips. Her stance is high. She shoots. I sprawl on her head, circle, and take her back for two points.

"Leg lace," Coach shouts.

I get her up on the table and set up the move. After three successful turns and six points, Coach hollers, "No more."

The ref stands us up. Whistle. Shoulder throw to pin. Match. My arm is raised. I shake the other coach's hand and glance at my dad. He looks like he might float to the rafters. I smile and go to Coach. He slaps my back. "Good commitment on the throw. You're up again in fifteen."

I drink some water. Getting through the first match is always the toughest. It's hard to break the seal. I watch a few matches and then resume my routine of pacing, visualizing, panicking, drinking too much water, wishing I hadn't drunk too much water, and skipping through my playlist to find the right song.

Before I know it, I'm up in two. I don't see Coach. Sometimes he deliberately stays out of my corner. He doesn't want me to get comfortable with him always calling the shots. *So much of wrestling*, he always says, *is instinct. You can't hone that if I'm always standing there telling you what to do.*

I've wrestled my next opponent before. Her club focuses more on recreation than competition and I make quick work of the match. Sweep single, drive, back trip. She manages to fight her way to her stomach. I set up a Japanese leg ride. She curses under her breath. I make myself heavier. She groans. I switch positions and get a cradle. Pin. Two down, two to go.

After the match, I scan the crowd for Ozzy. I know he's not coming. Sometimes his dads come to watch, but today they're on a jobsite west of the city, building some custom monstrosity on a man-made lake. Ozzy had to send pictures of the design because it was too extravagant for him to describe.

I check the bout sheet for my next match. Mom comes up beside me and peels a hair off my singlet.

"You look good out there, Row. I don't know, like extra tough or something. Your dad's having a blast."

I glance back at my dad. He's in a reclined position, head back and legs extended, like he's about to have dental surgery. Ike scrolls through his phone beside him.

"He loves watching you wrestle," she says. "They both do."

I'm not sure about Ike, but she's right about my dad.

"K, I gotta go."

"Good luck."

I head back to Mat A. Shit, I'm already up next. Thrower has already pulled off her slouchy jogging pants and tossed her earbuds. Still no smile. She fidgets with her mouth guard as her coach, a short man with a rusty moustache and portly limbs, gives her last minute instructions.

The ref calls us to the mat. I blast a few tuck jumps to get my legs going and then drop deep into my stance. I channel Axel from his early UFC fights and stare into my opponent's eyes like I'm trying to exorcise her earliest childhood memories.

Whistle. She grabs my wrist and tries for a two-on-one. I break her grip, square up, and snap her down. Front head pinch. Caspian. Pause. *The guillotine drill.* Oh fuck, I'm on my knees. I can't get back to my feet. We get into a scramble. She takes my back but I'm able to reverse the position. Two-two. *Where's Coach?* Not in my corner. Thank God.

The ref stands us up, and we're back at it. This time *I* take the two-on-one, jack her up and walk her to the edge of the mat.

When I feel her push against me with the right force, I rip her down. She lands on her face and makes a noise like the wind's been knocked clear of her lungs. From the corner of my eye, I see Leo on Mat C nod. *I need to get the hell out of this match.* I get her into a quick pin. The ref slams his hand against the mat and then raises my arm in victory.

I make eyes at Pia. She saw me screw up. At least Coach didn't. I grab my hoodie and water bottle from beside the score table. There's a drop of blood on my wrestling boot. I bend to wipe it off with a bit of spit. When I stand back up, Coach is there like a fat avenger.

"What the hell was that?" he asks, face redder than a gas station hotdog. "You did a beautiful snap down, got her in front head position, and then you stopped." He throws up his hands. "You can't hesitate," he continues. "You do that in New York, you're gonna get taken down. What was going through your head?"

What was going through my head was that I had the perfect position to choke her out. "I don't know, I was just overthinking it."

"Well, don't. Wrestle with your body. You get the position, you do the move. Don't hesitate. You understand?"

"Yes, Coach."

"Give me two four-point throws and whatever else you want for two. Let's get a tech in this last match."

I nod and he storms off to the coaches' lounge. He'll probably stress-eat half a pizza. Once he ate six donuts when I lost an easy opening match. I go to the bathroom and check my phone. Ozzy's sent me a pic of him partially costumed. His green vest looks itchy. I message back asking if he'll have a hat to go with it. *Didn't they all wear floppy hats back then?*

My last match is anticlimactic. I do as Coach instructed, and get the 10-0 win in less than a minute. My opponent cries. Because it's a small tournament, there's no elaborate medal ceremony. No podium, no pictures. In fact, the medals look like they were forged in someone's basement. I string my gold over my dad's neck. He types on his device: *I'm proud of you, Peach.*

Peach. He hasn't called me that in years. It almost takes me out at the knees. I stumble. He used to say it when we did yard work together. A memory of him and me raking together in tandem floods my limbs. He never got mad when I pressed too hard and ripped out chunks of lawn.

"Thanks," I quietly reply.

"You okay?" Mom asks. "You won!"

"Yeah, I'm good," I say, still picturing our old backyard with the slanted swing set and the heady sunflowers and piles of leaves Dad would bury me in. *Peach.*

"Well, should we go somewhere to celebrate?"

Ike wanders into the conversation. "Can you drive me to Enzo's?"

"I have to stay," I reply. "I have to clean the mats and help set up for tomorrow. If I'm really hungry, I'll pick something up on the way home."

"Okay. Text me when you're on your way."

Ike spins Dad is in his chair, tipping him like he's a passenger in a wheelbarrow. It looks sort of horrifying from afar, but it's something they've done from the beginning. If there were wheelchair roller derby, they'd join and win.

I watch my family zigzag across the gym and out the double doors.

Coach tidies the scorekeeping tables with a slice of pizza in his hand. I find Leo and Pia in the officials' room. Leo offers a fist bump. "Nice rip down," he says. "Her face bounced off the mat."

"Thanks, I know. I felt kind of bad after. What time do you start tomorrow?"

"Nine." Leo yawns.

Pia hugs me. She's made an Adidas sleeve for her cast. Three stripes and probably ten thousand likes.

"Anyone know where the mop is?" I ask.

Leo takes off his wristbands and whistle and dumps them into a plastic bin.

"The guy with the beard went to get it. See you guys tomorrow. Good job, Row," he says before checking out.

"Want me to drive you tomorrow?" Pia asks. "We have to be here by eight thirty."

"Ugh, yes."

"I'll pick you up early and we can go to that bakery that makes those freakish cinnamon buns. Or we could just hit up Starbucks."

"Sounds good."

A hand and a mop appear in the doorway.

"Got it."

"I'm out," Pia says, sliding off the desk she's been sitting on. "I'll text you bright and early."

I wring the dirty mop in the bucket and start on Mat B. The guy with the beard is already halfway finished Mat A. Coach gathers abandoned water bottles and a mouth guard, whistling as he transfers them to the garbage and recycling bins.

Bearded guy is quicker than me. By the time I finish cleaning

Mat B, he's almost done the last one. He takes my mop and bucket. "I got it from here."

I wave goodbye to Coach, grab my backpack from the stands, and change out of my wrestling boots into sneakers. The pedway to the science building is locked, so I have to go outdoors. The air is cool, and the campus floodlights cast a bluish glow. A couple holding hands walks in front of me. The guy is built like Ozzy. *What college excels at women's wrestling and theater arts?* I suspect we'll have to shift our plans from the Midwest to the east coast. Maybe we'll end up in New York together, lining up for last-minute Broadway tickets and spending the weekend riding the Cyclone on Coney Island. Screw Jack in the Box. We'll be dining on lobster rolls and funnel cakes.

I turn off campus toward where I parked. I see the faded blue sign for the dry cleaner. The smell of deep fryer and malt or barley or whatever the hell it is they put in beer wafts from the pub. A figure stumbles from a doorway three buildings up. He is hunched, his hood tucked up over his head. He moves swiftly in my direction. I can hear his labored breathing. I see my car. I debate whether to step off the sidewalk and move onto the road, but he is closing in and the cars lining the street are parked tight. I'd have to roll over the trunk like a thug in an action movie.

I make my body small so he might pass without touching. Under my sleeves, I make fists. He is less than ten feet away now, hulking. Light from a closed textile shop trickles onto the sidewalk, illuminating gum stains and debris. Blood. I look up. A stream drips from the stranger's nose.

"Caspian?"

He lifts his face, hand cupped below his nose, nostrils flared. There's a gash over his left eye, bisecting a previous scar. There's so much blood I can't make out the graphic on his T-shirt. I slither out of my backpack and pull out a towel, used and damp, probably from last week. I hold it up to his face. He staggers back and partially sits on the hood of a black Honda.

"What the hell happened to you?" I ask.

It occurs to me that if he was jumped, his assailant could still be in the area. I do a quick scan of the street while applying pressure to his face.

He goes to speak but offers a wave instead. Like it's no big deal. I dig through my bag for a package of wipes. There's a cut on his knuckle. His shorts are ripped. *Why is he wearing shorts?*

I clean what I can of his wounds with the baby wipes. His hand shakes when I get to his split knuckle. *Damn.*

"What happened?"

"Just a … an accident. At work." He gestures toward the pub.

"You work at a pub?" *How old is he?*

"Dishwasher."

"And what, you got jumped by a dinner plate?" I pull the shirt away from his nose to see if it's still bleeding. "I hope you get danger pay."

A drop of blood soaks into the pavement. I rummage through my pockets and find an old napkin. "Here, put this on your forehead."

His breathing settles. With the bleeding mostly contained, he leans his head back and stares into a streetlight. His green eyes look more beautiful set against the wasteland that is currently his face.

I examine the cut over his eye. "I think you might need stitches. Can I take you to the hospital or something?"

"No hospital. I'm fine." He gestures to his forehead. "That always splits open."

"Then can I give you a ride home?" I don't even know where *home* is.

"Please," he replies, pushing off the car.

I say, "I'm just up here," and rezip my backpack. Caspian follows behind. *Frig, I hope he doesn't bleed on my seat.* I open the doors and he plunks inside, adjusting his own backpack onto his lap. One of Ike's basketball shirts is in the back seat.

"Here, put this on."

He doesn't argue, just pulls off his bloody shirt and stuffs it in his bag. His chest is red. A bruise is forming below his rib cage. His six-pack remains perfectly intact. He slides Ike's shirt over his head. "Thanks, Rowena."

Oh my God. Stop calling me that.

I start the car. "Where am I going?"

"You know Father Garth Weedon arena?"

"Yep."

"I live near there."

No one lives near there. Do they? I pull out and head north. I've watched Ozzy play hockey there a hundred times. Tall Dad was always scared of that rink and would triple-check that he'd locked the car doors.

"Are you going to tell me what happened?"

Caspian sighs. "If I tell you, do you promise not to tell anyone?"

I hesitate, wondering if I'm somehow going to end up in jail after this. "I promise."

"So, the pub I work at has a basement."

Oh, fuck. Here we go.

"And some Friday nights we host fights."

"What kind of fights?"

He glares at me. "Oh, Rowena, what kind of fights do you think?"

"It's Rowan."

"I said that."

"Illegal ones?"

"Underground ones."

"Like *Fight Club*?" It's one of my dad's favorite movies.

"Yeah," he replies. "Like that."

We drive in silence as I jump onto the ring road that circles the city. The Freeman industrial plant twinkles in the distance like a toxic Emerald City. Ozzy calls on the Bluetooth. I don't answer. Caspian doesn't comment.

"What's the point?" I ask.

"The point?" Caspian unzips the front pocket of his ratty knapsack and pulls out a wad of cash. I nearly drive off the road, tires flirting with the shoulder and spraying gravel.

My jaw drops. "You *won* that fight?"

"I always win."

"How much is that?"

He fans the bills and then folds them back into his backpack. "Twenty-six hundred bucks."

I don't ask what happened to the other guy.

"Take the first exit," he says, pointing at a green highway sign ahead.

I oblige and flick on my signal light.

"You can't tell anyone."

"Does Axel know about this?"

"Especially not him. He knows I did it once, but if he finds out I'm still doing it, he won't train me. He can never know." He grips his bag. "Turn left here."

I see the arena ahead tucked beside an industrial park. Bays and warehouses stretch out in every direction, selling machine parts and truck tires and modular kitchens. I'm not used to coming at it from this direction. A trailer park looms ahead. Oh my God. *Degan*. This is where I expect him to live.

"Turn right."

We pull onto a narrow side road littered with potholes and a row of dilapidated townhouses. The first one we pass is condemned, a faded telltale yellow sign from the city fixed to the front door. The next one has dirt for a lawn. A pint-size tricycle sits tipped over in the middle. Flower cutouts decorate the front window.

"Fifth one in." He points.

I don't look him in the eye in case he's embarrassed, and then I wonder if by not looking at him I'm implying that he should be ashamed and that I'm a privileged bitch.

The third and fourth townhouses have sheets for curtains. An old woman sits on a lawn chair in front of the fifth. *His* house. A trio of garden gnomes dressed in suspenders lines the walkway.

"Why do you do it then? If MMA means that much to you, why would you risk losing your coach?"

He opens the door so the interior light flicks on. He stares at me hard. "Come on, Rowan." He accentuates the correct saying of my name for effect. "Do you really have to ask that question?" He looks out at his house. A black mailbox hangs sideways off a hinge. An upstairs window is broken and the knee-high picket fence lining the yard is nearly completely flattened. At one time it was painted white.

How do I answer that? Caspian doesn't let me.

"Promise you won't tell?"

"I won't tell."

"My grandma will get this washed," he says, pinching Ike's shirt, "and I'll bring it to the gym Sunday. You practice Sunday?"

"Ten a.m."

"I owe you," he says. "If there's anything I can do, let me know. Just keep this all a secret."

Somewhere in the distance, a dog barks.

"There is one thing you can do."

Caspian pauses, one foot already out the door. "What's that?"

Another missed call from Ozzy. I scroll through my photos and stop on Popcorn sitting proudly in the front seat of my car, where Caspian sits now.

"I need you to help me find this dog."

Caspian takes my phone and studies the picture under the dome light.

"Deal. Give me your phone number."

"What for?"

"In case I find it," he snaps.

He pulls out his cracked phone and I give him my number.

He climbs out of the car. "Thanks for the ride. Rowena."

CHAPTER 14

Pia picks me up just after seven and we drive to another quadrant of the city for cinnamon buns she saw on TikTok. A block away, she rolls down our windows. Her hair dances in the draft. Mine whips in my face.

"Smell that," she says.

I inhale and get a mix of diesel, grass clippings, and Christmas morning. December is the only time of year my mom really bakes, and I consider the possibility my dad might not make it until Christmas, and what that would look like without him. Ike would use a chain saw to carve the turkey, and our tree would be artificial. And no matter how much food we make or decorations we display, the table will always be too big for three.

At the drive-through, Pia orders a dozen assorted rolls. We spread the box between us.

"Which one would Coach want?" I ask.

We leave him the brownie one. Pia chooses coconut. I take butterscotch. When we get to the campus, she parks a few streets over from the pub where Caspian washes dishes. And where he beats the shit out of people for cash. I want to tell Pia about it. How his face and shirt looked like a crime scene, his townhouse a movie set. His grandma on the front step waiting for him to get home like a sad war widow.

We pass the university arts building, sustainably designed and sprawling. The morning sun blazes off the glass and we both have to squint. Pia stops in front of a sculpture featuring half a dozen polished stone people. They're all headless. She poses with a cinnamon bun and films a quick TikTok.

"If wrestling wasn't a factor, where would you want to go to college?"

Pia swings open the door to the rec complex. "Well, my mom still wants me to become a vet like her, so I guess some prestigious vet school, and my dad says I can do anything I want as long as it's engineering."

We both laugh, but her laugh is measured. She should be going to New York or Paris for fashion design.

When we get to the gym, Coach is yelling at Leo for something. Pia and I take the long way around the mats to the officials' room to avoid him. There's a chart on the wall that indicates our assignments. Pia is scorekeeping on Mat B, and I'm timing on Mat D.

We drink shitty coffee from Styrofoam cups and head back out to the mats.

"Why's he here?"

I follow Pia's gaze to the stands, which is already brimming with nervous parents and sleepy wrestlers with bed heads and crusty eyes. One of our teammates doesn't even have his wrestling boots on. Near the back lounges Axel, dressed for a nightclub and balancing a serious metal clipboard on his lap.

"Probably recruiting," I say.

"He wasn't here yesterday."

"Maybe he doesn't want girls."

Axel notices me staring and offers a wave.

Pia raises her eyebrows. "Or maybe he's already found the only one he wants."

I shoot her a look.

"What?" she says. "You know it's true. That's all everyone's talking about at the gym."

"Not Coach though, right?"

"No, but he's not stupid. He sees the way Axel looks at you when you get a nice takedown."

"I have no interest in MMA," I blurt.

"None?"

"I mean, striking is fun but I have no desire to get into a real fight." I think of the blood pouring from Caspian's nose, the bruises on his body like the bad sponge art my mom used to do. "It's good cross-training."

"Well, if there's any girl I know who could pull off cauliflower ears, it's you."

"I do *not* want cauli-ears." They look like the kind of prosthetics people use to be monsters on Halloween. "My ears are ugly enough as they are."

She pinches my earlobe, the piercing long grown over from when I gave up matching best friend earrings for headlocks. "Your ears are cute."

"Then maybe I can take up ear modeling."

Pia giggles.

"Rowena," Coach hollers, making us both jump. "Come here."

"Uh oh." I set my coffee on the score table. *What does he want?*

"Get in there and let Leo get a few throws. Looks like he went to bed last night and forgot how to wrestle. He's throwing like a blind garbage man." He stares at my skinny jeans and crop top. "And why are you dressed like that? You think you were timing a fashion show?"

"I didn't think I'd be wrestling."

Pia tosses me a team jacket.

"Ten throws and give him a lot of resistance."

"Yes, Coach."

I find Leo in the corner, head down and out of breath. "You all right?" I ask.

"I can't focus," he says. "Coach is on my ass. I'm getting all my setups wrong."

"Basic arm throw. Let's go."

We square up and Leo goes in, slips his arm under mine, spins, drops to his knees. I go up and over.

"Not bad, but you got to be tighter. And when you turn, you should have my upper arm. You're kind of low." I demonstrate by taking the position of the thrower. "Got it?"

He nods. Each successive attempt is better. We cycle through a few more moves until I feel my jeans might split.

"You good?"

We slap hands.

"Thanks, Row."

I head back to Mat D. My coffee is cold but I drink it anyway. The tournament organizer calls the wrestlers to the mat and goes through the same spiel he did yesterday. An alert signals from my phone and I realize I never called Ozzy back last night. I go to my texts.

Good night I guess.

It's unusually passive-aggressive. That's my territory. I think about texting back, but if he's left his volume on, he'll be pissed

I woke him so early on a Saturday. Unless he has rehearsal. *Does he have rehearsal?*

I swipe to the news alert from the Global Institute for Neuro-degenerative Diseases and read the headline: *Clinical Trial Suggests Breakthrough Treatment for Patients Living with Sporadic ALS.* Other than therapeutics, there hasn't been a new drug to halt or limit the progression of ALS since before I was born. Reluctantly, I click on the link.

I skim through the first few paragraphs when the first match is called. I replace my phone with the stopwatch. Both wrestlers are small and wear singlets that sag. One of the boys has a mullet. They shoot at the same time and crack heads. At the end of the first round, it's tied 4-4.

I refresh my screen and read the next paragraph. The science around ALS is complicated but the drug in discussion sounds different from the others. At least it does at nine o'clock in the morning. I copy the link and text it to my mom: *Did you see this?*

The whistle blows. I start the timer and tuck my phone away. Leo is up on Mat C. Coach is in his corner, kneeling, trying to act casual. Leo doesn't respond well to standing Coach. He gets a solid fireman's carry to barrel roll. *Nice.* The match in front of me goes to a decision. The mullet kid loses and has a fit. I yawn my way through the next fifteen matches.

The morning session ends around noon. Pia and I eat pizza in the coaches' lounge. We sit side by side on an old wooden teacher's desk and swing our legs. Leo texts and asks me to smuggle out a piece of Hawaiian. I wrap a piece in paper towel and find him in the stands, silver medal dangling from this thick neck.

"What happened in your last match?" I ask, setting the pizza beside him.

"I tried a lat drop but I fell and pretty much pinned myself."

"That sucks."

He shrugs. "You ever hate wrestling?"

"Sometimes," I say. "But I think that's part of any sport. It's hard to be on top of it all the time."

"Yeah." Leo wipes his forehead with a towel and eats the pizza in three bites. "Thanks." He packs his bag and climbs down from the bleachers. I watch the next session of wrestlers warm up. Little kids. Kill me. Maybe I can find someone else to take over timing on Mat D.

I stand to go back to my post when Axel calls my name. He sits in an empty row one section over, sunglasses on as if he was up all night and the lights are too much.

"That guy you were just talking to. He's your training partner, correct?"

"Sort of. Pia's my actual training partner, but she has a broken arm. So yeah, right now I'm drilling a lot of Leo."

"He's pretty strong?"

"Very."

"Do you know whether he's done any jiu jitsu before?"

"I don't think so. He did judo as a kid."

"Thanks." He flips a page on his clipboard and makes a note. "Listen, I'm sorry about the other day. I didn't know about your dad."

"It's okay. I think it actually kind of helped me. The striking. It's like I know he's going to die but if I don't say it every now and then … if I don't acknowledge it, I go right back to the day he was diagnosed. I hate reliving that."

I spare him the details. The color of my mom's face when she walked in the door, the hole Ike punched in his wall, which is still there but covered by a flimsy *Space Jam* poster, and the look in my dad's eyes. A little part of him had already died. Friends and family saying *everything will be okay*. Total bullshit. There's nothing okay about ALS.

"Do you think we could do it again? The pad work and sparring?"

Axel opens and closes his mouth. He pulls his sunglasses up to rest on his shorn head. A gold chain with an exaggerated cross hangs from his neck.

"Rowan, I'd love to train you. You have a real talent for mixed martial arts: the striking, the wrestling … you have all the instincts of a fighter. Things I can't even teach. You're a coach's dream. But you have a real opportunity to get recruited at a top US college. With two different NCAA divisions having voted to approve women's wrestling as an Emerging Sport, you're going to be graduating right at the perfect time."

"I didn't say I wanted to do MMA. Coach is always telling me to look for opportunities to cross-train. I thought this was a good fit."

He sighs. "Rowan, Coach doesn't want me training you."

"Why not?"

"He wants you to focus on college, specifically this tournament coming up in New York. It's no small deal, Rowan. It really will be crawling with recruiters. Look around."

I glance at the mats where the kids are still warming up. A boy and a girl compete to see who can put their leg behind their head. No wrestling.

"Because they sure as hell aren't coming here."

I sigh. "I don't think that's up to Coach. He can't encourage me to cross-train one minute and then tell me not to the next."

"He wants you to focus."

"Please, Axel?"

"Rowan, I literally can't. Coach threatened to take the space away and rent it to someone else if I didn't comply." He tucks his clipboard under his arm. "Look. Get through New York. I may know some coaches who'll be there. I'll make sure you meet them. You go and kick some ass at that tournament, and we can talk later. Coach may relax a little if you bring home some hardware."

I frown.

"Cheer up," he says, lightly smacking my arm. "You'll love collegiate wrestling. Look where it got me." He winks and jogs down the stairs. I follow at a safe distance, fuming. Coach high-fives a little wrestler for taking a single leg in warm-up. *I'll train if I want to.*

I go to the score table fifteen minutes before I have to. I still haven't texted Ozzy. I Snap him a pic of me holding up the stop-watch.

What happened last night? he types.

I had to drive a teammate home. It was late.

Who?

Do I tell him the truth? I start to type "Caspian" and then delete it.

Just some new guy.

He drops it.

Did you win??

Yes, shit. I can't believe I didn't even tell you that. Oops. What r u doing?

About to leave for rehearsal. Juliet's picking me up.

Ugh. *Nice.*

You want to hang out tonight?

YES. *Maybe. Text me later?*

Heart.

I look away from the screen and rub my eyes. My neck and shoulders kill from yesterday. On cue, Pia comes up behind me and starts rubbing the back of my head. Even with one hand, it feels great.

"Oh my God, don't stop," I say, closing my eyes. "I'm so sore."

"I don't miss that one bit. Look at this." She holds her phone in front of my face. I read: *You want to come watch the Rebels play tonight?* The Rebels are a top tier soccer team. The best in the city.

"Who's it from?"

"Ahmed!"

"Did you say 'yes'?"

"Well, yeah, obviously."

With a dreamy smile, she wanders back to her table.

I clear the timer and prepare to be bored for three hours when my phone chimes. I need to turn off the volume before the first match starts and the ref gives me a dirty look.

It's from my mom. *Rowan, I just got off the phone with Dr. Patel. That article you sent … the new drug really is groundbreaking. He thinks it would benefit your dad. He'd already contacted the doctor who ran the clinical trials.*

I sit up straight, my heart in my throat. *That's amazing,* I type. *So can he take it?*

He'd been watching this study for a while. The only drawback is the cost and he'd probably have to go to Sweden for it.

Sweden?

It's a long story. He'd have to undergo a pre-treatment procedure before he could take the drug.

The ref calls the first two wrestlers to the mat. A girl with taped sneakers and a boy's singlet on backward, and a boy in a Thanos shirt.

How much?

Fifteen thousand.

I don't reply. I know my parents have already re-mortgaged the house. A GoFundMe campaign was the only way we could pay for his new chair, and an anonymous donor covered the cost of his communication device. Beryl bought Ike his last pair of basketball sneakers. All this and I flew to Vancouver twice and still went to a training camp in Fresno, California.

The whistle blows and within thirty seconds the girl gets a bloody nose.

* * *

Mom invites Ozzy for dinner. I check the fridge and ask if we can order takeout. I have nothing against her cooking, but compared to Tall Dad's, it's kind of embarrassing.

"I was going to make a Hungarian stew."

With what? I rifle through the cupboards. *Cinnamon Toast Crunch, creamed corn, and canned pineapple?*

"Please can we get takeout? We can have stew tomorrow."

She crosses her arms and leans on the counter. "It's expensive."

"China Kitchen has free delivery."

She can't say no to chow mein.

"Fine." She throws up her hands. "Ike, come set the table. Rowan, get extra wontons."

I order from my phone. Extra wontons for Mom, ginger beef for Oz. I check the clock on the microwave. He'll be here in fifteen minutes. Dad watches a show on North America's best climbing peaks. A few of them he summited before I was born. Most are on the West Coast. Half a dozen are ice climbs. He hates those.

I pick up one of his *National Geographics* and open to a double-page spread on the Sami reindeer herders of Sweden. I picture my father there, cloaked in red and blue, pre-treated and drugged up, feeling returning to his muscles the way feeling returns to your toes when you've come in after being outside too long. Of course, he'll be nowhere near the north or the reindeer. He'll be at some architecturally designed hospital in Stockholm. We have to get him there.

Short Dad drops Ozzy off in the work van. I wave from the front porch and kiss Oz like I haven't seen him in weeks. He blushes, seeing my dad in the background.

"Hey, Mr. Harper."

My dad types, *Hello, Benvolio* on his device.

It sounds like a hipster song title. Ozzy smiles and responds in Shakespeare. My mom giggles from the dining room where she's pouring water. Ike says, "No Shakespeare at the dinner table."

"Only 'cause you're failing *Macbeth*," I chirp.

My dad types, *Out damned spot*, and I think of the blood droplets on the wrestling mat, the pool of blood in Caspian's cupped hand. *What's a little blood?*

The Chinese food arrives, and Ike eats an egg roll before everything else is even unpacked and set on the table. My mom slaps his hand and shoves a wonton in her mouth. Tall Dad would be horrified. Dad joins us at the table though Mom's already fed him. Chinese food always gave him IBS, so it's an easy meal to indulge in without feeling guilty that he can't participate.

After dinner, Ozzy and I sit out back. I build a fire in the fire-pit and we sprawl on faded loungers. Wispy clouds drift across the sky. Ozzy rests his hand on his gut. No one in the history of humankind undereats Chinese food.

"We should go somewhere this summer," I say.

"Where?" he asks. "And when? Don't you have a whole bunch of training camps lined up?"

"A few."

"I applied for a theater intensive. In South Carolina."

"South Carolina?"

"Mr. B said it's one of the best programs in North America. He helped me with my audition."

I can't think of any training camps in South Carolina. "That's good, Oz. I hope you get in."

"We'll see. I applied late but they still had a few spots left for boys. All of their faculty has been on Broadway, including this guy." He shows me a picture of an actor in heavy stage makeup. I have no idea who it is, but I reply, "Cool."

"Juliet said they have wicked white sand beaches. She's gone there the last three summers."

How convenient. "Ozzy, you literally hate sand. Since when do you care about beaches?"

"You always say I look good with a tan."

"You're half Lebanese. You're pretty much always tanned."

He reaches for my hand. I want to bend his fingers back, imagining they're Juliet's.

"Is acting something you can even *learn*? Don't you have to be born with it?"

He lets go of my hand, hurt. *Fuck.*

"I'm not saying *you* weren't born with it, Oz. I was just wondering."

"Yes, you can be 'born with it,' but like anything you can also learn. Just like you with wrestling. I'm sure you were always good at starting fights, you just needed to learn how to finish them."

"What's that supposed to mean?" I chuck another log on the fire. It snaps, shooting embers into the air.

Ozzy leans heavily in his chair. "Look, I don't want to fight tonight."

"I'm not fighting."

"Can't you just be happy for me?"

"I am happy for you."

Ike steps onto the back deck with a bag of marshmallows. "You guys want some?"

I open my arms to receive a pass. Ike twists off the top of the bag and hurls them over. I yank a piece of kindling from the edge of the firepit, blow it, and slide a marshmallow onto the tip. Ike jumps off the side of the deck into the yard.

"Where are you going?" I ask.

"Beryl's." He crosses the rear end of her driveway and raps on her back door.

"She gives him cigarettes," I tell Ozzy, turning my stick.

He screws up his face like he doesn't believe me.

"Just watch," I reply, pulling off the top golden layer of the marshmallow.

My phone buzzes from the pocket of my hoodie. I hand Ozzy the stick. He leans forward and jams the end of it into a smoldering crevasse. There's a picture of a chihuahua on my screen. From Caspian. The accompanying text asks *Is this it?*

Oh my God. How can he think Popcorn is a chihuahua? And he said Degan had been hit too many times in the head.

Um, no, I reply. *It looks like this.* I forward the picture I showed him the other night; the one I took from the car, of Popcorn riding shotgun.

Ozzy glances at my phone. "Who's that?" he asks.

"Caspian."

"That douche from your club?"

"He's not a douche."

"Why's he sending you pictures of his dog?"

I dig another piece of kindling from the pit. "There's been a new ALS drug just approved."

Ozzy brightens. His marshmallow catches fire. "One that'll help your dad?"

"Supposedly."

"That's great, Row." He massages my knee and I feel guilty for not being as supportive of him as he is of me. "So can he take it?"

"He'd have to go to Sweden."

"Sweden's nice," he offers.

"It's expensive."

"Your mom will come up with the money. You know she will."

"I hope. She's been discussing it with Dad's doctor." I rest my head on his shoulder. "Sorry, Oz. I know I've been a bit bitchy. Everything just feels like it's happening all at once: Dad, the tournament. Us."

"Don't worry about *us*," he says, kissing me, the sticky sweet of burnt sugar on his lips. "We're good."

Are we?

I kiss him back as Ike hurls a leg over the deck railing.

"Get a room," he heckles, butting his cigarette in Mom's dead tomato plant. He sprays Listerine in his mouth.

"See?" I say nodding toward Beryl's.

Ozzy shakes his head and smiles. Ike snatches the bag of marshmallows from my lap and stuffs a handful in his mouth before going back inside.

"Tickets for *Romeo and Juliet* go on sale Monday," Ozzy says. He runs his fingers through my hair. "I can't wait for you to see it."

I still haven't told him it's the same weekend as New York.

"There's wheelchair seating," he adds, hopeful.

"Dad will totally go. How much do you think airline tickets to Sweden cost?"

Ozzy hums. "Geez, probably a couple of grand at least."

Fifteen grand for the treatment, plus another four or five for travel. Twenty thousand dollars.

I lay my arm across his body. The wind shifts and blows smoke in my eyes.

How much are tickets to an underground fight when there's a girl on the card?

CHAPTER 15

Coach is on the treadmill when I get to practice the next morning. His wife must be on him again to lose weight. His T-shirt is sweat-drenched. A bottle of Gatorade is nestled in the cupholder. His seventies-style headband pulls on one of his eyes, giving him a permanent look of surprise.

"Three kilometers at six point one? My dad could run faster than that and he's in a wheelchair."

"Very funny, Rowena," Coach laughs. "But this is my third set. Wasn't that your excuse too?"

I think about fist-bumping him, but any distraction and he might fall on his face. A group of fighters congregates in the corner by the heavy bags. I don't see Caspian, but Axel sorts through a box of shin guards. Leo is already running laps. It's staged. This is his way of showing Coach he's not satisfied with second place. Coach loves this Karate Kid shit. I've done it myself. Shown up early after an unnecessary loss, to get back on the proverbial horse. Stay late to do more reps. Extra push-ups.

I slip into the changeroom. The metal lockers are cool against my spine. I miss Pia. She'd normally be sitting across from me right now. We'd both lace up our wrestling shoes and then we'd bring our feet together, boot-to-boot. Hers are a tiny size seven, mine a whopping size ten, though I've lied that they're nine and a half.

I hear a rustling noise behind me. Scratching? I shove my feet into my boots, stand, and open the lockers. Empty. It happens again. I check myself in the mirror and gather my hair into a high ponytail. My stomach groans. Leftover Chinese food was probably not a good idea for breakfast.

As soon as I open the door, Caspian grabs me by the hand and whisks me to the front entry. It might be romantic if he wasn't squeezing so hard. I wince and pull away.

"Sorry," he replies. There's tape over his eye.

"Are you wearing makeup?" I study the shading on his cheek and the swath of concealer on his forehead.

"Is it that bad?"

"You just have to blend it. You shouldn't be able to see the lines."

He leans in and whispers, "Can you fix it?"

I gently run my thumb along the makeup line. It zigzags like the border on a map. I make it invisible.

"Thanks," he says, checking his reflection in the window. Then he turns to rest his paw hands on my shoulders. I sink an inch into the floor.

"I got your dog," he says.

"Popcorn?"

"The dog in the picture."

"But how?" When I asked him to find Popcorn I didn't actually expect him to *find* Popcorn. There are probably a thousand strays in the city. "Are you sure it's him?" Or her. I think of the chihuahua photo he sent.

"Positive."

I hug him. He stumbles backward, unsure what do with his arms since I've locked them against his body. My ponytail just grazes the top of his ribcage.

"How did you get him?"

"He likes chicken wings."

I raise my eyebrows.

"Your dog hangs out behind my work. Right after you sent me the picture last night, he came wandering down the alley. I recognized him by the dark spot on his back. He stinks, though."

"That's definitely Popcorn."

"And he prefers honey barbecue."

I picture Popcorn curled up on my dad's lap, watching *Great Migrations* and eating a plate of boneless wings. Dad also always preferred honey barbecue.

"I'll pick him up after practice. I can drive you home."

"No need. Grandma would've killed me if I brought a dog into the house. Popcorn's here."

"What do you mean here?" I scan the front entry as if Popcorn might be somewhere obvious.

"He's in the storage room."

"You can't leave him in the storage room. Coach will kill you."

"Then keep Coach out of the storage room."

Oh my God. Popcorn barks. We both hold our mouths to stop ourselves from laughing. "Make him shut up," I say.

"He's your dog."

I check the clock. If I'm not on the mat running in two minutes Coach will lose his shit. "Okay, I'll go tell him to stop barking."

I race alongside the mat and head to the back of the gym. Coach wipes down the treadmill. I slip inside the storage room.

Popcorn wags his tail and totters over. I scratch the top of his head.

"No barking, okay?"

Popcorn barks.

"No, I said *no* barking."

Popcorn turns a circle and then sniffs a blue vinyl wrestling dummy.

"Be a good dog," I say, easing away. I yank the door shut and hear Popcorn whimper.

I immediately step onto the mat and start jogging, willing the dog to be quiet with each lap. From across the room, Caspian grins. I can't wipe the smile from my own face.

"What's so amusing, Rowena?" Coach yells. He wipes his red face with a towel and peels a banana. "We doing stand-up comedy today instead of snap downs?"

I shake my head.

"Then stop smiling. You got fifty burpees to do, and that's just for warm-up."

I make a *bring it on* gesture, and switch from running to walking lunges. The rest of my teammates file onto the mat. At precisely ten, we start burpees. Coach makes Leo count them in descending order.

"That's not a jump, Snyder," he yells at a kid. "That's a heel lift. You look like you're doing the wave. You think you're at a hockey game? Jump!"

I'm not even tired when Leo squeaks out, "One." Some of my teammates resemble beached starfish. Coach plays White Snake or Poison or whatever mid-life crisis music he has on the playlist today. We get water and he calls us in.

"Snap down, slide by, ankle pick," he says, motioning Leo to join him at center. He demos the move, freezing after the slide by. In the pause, Popcorn barks. I look for Caspian. He's bent over, heaving, recovering from a drill.

"Did I just hear a dog bark?"

A couple of wrestlers shrug. Caspian smoker-coughs, like Beryl, loud and sputtering as if he's trying to dislodge a tank stuck in the mud of his ribs. Axel watches him, puzzled. Coach shakes his head, returns to his demonstration, goes through the move two more times, and sends us off in pairs to execute.

"There are always dogs hanging out behind the KFC," I offer.

I snap down hard on Leo and he curses under his breath. Popcorn barks. *Damn it.* I clear my throat and finish the sequence. Coach heads toward the storage room.

"Coach!" I say as Leo lines up to take his turn. "Can you watch?"

He stares with beady eyes.

"Why are you calling him over here?" Leo mumbles.

I whisper, "Just go with it."

Leo goes for the ankle pick and I deliberately do a terrible job defending it.

Coach jumps in. "The hell was that? You gotta sprawl, Rowan. This is base-level wrestling. You think I'm flying all the way to New York just to see a musical? Do it again and react to his attack appropriately."

Leo and I square up. Silence. Coach forgets he was headed toward the storage room and watches with crossed arms. He grumbles, "Better," and moves on to the twins wrestling beside us. "What, did your parents have two of you so they could eventually pick which one was better?" The twins laugh in unison.

"Because if you wrestle like that, neither of you are winning that one."

Midway through practice Coach cuts live and switches to conditioning: push-ups, sprints, tuck jumps, sprawls, chin-ups, bear crawls. Axel watching is the only thing that gets my chin over the bar. By the time Coach calls practice, I can barely stand. Leo pukes in a garbage can. The twins hate each other.

When Coach heads back toward the storage room, I search for a distraction.

"Coach there's someone out front," I holler.

He looks suspiciously over his shoulder.

"By the desk."

He turns back and I grab Leo. A string of drool hangs from his face.

"Help me."

He stumbles behind. I open the storage door. Popcorn stands on an old throwing mat and does the dog equivalent of smiling.

"What the hell?" Leo says.

"Just cover me while I move him to the girl's changeroom."

I pick Popcorn up. "Oh my God. You friggin' stink." He tries to lick my face, and I gently bat him away. Leo shelters me as we sidestep around the perimeter of the mat and I throw myself into the girl's locker room.

"Thanks," I say as the door wheezes shut.

Popcorn wags his tail with so much force his entire back wiggles.

"Sit," I command. He jumps up on the bench.

I strip out of my training gear and shower, the curtain only partially drawn so I can keep an eye on the dog. When I'm dried off and dressed, I call Pia.

"Is your mom at the clinic today?"

"I don't know. She had a farm call earlier. I don't think she does regular appointments on Sundays."

"Can you call her and ask?"

"Why? What's going on?"

"I rescued a dog."

"How and what for?"

"It's the stray from the alley. Remember? Last week? By the bubble tea place, the brick, the dog?"

"You found *that* dog?"

"Popcorn."

"It has a name?" She pauses. "What if it's just missing or lost?"

"I'm pretty confident it's a stray."

"How do you know it doesn't have some disease?"

Popcorn circles and lies on my feet.

"I don't. That's why I need your mom to look at it."

Pia sighs.

"Please, Pia? It's for my dad."

"Like a therapy dog?"

"Yes," I reply excitedly. "Exactly."

"You know therapy dogs actually receive training to become therapy dogs, right? Like police dogs? Not all dogs are the right fit. You can't just make a dog be a therapy dog."

Popcorn jumps up on my leg. "Sit." Popcorn barks and bites my pants. "Bad, Popcorn," I whisper, deflated.

"You know if you really want a therapy dog for your dad, I'm sure my mom has contacts."

But I want *this* dog. "Please, Pia," I beg again. "Even if I can't keep it, maybe your mom can just fix its leg?"

"I'll call her."

We hang up and I pry open the door to see what's going on back in the gym. Axel and his athletes have taken over the wrestling mat. The storage room is open, Coach probably inside looking for a hidden cheeseburger.

"Caspian." Axel snaps his fingers. "Pay attention."

I dig through my bag for my keys, gather my belongings, and wrap the dog in the wet towel. With my back to the mat, I smuggle Popcorn out and wrangle him into the front seat. Caspian watches through the window.

I start the car and turn on the vents, waiting for Pia to call back. Her mom's clinic is at the edge of the city, out by Leo's, where she can service the farm animals that she specializes in treating and the occasional urban rescue.

My phone rings.

"Okay," Pia says, "my mom's just leaving a farm in Brooks-field. She can meet you at the clinic in half an hour."

"Thank you, Pia. I love you."

CHAPTER 16

I drive with the windows down. Popcorn's tongue hangs out of his mouth. He sits for most of the ride, but curls into a ball as the suburbs give way to range roads, blond fields, and threshers. I pull into the clinic, a squat building with a pitched roof and aluminum siding. The cabinet shop next door is closed.

Pia's mom is parked out front in the Choudhary family Lexus. She is small like Pia with thick black hair that she wears braided down her spine. She gets out of the car in her lab coat and Skechers.

"I hear you've brought me someone to look at," she says, coming around to the passenger seat. She stoops and peers into the open window. "Aren't you a gnarly little thing?"

Popcorn wags his tail.

"Let's go." She motions toward the clinic. I wrap the dog back up in the towel and wait behind Mrs. Choudhary as she unbolts the front door. "Take him to room three. Last door on the left. I'll be right there."

I can barely handle Popcorn's breath. *Frig, Popcorn.* This honey barbecue thing isn't going to work. We settle into the observation room. Bovine anatomy charts hang beside tick posters. A bulletin board of thank-you cards and pet portraits lines the back wall. Horses, lop-eared rabbits, homely cats. No Popcorns.

Dr. Choudhary comes into the room. She washes her hands and pulls on a pair of sterile blue medical gloves. Before she starts, she takes a long hard look at me. I wonder if she's going to ask about the Chinese beer Pia and I drank.

"How are you doing, Rowan?"

It's a weighted question. The same I've heard a million times, but coming from my best friend's mom, it makes me break. My eyes immediately get teary. I want to go back to a simpler time when Mrs. … *Dr.* Choudhary asked me easy things like whether I wanted chocolate milk with dinner or ketchup for my fries.

"I'm okay," I sniff.

"You know you don't have to be okay." She scoops Popcorn from my lap and sets him on the table. "Oh my," she says giving him the once over. "It's like he's been sleeping under a car."

She takes Popcorn's vitals, stethoscope strung up under his heart, running her fingers up and down his belly. She examines his nails, manipulates his wonky front leg. "It was probably broken at one point and healed incorrectly." She opens his mouth with animal pliers. "Mercy," — she turns away — "a broken leg and a few rotten teeth. These two," she gestures, "will need to come out."

"Is that why his breath stinks?"

"That's part of it." She feels around his neck and looks inside his ears. "I don't see any tattoos or microchips and obviously no collar. You didn't happen to bring a stool sample, did you?"

I cringe. "No."

"Popcorn'll need to be dewormed and we'll want to start him on a flea and tick treatment right away, but first, I think we need to give him a bath and a shave. I need a better look at his skin."

"But he's okay?"

"Looks to be. You want to carry him around back? There's a wash station."

I cradle Popcorn in my arms. "Do you think Pia will be ready for New York?" I ask.

"We sure hope so. Unlike Popcorn's leg, Pia's arm is healing up nicely. One more week and she'll be out of that cast. But really it depends on how quickly she can get back to wrestling." She plugs in a set of clippers, and motions for me to place Popcorn in a raised tiled enclosure. Popcorn lies down.

"Stand up," I say. Popcorn rolls over.

Mrs. Choudhary laughs. "You'll have your work cut out for you with this one."

She begins to shear off his fur. The dark spot comes off entirely. A scar the length of a French fry is revealed near his left haunch. She sets down the clippers, sweeps away the fur, and turns on a handheld shower sprayer. Popcorn cowers under the stream.

"You want to help?"

"Sure."

"Put a little of that into your palms and give him a good lather."

I pick up the industrial-size white container she points to on the counter, and pump some of the soap onto my hands. He's got more hair than a drag queen. Popcorn seems to enjoy being washed. Now if only I could brush his teeth. Once he's rinsed, we towel him off together. She dries him with the same kind of hairdryer you'd find at a salon, sleek and powerful.

Dr. Choudhary leaves and returns a few minutes later with a dog biscuit. "We can deal with the tooth extraction later." She administers a few oral medications and then gives him a shot. "There," she says pulling off her gloves and disposing of them in a flip-top trash can. "That's all for today. We'll wait a few minutes to make sure Popcorn doesn't react to anything I've given him."

She slumps down in a patient chair beside the bath enclosure and gives the tile a rinse. "I'll send you home with some food. I don't see many dogs, so I have a ton of free samples taking up space in the storage room."

"Thanks, Mrs. Choudhary."

She smiles. "Pia said you were hoping Popcorn might be a therapy dog."

"That was the plan. I never considered that you couldn't just turn any dog into a therapy one."

Popcorn jumps up, placing both paws on my knees.

"I have high hopes you just might." She smiles. "My question is, is Popcorn a therapy dog for your dad, or for you?"

I'd never thought about it. Of course my intent was for my dad. I imagine he's lonely when Mom's selling a house and Ike and I are at school or basketball or wrestling, and he's stuck at home watching the same *National Geographic* specials about ancient megastructures or Genghis Kahn or *How to Stop a Hurricane*. Why isn't there something useful like a *How to Stop ALS* documentary or a *How to Train a Stray with Bad Breath* one?

"I guess it's kind of for both of us."

"I think that's a good idea, but there's something you'll need to do."

I know what's coming. The same lecture my parents have given every time we've asked for a dog. *You'll need to clean up after it. Pets are very expensive. You'll have to walk it regularly. Even when it's minus thirty. Check it for fleas. Check it for ticks. Bathe it. Make sure it has water. Train it. Keep up with its vaccinations. Give it lots of attention. It's different than a cat.*

"What's that?" I ask.

"You'll have to get used to calling it *her*."

"Wait, what?"

"Popcorn's a girl."

I look down at the mess of dog licking my shoelace and ask, "You're a *girl*?"

Popcorn barks.

* * *

Panic begins to rise in my chest as we near my neighborhood. Sensing we're nearly home, Popcorn wags her tail and stands. Beryl weeds the flower bed in her front yard in fatigues and the kind of sunglasses worn by New York socialites. A heap of dandelions and leaves and wilted grass is spread out at her knees. Her garden gloves are Ike's old winter ski gloves.

I get out of the car and carry Popcorn up the drive. It takes Beryl ten minutes to stand, but when she's up she crosses the yard with the discipline and speed of a soldier commanded to advance.

"What do you got there?" she asks, a smattering of earth on her cheek.

"This is Popcorn."

Popcorn wiggles.

"Breath smells like Hitler."

"She needs a few teeth pulled."

Ike appears from around the side of Beryl's house. He holds a paper compost bag and wears his court shoes. He gathers the pile of weeds Beryl pulled and shoves them in the bag.

"How come you're wearing safety goggles?" I ask Ike.

Beryl pulls off her gloves. "The thorns on my rose bushes are bayonets."

"How come you have a dog?" Ike's smile rivals a supermodel's.

"She's a therapy dog," I whisper.

"Her name is Corn Dog," Beryl adds.

"Popcorn."

"Can I hold her?" Ike asks. The compost bag drops and tips over. His arms are already peeling her away.

I pass her over. Popcorn licks Ike's face. "How did you ever convince Mom to get a dog? I've been asking since grade one."

I glance up at the front window. The blinds are closed.

Ike follows my gaze. "Holy shit, you never told her?"

"It's a … surprise?" I stammer.

Beryl bends to pick up an old seedpod. "Did that with my first husband. Didn't go over too well."

"How come?" Ike asks.

"Because he was German! My father chased him out of the yard and down the street." She turns and sizes up her garden. "I think we should take out that whole bush."

"That one?" Ike points to a mossy jumble creeping over the wall.

"Yep." She makes the universal sign for cutting off a head, hand to the neck. Sound effects. "It reminds me too much of his beard."

I don't know if she's referring to her first husband's beard or her father's. I don't ask. Ike passes me the dog and begins the task of removing the straggly bush. I stare up at the front door, Popcorn nestled in my arms.

"Wish me luck."

"Plug your ears," I hear Ike tell Beryl. "It's about to get ugly."

She shrugs. "I can't hear half of what you say anyway."

When I walk in the front door, Mom is giving Dad a haircut. He and Popcorn will match. A smile escapes my mouth as I whisk the dog down the hall to my room. Dad wears a towel around his neck. It's secured below his chin with a chip-clip. Mom is cleaning up around his ears, her eyes practically crossed as she zooms in with the clippers and tries to exact the perfect curve.

"Hey, Row," Mom says, examining the line with her thumb. "How was practice?"

My dad goes to type something in his device, but Mom tells him to "stay still."

He rolls his eyes.

"Do what the woman says," I joke, pointing to a spot my mom's missed.

She cuts the rogue patch and turns off the clippers, brushing the hair from my father's neck with a tinted blusher brush.

"How was practice?" Mom repeats.

"It was good. I got a dog." Boom.

"You what?"

"I got a dog."

"Rowan," she cautions, "tell me that's a wrestling move." She yanks the plug from the wall and rips the towel away from my dad like an angry magician.

"It's not a move, Mom."

"Rowan?" She stands, hand braced against the dining room table, gaping. "How could you do this to me?"

I step back and swallow. Her reaction is worse than I expected. Maybe if she just sees Popcorn, it will change her mind. I rush to my room and open the door.

"Come here, Popcorn," I call.

Popcorn wanders out with a wrestling boot in her mouth.

"Those are your new boots," Mom says. "You think we can afford to just buy you another pair on demand?"

"Let go, Popcorn." I toss my wrestling boot back into my room and close the door.

"Who's going to look after it?" Mom shouts.

"I will. So will Ike."

"Ike is sixteen and he can't even make a sandwich. And you're never home." Mom paces, grabs the broom from the kitchen, and aggressively sweeps Dad's hair from the floor. My father puts his chair in reverse. He backs away like a pallet jack and situates himself in the living room. Popcorn bites the back wheel.

Oh my God, Popcorn. NO.

"This was a really selfish thing you did." She fights tears. Mine come freely. "I'm trying to figure out how we can get your dad to Sweden for a treatment that might save his life, and you bring home a dog?"

She crumples into a dining chair, elbows crashing against the table. She sobs.

What have I done?

"She's already had her vet check," I say. "I have a bag of dog food and Pia's mom gave me a whole bunch more."

Mom looks up from the table, filmy makeup-stained tears on her face. "It's not just the money, Rowan. It's the time. I can't look after anyone else. I can barely look after myself right now." It comes out as a whisper.

I hand her a Kleenex. "I'm sorry," I say. "She's a therapy dog. I thought it might help."

Never mind Dad. Mom needs a therapy zoo.

Popcorn stands on the couch, her front paws on the backrest. She stares at us with her head tilted. The cuckoo clock, which works intermittently, chooses now of all times to discharge. The bird only has one eye, and it springs from the door with a ghoul-ish quiver. Mom covers her face.

In the living room, my dad types something on his device. He's written, *You should have asked first.*

"I know," I say, rubbing the tears with the heels of my hands. "I'm sorry."

I see his hand flicker toward me. Fatherly instinct. Make it better. The way he did when I was a kid and I fell off my bike or got stung by a wasp or hit by a pitch. I don't let him.

The next thing I know, Popcorn is standing on the dining room table, perfectly positioned on one of Beryl's hand-me-down woven placemats, as if she's the centerpiece. The tiny clock door shuts.

For fuck's sake, Popcorn. Can't you just do what you're sup-posed to for once?

I storm across the room to get her off when she begins licking my mom's cheeks, methodically, like her face is a dozen chicken wings. Mom gently bats her away, turning her head.

I slap my thigh. "Come, Popcorn."

Popcorn continues licking Mom's face like her life depends on it. *It does.* I'm about to tug her away when my mom starts laughing, hearty and hysterical, her whole upper body bouncing.

"She won't stop licking me," Mom squeaks.

Again, I go to remove the dog, but Popcorn persists. Mom laughs harder.

"What?" I ask, my shoulders and jaw beginning to relax.

"Her breath," she says. "It's terrible."

Across the room, Dad smiles.

"Some of her teeth are rotten."

"Only some?" She laughs so hard her eyes squint, and she makes a high-pitched witchy *hee hee hee* sound. "It smells like your mouth guard."

"Okay, my mouth guard doesn't smell that bad."

I see my dad typing. He writes, *it does*.

"You can't even smell her!" I argue.

When my mom is soothed, Popcorn jumps down from the table. I sit down.

"I'm sorry," I say. "I know I should have asked, but after I saw those dogs at the hospital, I just thought it might be a good idea for Dad to have his own therapy dog. And Popcorn … she kind of … found me."

My mom wipes her face, remnants of laughter still visible in the occasional shake of her shoulders. "I'm sorry, Row. I know you meant well. It's just a dog is a lot to take on right now. Between your dad and New York and Ike … You know I caught him smoking on the roof the other night? And I have houses to sell."

"I promise I'll look after her. And Ike will take her for walks. That way he can smoke so you don't have to see him."

She rolls her eyes.

"I'm serious, Mom. None of the burden will fall on you. Pia's mom is covering the vet bills. I already have food. I just need to get her a leash and a collar." *And a dog bed. Some toys … Ugh.*

"I'm not scooping any poop."

The mechanical voice of my dad's device sings, *Neither am I*.

"Very funny," I say.

My mom's expression changes from comic relief back to worry. "We can try her out," she says. "But if it doesn't work, you have to be prepared to rehome her."

"Promise."

She takes a sip of tea. It is likely long cold by now and she stares out the back window. Ike leans on the deck with a shovel.

I lower my voice. "Is Sweden really possible?"

"Dr. Patel has a call scheduled with them at one o'clock in the morning our time. He's trying to make the necessary arrangements. They'll need to ensure your dad fits the profile for this drug. It's risky if not. If he does meet all the requirements, then it's just a matter of money." Her shoulders fall. She sets down her tea.

"And is that part possible?" I ask. "The money?"

"Well, I got a new listing in Brookside Estates, so that's a start."

The door on the cuckoo clock suddenly bursts open. The bird tips forward, a stalled automaton. The spring on which the bird is attached hangs limp.

The hell?

Mom removes the placemat that Popcorn stood on and folds it in thirds on her lap. "If this drug works, he may make it until Christmas," she says. "He may even see you graduate."

I rest my hand on hers. In the living room, Popcorn is asleep on my father's chest. Dad's eyes are closed but I have no idea if he's awake or asleep. Either way, he looks peaceful. I stand in the hall, study his crippled hands and crooked neck. It's easy to forget he's only forty-four. The same age as Axel. The same age as Short Dad. The same age as men who can still take other men down or strip houses to their studs or install heavy bags or kitchen sinks or track lighting. Men who can make it to graduation.

I go to my room and text Caspian. *Can you get me a fight?*

CHAPTER 17

Caspian doesn't reply until morning.

Lol.

Why is that funny? I reply.

Ike braids my hair.

First, I can't just "get you a fight," and second, you'd lose.

I slam my phone on my desk.

"Whoa," Ike says. "Hand me an elastic." He twists off the end of my braid. "Why are you raging?"

"Never mind. Can you take Popcorn outside?"

Ike tosses my hairbrush on the bed. "Where is she?"

"In the kitchen."

Ike leaves and I text Caspian again. *Why would I lose?*

You think you can win a street fight with one striking practice?

I beat Degan.

Degan's not right in the head. You saying that would be like me beating my grandma and bragging about it.

I slide into a pair of jeans and an old shirt of Pia's, low-cut to match my mood.

Why you wanna fight so bad?

I need the money. I don't know why I admit this. It makes me sound like a meth-addicted prostitute.

What for? You want to get that mutt a fancy collar?

Popcorn prances into the room with one of Dad's collector's edition *National Geographics* wedged between her teeth. *Secrets of the Titanic.* Not anymore. *Shit.* I follow the trail of secrets down the hall, collecting the ripped pages. Popcorn drops the magazine, and I stuff the severed pieces back inside.

I just need it, I reply.

Ike pours me a bowl of Cinnamon Toast Crunch. We eat at the dining room table. Water surges through the pipes overhead. Mom's helping Dad shower.

You need skills, Caspian types.

Can't you just meet me before practice tonight? Fifteen minutes.

Milk drops from Ike's chin. "Who are you texting?"

"Caspian." I add an extra handful of cereal to my bowl.

"What the hell kind of name is that?"

I shrug. Popcorn pees in the hall. Oh my God. I use half a roll of toilet paper to sop up the mess and then spray the floor. Lysol seeps into the hardwood.

I add to my previous text. *At the KFC.*

Will you buy me a Big Crunch Sandwich?

Will u get me a fight?

He texts back, *5:45.*

Ike drives us to school. Neither of us bothered to pack lunch, so we divide the dirty coins in the cup holders. There's enough for us each to get a kebab at the 7-Eleven, or a yogurt parfait from the cafeteria. Pia's waiting at my locker.

"How was your first day as a new mom? Did Popcorn sleep through the night?"

"She peed on the floor this morning." I take out my physics book. "And she ate one of my dad's *National Geographics.*"

"Not the Yellowstone one."

"*Titanic.*"

"Thank God. Nice shirt. A little Monday morning cleavage."

"They'll never dress code me when my hair's in French braids."

"I wore that shirt for my first post. It looks way better on you than me."

We head down the south hallway toward first period. Pia gives me a Tic Tac.

I ask, "How was your date with Ahmed?"

"Good, but weird. Good because we're going out again next weekend, weird because he brought his older brother."

"He brought his older brother?"

"Right? Weird. I mean maybe he just wanted to see the game, but he sat with us the whole time and Ahmed was super shy and awkward. Four free kicks and a yellow card before he made any real eye contact."

"Did you do anything?"

"Yeah, I made out with him while his brother filmed. No!"

I laugh. She smacks me.

"He did hug me goodbye."

"And?"

"And I'm not going to lie, it was pretty intense."

"Intense hugging."

"Trust me, it's a thing."

"Namaste," Mr. Williams says as we enter the classroom.

Pan flute music spills from a speaker on his desk. Study period. Pia and I sit in the back and pull out our textbooks. The guy who sits in front of us says, "What kind of hippy shit music is this?" And puts in AirPods. I don't admit it, but I find it relaxing. It reminds me of a recurring dream I have of me and my dad summiting a mountain somewhere in the clouds. We both raise our arms in victory and then I slowly turn to take in the view. North, east, south, west. After I complete the rotation, I am alone.

Mr. Williams hands out a worksheet. I slip my phone underneath it and watch muted YouTube videos of Axel and Ronda Rousey. Amanda Nunes. I study their technique. Occasionally, Pia interrupts to show me pictures of herself and Ahmed from Saturday's game. He's dressed head to toe in Adidas. His hairstyle could cut diamonds.

Ozzy and I meet up after class. He takes my hand and leads me down the hall to the school theater. Sometimes I wish the hall could just open up, the bricks crumble away, and we could keep going off into the proverbial sunset. Before we get to the ticket booth, I give his hand an extra squeeze.

"Cast members get priority access," he says. "They go on sale to the public after lunch."

I nod with enthusiasm and try to shake the feeling that one day an understudy might take my place. That after graduation there's a good chance Ozzy will be rehearsing lines in some shitty Brooklyn flat with nothing more than a hot plate and a dream, while I'm practicing suplexes in a Colorado gym full of Mormons.

"Is Ike coming?" Ozzy asks. "Three tickets or four?"

"Two."

"Two?" His body language deflates. "Just you and your mom?"

"My mom and my dad."

"You're not coming?"

"Sorry, Oz. I've been meaning to tell you. It's the same weekend as my tournament in New York."

The girl selling the tickets looks down, busying herself with a spreadsheet and a highlighter.

"Oh," is all Ozzy says.

"Maybe I can come watch the dress rehearsal?"

"Maybe." He turns to face the ticket girl. "Make that only two." He hands over a twenty-dollar bill. "One for wheelchair seating."

The girl fishes two orange tickets from a container, marks the row and seat numbers in the corners, and slides them over.

Ozzy places them in my hand. "Have fun in New York," he says.

"Oz, it's not like I had any control over the tournament schedule. You know I wish I could."

"I have to go," he says. "I have another fitting."

How many frigging fittings do you need for one play?

I stand there, frozen, tickets in hand, and watch Ozzy disappear down the aisle toward the stage. A tall girl waits with a measuring tape. Ozzy spreads his arms like he's getting screened at airport security.

My phone buzzes in my pocket. My mom sends a picture of the *National Geographic* that Popcorn destroyed. I'd meant to hide it. I type, *I'm sorry.*

What else can I say?

When I look up, Ms. Foy is there with her floral travel mug and Bell "Let's Talk" face. *Oh my God. Now what?*

"I have some information on writing the SAT," she says. A brochure is tucked under her arm.

"Do I need to be thinking about that right now?" I ask. I'm only in grade eleven. I have a whole year before I need to start worrying about SATs.

"Rowan," she says, frowning. "You really should've already written it if you want to be considered for early admission. You'll have to write it in the fall. And again in December — at the latest — if you don't do well."

She hands me the brochure. *SAT Prep Courses for Canadian High School Students.* Wow. *I can't wait.*

"Thanks, Ms. Foy."

"If you need help registering, let me know." She pauses. "Everything else okay?"

How can I make her go away?

"I got a dog," I say. "Her name's Popcorn."

"That's wonderful, Rowan! Pets can be great study companions."

I smile. "I'll remember that when I'm cramming for my SAT."

She looks like she might want to continue the conversation, but someone down the hall yells "motherfucker" and she promptly leaves to investigate. I head to the 7-Eleven for a kebab.

Ike has a basketball game after school. I drive home solo, anxious to see how Popcorn made out for the rest of the day. Mom sits barefoot on the couch in lumpy Costco spandex, sock dents around her ankles.

"Your dad and I just took her for a four-k walk."

Popcorn lies on the floor, her upper half in a brand-new dog bed.

"Do you like it?" she asks. "We stopped at the pet store this morning. Your dad picked it out."

My dad looks sunburnt and content.

"Was she good?" I ask, bending to scratch Popcorn's ears.

Dad types, *She tried to eat a dead pigeon.*

"Gross."

There's stir-fry on the stove. I serve myself a bowl and take it to my room. Mom follows me.

"How was school?"

"Ozzy's mad because I'm going to miss his play." It's not what I'd planned to say.

"I'm sure he's not *mad*, Rowan. He's probably just disappointed. Weren't you upset when he couldn't make Nationals last year?"

"Yeah, but I didn't tell him that. I didn't make him feel guilty."

"He'll get over it," Mom says. "It's obviously just very important to him."

She looks younger with her hair tied back in a ponytail.

"Well, so is New York to me."

"Speaking of which, Coach emailed your ticket. Did you know the club has a new sponsor? They covered the cost. Barrett something?"

Axel.

"Sounds like an insurance company. I'll forward you the ticket. Coach has you leaving at six a.m. Why does he always book the earliest flights he can get? I told your dad he can drive you to the airport this time." She laughs at her own joke.

Three weeks. I finish my dinner and leave the bowl on my dresser. I wonder if I can get a fight before then. I change into leggings and fold myself into a sports bra that's thick as armor.

Mom loads Dad into the van. They're going to watch Ike's game. I wave from the driveway. Popcorn watches from our front window, Beryl from hers. I pile into the Civic, and head for the KFC.

Caspian loiters like a well-dressed homeless person outside the strip mall. He approaches when I pull in, opens my door.

"Rowena," he says, bowing like a chauffeur.

K, that's weird.

"What?" he continues. "My G-Ma told me always open the door for lady wrestlers."

"Haha. Your *G-Ma* told you that? How oddly specific."

We stand in line with the after-work crowd, weary mothers and tradesmen with wool socks and whale bellies, ordering buckets of chicken and six-packs of gravy, and photoshopped coleslaw.

"You seriously want a Big Crunch Sandwich?" I ask, digging my debit card from my wallet.

"G-Ma also told me never to work for free."

"I'm glad you consider this work."

"You have any idea how hard it will be to get you a fight?"

I order him the sandwich. He carries the red tray to a corner table and empties half a dozen packets of ketchup onto the paper liner.

"Seriously, though. Why do you want a fight so bad? You don't look like the kind of girl who urgently needs money. Tell me you're not in some sort of trouble."

"My dad's dying."

Caspian stops eating mid-bite, sets down his sandwich, and folds his hands.

"Of what?"

"ALS."

"Is that what Stephen Hawking had? He lived forever."

"It affects everyone differently. Largely depends on the motor neurons running the diaphragm, and the swallowing muscles."

"That sounds very science-y."

"Or, depending on how you look at it, very deadly."

A child at the table beside us stares, swinging a french fry through the air like a conductor's baton. Her mother breastfeeds a sibling. Caspian waves. The little girl waves back. Caspian initiates peekaboo, and they carry on for a good five minutes.

Maybe his fight name's the Child Whisperer.

"There's a new treatment in Sweden."

"So you need the money to get him there." He picks up his sandwich. "Look, I'll try to get you a fight, but you need to train. Ask Axel to help you get a few reliable strikes. You need a good combo. Otherwise, you rely on your wrestling."

"He won't train me."

"Why not?"

"My coach won't let him."

"You're fucked then." The breastfeeding mother looks up from the table. "Sorry," he says. "Screwed. You're screwed."

"Can *you* train me?"

"I don't have a lot of time."

"Neither does my dad." I squeeze my hands into fists.

"You any good at math, Rowena?"

"What does math have to do with it?"

"I'm trying to get my GED."

I look at him pityingly as a trio of delivery drivers swarms the counter.

"Don't look at me like that," Caspian says.

"Like what?"

"Like a judgmental bitch."

I sit back in my chair.

"You think I'm some white trash Eminem dropout who lives with his grandma?"

I do. "I didn't say that."

"You thought it."

"I'm really good at math."

"We start tomorrow."

"Tonight," I say standing, noting the time.

"Tonight? You got problems, Rowena."

"I sure do." I pick up his Big Crunch and take a fat bite. "I'll see you after practice." Trapped by the nursing family, I practically crawl over the table. The drivers clear a path. Caspian gapes. I don't look back.

CHAPTER 18

Coach is in a good mood. He must have lost a pound. Pia, still in her cast, joins in the warm-up. We jog side by side.

"Did Coach send you a ticket for New York?" I ask.

"He's reserved a seat on the flight but hasn't paid for it. I'm trying to convince my parents to let me go, regardless of whether I can compete or not."

"That would be awesome," I say. "I'll go to all the thrift shops you want. I'll even try stuff on."

After warm-up, Pia heads to the squat rack. Caspian slinks through the front door, hair standing on end, cheeks aglow with KFC. I ignore him and settle into the comfortable routine of drilling with Leo.

We practice double legs. Leo drives hard, and Coach praises him. Occasionally, I catch Axel watching. He nods when I get a strong takedown. My practice ends half an hour before his. Pia and I go to the changeroom together.

"Want to grab something to eat?" she asks, leaning against the far side lockers. Her once fancy nails are chipped and back to a wrestling roughness. I can't wait for her to get the cast off.

I debate whether to say anything about Caspian. She'd lose

her mind if she knew I was planning to fight for cash in some shit basement pub.

"I'm going to do some extra training," I reply.

"With Coach?"

"With Caspian."

"*Caspian*? Hot fighter boy? Define *training*."

"He's really good at high crotch defense. Knows how to sit the corner."

"Leo's good at that too, no?"

"He's already left."

"What would Ozzy think?"

"I don't care what Ozzy would think. It's just training. I'm not going to get any better if I do the same things all the time. And don't say anything to Oz. I'm not telling him because he already thinks Caspian's a douche."

Pia unbraids her hair. "He kind of looks like one."

"He's not, really. And he knows his stuff." *Except for math. Possibly science. English.*

"I'm sure Ozzy wouldn't care. He's used to you training with guys."

Not this kind.

"Maybe. He's just acting unreasonably right now. I mean he's pissed off because I'm going to miss *Romeo and Juliet*."

"Only because he cared enough that you were going in the first place. He wants you to be proud of him."

"Did he say something to you?"

"No." She runs a pick through her hair. "I can just see it."

"Well, I tell him that all the time."

"Then he'll get over it." She slides her water bottle into the pocket of her bag. "By the way, my mom said she could pull

Popcorn's teeth on Friday. She teaches at the university that day. Just bring her to the lab after school."

"Will you come?"

"Sure."

"Sleepover after?"

"Yeah. Let's do that." Her hair gets caught in her backpack. She flicks it away. "Be careful, okay?"

Be careful? "What do you mean?"

"With Caspian."

I don't ask her to clarify. Either she's implying that he's a white trash dirtbag who'll teach me to hot-wire cars and shoot cheap vodka, or a white trash Thor who'll buy me dollar-store lingerie and fairground teddy bears. Both scenarios: trouble.

"I'm good."

After Pia's gone, I fix my hair and wait. Caspian comes out exhausted. We climb into my car. He doesn't open my door. Neither of us talks until we hit the highway north.

"Why didn't you finish high school?" I ask.

"Do you want the short version or the director's cut?"

"Short."

"I had to look after my grandma."

We drive for a quiet minute, past warehouses and roadkill and RV stores. Caspian fiddles with the Spotify playlist on my phone. He skips to a new song. One of Ozzy's and mine.

"Now you're wanting the director's cut," he observes.

I laugh. "Kind of."

"So, my dad got addicted to fentanyl after back surgery. Once he finished his prescription, he turned to some illegal shit to get more. Somehow, my mom got involved, and now she's in jail, he's in rehab, and I'm a high school dropout."

"Oh," I reply.

"Yeah. Oh."

We pull onto his street if you can call it that.

"Park around back," he gestures.

I triple-lock the doors like Tall Dad and follow Caspian through the ramshackle yard to the back door. The screen bulges. My heart dips as I imagine what's inside: a hoard, a bag of meth, a dead body. But instead, we step into a tidy yellow kitchen, not a dirty plate or used needle in sight.

"I got to eat first."

Caspian pulls out a blender and a tub of protein powder. He works with the finesse and speed of a seasoned bartender, adding ice cubes and chunks of frozen fruit, blending, adding, blending. I haven't touched our blender since Ike nearly killed Dad.

"Do you want some, Rowena?"

He pours himself a cup.

"Sure."

He takes a second glass from the cupboard and fills it to the rim.

"I have to check on my G-Ma."

I nod, sipping the shake. On the counter is a picture with the phrase *together we make a family* burned into the wooden frame in a frilly font. I study the photo inside: a boy, unmistakably Caspian with his green eyes and contest-winning smile, a mom with soft shoulders and white teeth, and a dad. In a suit. He looks like a CFO or the Director of Sales for a tech company. He does not look capable of home invasion or armed robbery, or whatever illegal activity Caspian implied. *What the hell?* This is the opioid crisis Ms. Foy preaches about.

I still have the frame in my hand when he returns to the kitchen, remnants of drink on his upper lip, and by his side, an older lady dressed for winter in a thick cardigan and hundred-dollar slippers.

"Rowan, this is my G-Ma, G-Ma this is Rowan."

"Is she your girlfriend?" G-Ma asks hopefully.

"Hard no," Caspian replies.

I'm a hard no? My face flushes with heat. I set the picture on the counter.

"We're just friends," Caspian clarifies. "I'm helping her with MMA; she's helping me with math."

"Don't get that pretty face smashed in," his G-Ma says.

Thanks for the vote of confidence, G-Ma.

"I'll try not to," I reply.

Caspian opens a cupboard and hands his grandma a pill and a glass of tap water. "Did you take your blood pressure today?" he asks.

"One thirty-eight over ninety."

He nods and makes a face like he's synthesizing data.

"K, we're going to the basement."

"No kissing or touching," she says.

"Oh my God," Caspian replies.

I follow him downstairs.

"Sorry about that." He tosses me a pair of thin and fingerless MMA gloves. They're nothing like the rose gold boxing ones I used with Axel.

"First, fix your stance. We ain't wrestling. Take your feet narrower. Now jab into my left hand."

I punch.

"Too slow. You gotta pull back fast. In and out." He demos.

I repeat, and then we switch to hooks. I pour sweat and my mouth gets so dry I can barely swallow.

"You need some water?"

I nod, yes.

Caspian bounds up the stairs and I take a moment to survey the room. The walls are wood-paneled and covered in embroidered birds hung in staggered formations. The water tank and furnace are tucked into the corner, partially concealed by a folding screen. The mat beneath my feet is worn and sun-faded. Holes pepper the surface as though someone has walked across the mat in stilettoes.

"Thanks," I say when Caspian returns with the water. I drink in panicked gulps, the water dripping down my face.

"Okay, because you're a wrestler, you're most likely going to want to take the fight to the floor, but since you don't know a lot of jiu jitsu, you'll need to do ground strikes. Go down." He points to the floor.

I get on my back and he straddles me, high above my hips.

"You want to just throw, aiming for the temples, anything you can get, because your opponent will be covering up. You catch an ear, side of the jaw. Hammer fist her nose. You just keep going."

"Until?"

"Until you knock her out."

The air is ripe with his signature Old Spice and the faint scent of protein powder. A single dangling light bulb interrogates us overhead. We switch positions so I'm on top just below his rib cage, and I have a sudden longing to be with Ozzy in his small room with the plaid sheets and ticket stubs and chopsticks.

Instead, I'm caught between Caspian's hypnotic eyes and the judgmental gaze of a needlepoint peacock.

Caspian takes my wrist and pulls it to the back of his ear.

"Here," he says. "This is where you want to connect."

Connect. My fingers graze the soft spot of his neck. He takes a breath. If he looks any deeper into my eyes, one of us might combust.

"Anything else?" I ask.

He reaches up, thumbs my bottom lip. Behind us, the furnace kicks in, sputtering, choking. "Protect your face, Rowena," he says.

"Protect my face," I repeat, untangling my body from his.

Protect my heart.

CHAPTER 19

I spend the remainder of the week training with Caspian. Trig-onometry and popcorn chicken before practice, ground and pound and protein shakes after. He picks up math quickly, working the calculator like a bona fide accountant. I make him a cheat sheet with all the formulas carefully printed out, and tips on when to use them. We blow off one training session early and play modified road hockey in the middle of his street where there are no cars or kids or nets. A single streetlight illuminates the playing area. There's no one to hear us laugh, no referee. Afterward, we eat microwave popcorn and binge watch *The First 48*. He plays with my hair. It's the most relaxed I've been in weeks.

Still no word of a fight, still no tickets booked for Sweden. I barely talk to Oz.

Pia drives me home Friday after school to pick up Popcorn. It takes a piece of cheese and three Milk Bones to get her off Dad's lap and into the crate Pia's mom has loaned us. Halfway to the university, Ozzy calls. *Why didn't he just text?*

"Rowan," he says, barely able to contain himself, his voice a new radio frequency.

"What is it?"

"You'll never guess what just happened."

"You got into that summer theater school in South Carolina."

"Romeo has pneumonia."

"Shitty for Romeo."

"Rowan, I'm his understudy."

"What about Benvolio?"

"Who cares about Benvolio? I'm Romeo."

"Wow, Oz. Your first lead. That's awesome."

"I'm so nervous."

"You'll be great. I know you will be. Did you tell your dads?"

"Not yet. Tall Dad's going to freak out."

"Oh my God, Tall Dad's going to cry."

"He'll make a scrapbook."

Popcorn barks from the back seat, as we pull up to the university vet lab.

"K, gotta go. Popcorn's having some teeth pulled, then Pia's sleeping over. I'll call you later."

"Congrats, Oz!" Pia yells. She puts the car in park. I attach Popcorn's leash to her collar. Dr. Choudhary meets us at the receiving doors so we can avoid the labyrinth of beige hallways leading to the lab. She has a pair of third- or fourth-year students with her. They both look equal parts nervous and eager.

"Why don't you girls grab some dinner?" Dr. Choudhary says. "Pia, I'll text you when Popcorn's ready to be picked up."

I give Popcorn a quick nuzzle before Pia and I head for the campus food court. My phone chimes in my pocket as we line up for shawarma. A math meme from Caspian. I laugh, and punch in an equation. He replies with another meme. I heart it.

"Oh my God," Pia says, reading over my shoulder. "He's totally into you."

"They're *math* memes, Pia," I say, ordering a shawarma wrap with extra sauce. "We're just friends. But if he was into me, I sure hope he'd show it by sending something other than triangles."

"I think he's hot." Pia orders a platter, pays with her phone.

I blush, change the subject. "There's a new experimental treatment for my dad's ALS." Nothing kills a conversation about hot guys like dying dads.

Pia's eyes grow. "For real, Row? That's amazing."

We find a table in the corner of the food court.

"There are a lot of details to work out, but Dad's always said when his condition got to a certain point, he'd try anything."

The premise of him not making it through the treatment hangs in the air like a blimp. I'd been so caught up in figuring out how he'd get to Sweden I never considered the possibility of him coming home in the plane's cargo hold.

"This is huge," Pia adds. "There's been no promising *anything* since his diagnosis."

"I know. But he has to go to Sweden."

She sits back. "Sweden? Is that like that the new hotbed of neurodegenerative research?"

"Apparently so."

We scarf down our food and play on our phones until Pia's mom texts a photo of Popcorn's rotten and newly extracted teeth. Pia cleans the table and I clear our trays. Caspian sends me a Snap. Instead of a meme, it's a selfie. He's doing trigonometry in a rash guard. I stuff my phone in my pocket.

"I'm so nervous about New York," I blurt.

"Oh, Row." Pia puts her arm around me. "I think the real

problem here is that you have not one, but *two* Romeos vying for your affection."

"Pia! That's not true."

She shrugs, unconvinced.

I think of Ozzy. *If Benvolio wore a green vest, what color does Romeo wear?* Oh my God. There'll be more fittings. There'll be more rehearsals. There'll be more Juliet.

Pia and I cross the quad toward the sciences building.

"Did you actually read *Romeo and Juliet*?" I ask.

"Yeah," Pia replies. "You didn't?"

"I read the summaries." We take the wheelchair ramp up to the veterinary school. "Do Romeo and Juliet kiss in the play?"

"Oh, Rowan." Pia puts her face in her hands. "Only like ten times."

Ten times, multiplied by four shows. Forty kisses. Even Caspian can do that math.

By the time we get Popcorn into the car and pay for campus parking rush hour's pretty much over, making the commute smooth and uneventful. Pia carries Popcorn to the living room where Mom has the dog bed set up near the footplates of Dad's chair. My parents watch their first movie in decades that doesn't involve space junk or fossils or a lost civilization. They hold hands, my mom's arm stretched awkwardly across a stack of pillows.

Pia and I lie on my bed and watch an old-school romance on Netflix. We use the polar bear Ozzy gave me as an armrest. Around midnight, we switch to a fashion-themed reality TV show and Pia falls asleep. I swipe through old UFC fights on Instagram. *TOP TEN SUBMISSION FINISHES OF ALL TIME.*

Guillotines, D'Arce chokes, arm bars, rear nakeds, arm triangles. I have to work on my jiu jitsu.

I'm about to fall asleep when I hear a rapping on my window. *What the hell?* I climb out of bed and peer through the blinds. Ike. I slide open the window.

"I locked myself out," Ike whispers.

"Where were you?"

"Out with the boys." He sips a supersize McDonald's drink.

"I'll meet you around back."

The light is still on in my parents' room. I quietly unlock the back door and Ike slithers in, smelling of weed and fries. I recoil.

"It wasn't me," he says, defensively. "I just went for the food."

"Sure," I say, through a yawn. "I'm going to bed."

* * *

I wake up the next morning with a shawarma hangover. Popcorn is groggy but takes her medicine like a champ. She can't eat her regular hard kibble, so Mom makes some wet concoction Pia's mom recommended.

Pia takes an old pair of my jeans she'll construct something new and wild from and drops me off at the gym. Practice is heavy on technique but light on live wrestling. Coach focuses on the details: stance in motion, positioning. Despite my gut rot, I feel fast. I feel ready. Leo gives me a ride home.

With Caspian working and Ozzy at rehearsal, I have the afternoon off. My dad sits in his favorite spot in the living room, lit up by a beam of sunlight. An out-of-control houseplant acts as a canopy over his head. His eyes are closed.

I chop up some vegetables and boil an egg for lunch. Mom comes in the door with Popcorn.

"It's beautiful out there," she says, kicking off her sneakers. She unclips Popcorn's leash. The dog pads down the hall and curls up on her bed. "You should get outside today."

I sniff the hummus in the fridge to make sure it's still good and take my food to the couch. My dad's wheelchair jerks, and he moves closer to the window.

"Dad," I say, holding up a red pepper. "You want to go get some fresh air?"

Mom jumps on this. "That would be an excellent idea," she says. "I have an open house this afternoon. I'm going to get Ike to help."

Good luck with that. What's he going to do? Blow smoke rings in a potential buyer's face?

"You can take the van," she continues. "And I'll take the car."

She takes a snap pea from my plate.

Don't you have homework? Dad types into his device.

"Some," I reply. "Nothing urgent."

"I'll get you some socks," Mom says to him, noting his bare feet.

She returns with tube socks and suggests a good pathway to walk. She complains the usual places are too crowded. "The cyclists drag mud everywhere."

I sit cross-legged and fold my dad's socks over his feet. I try to be quick, straightening my own socks at the same time. He hates when we dress him.

"Do you want a hat?" I ask.

A toque should be fine.

I help him into a spring jacket and pull the toque down over his ears.

"He'll need his sunglasses," Mom shouts from the hall.

I find my dad's Ray-Bans in the kitchen. They've got to be ten years old. I remember building snowmen in the backyard of our old house and always finishing them off with Mom's terrible handknit scarf and his glasses, and how he'd get so mad when he couldn't find them.

I slide them onto his face. They don't sit straight anymore.

Mom has dragged Ike out of bed. His hair is the shape of a campfire. He wears one of Dad's old triathlon shirts.

"Can you help me get Dad in the van?"

Ike grabs a handful of chips from the cupboard and then takes Dad outside. Mom comes down the hall in the midst of putting an earring in, her lobe red as a poker chip. "Text me if you need anything," she says. "I'll be in Aspen Creek until about four or five."

"I'm good," I say. "We'll just go for a short walk and then I'll come home and get supper ready."

"Your dad's dinner is already in the fridge. Blue Tupperware." She blows a kiss. "Thanks, Row."

I play Queen for my dad's sake and follow Mom's directions to Havelock Park. It feels like summer. Two ice cream trucks compete for business, though both serve crowds. Baby ducks waddle in a conga line from the slough that flanks the parking lot.

We stick to a paved path that winds through a wooded area. I occasionally need to kick a pine cone out of the way; otherwise, it's clear and not very crowded. Somehow the silence is comforting. People don't always need to talk. I feel like telling Ms. Foy this.

After a mile, the river comes into view and Dad seems to brighten. The trees begin to thin. It takes me a minute to realize we are on the opposite bank of *my* river. Specifically, where I normally come alone after practice. We are just downstream and in the shade.

I find a bench in the sun, but it requires Dad to go a bit off-road. I help him park so his wheels don't get caught in a rut. I fix his lopsided sunglasses and sit down on the end of the bench nearest him. An *In Memoriam* plaque is screwed into the back-rest. I don't bother to read it, choosing instead to imagine who sat here and whether they watch me now in a new form: the crow squawking from the tip of the blue spruce, the cumulus cloud hovering above like an enormous bird's nest. The river.

"What do you think of this new treatment in Sweden?" I ask. I shield my eyes from the sun, wishing I'd brought my own sun-glasses.

It's expensive, he types.

"Do you think it will work?"

He hesitates.

"You don't have to pretend if you don't think it will," I say.

Dr. Patel said it sounds promising.

"Then you have to try it."

I don't know if it's worth the money.

"What do you mean?" I slide to the end of the bench and face him. "Are the side effects bad?"

There's a US world team camp in Colorado this summer. I think you should go.

"Whoa, whoa, whoa," I say. "Instead of you going to Sweden for treatment that might extend your life?" Even agitated I'm careful not to say *save your life*. There is no saving. "That's ridic-ulous. Especially if Dr. Patel says it sounds promising."

I jump from the bench and pace. My dad looks beyond me to the river. Maybe even beyond it.

He types, *Nothing is promising.*

"Dad, that's bullshit. You know Dr. Patel. He wouldn't get behind something if he didn't think you had a chance to benefit. You have to go."

Your wrestling career is more promising than any ALS treatment.

"No." I shake my head.

Do you know three different colleges have already contacted Coach?

"They have?"

You have to go for it, Row.

"*You* have to go for it."

He stops typing. Across the river, a father swings his daughter in circles, while their dog bounds around them in approval. I wish Popcorn were here. I pick up a disc-shaped rock and hurl it toward the water. It skips three times before disappearing.

"I think you're getting a sunburn," I say, aware of the heat in my own face. "We should head back."

I place my foot on the bench to tie my shoelace and read the inscription on the plaque. There is no name, no birth date, no date of death, just the quote: *Death is not the greatest loss in life. The greatest loss is what dies inside us while we live.*

CHAPTER 20

I spend most of Sunday afternoon at Caspian's house, working striking defense: blocking, guarding, parrying. Slip, duck, weave, clinch, move away. We stop precisely at three because he has to work. No math. I hang out with G-Ma while he showers. She tells me about the time Caspian got lost in a shopping mall, and how security had to lock all the doors. I swear Tall Dad told me the exact same story about Oz.

I drop Caspian off at the pub on my way to pick up Ozzy from rehearsal, but Ozzy's not ready when I pull into the school parking lot. *We have to redo one scene,* he texts. I park and go to the front doors, but they're locked. I'm about to head back when one of the school janitors comes down the hall pushing a cart stocked with toilet paper and garbage bags. He lets me in.

"Thanks," I say. The janitor nods and bends to sweep up some debris. I head down the hall toward the theater. Inside, it's dark. Only the stage lights are on, casting a bluish hue. Mr B., the drama teacher, stands on one of the seats in the front row, script tucked under his arm, the other arm gesticulating wildly toward stage right. The balcony scene.

"So thrive my soul," says Ozzy.

"A thousand times good night!" Juliet cries. She gazes down at Ozzy, her face a full moon, radiant and bright, hair falling from her shoulders in never-ending waves. A medieval painting come to life. *A thousand times fuck off, Juliet.*

"Cut, cut, cut," Mr. B yells. "Ozzy, this is where you need to move closer to the balcony."

Ozzy takes a few steps over. "Here?"

"A little more to the left," Mr. B waves. "Now keep going from there. Lots of emotion, Oz."

Ozzy continues his lines, while Juliet, who's temporarily left the balcony, returns like some needy bitch. The scene is ridiculous, both characters going back and forth, whining, pledging, professing. *For fuck's sake, just tell her you'll see her tomorrow in the courtyard.*

Ozzy delivers the final lines of the scene.

"Yes," Mr. B shouts. "Yes, yes, yes." He throws his script in the air, tilts his head to the ceiling, arms outstretched like Jesus on the cross. "That's it, Ozzy." He jumps from the chair and scrambles up on stage. "That's the emotion I need from you every time. You were brilliant."

Brilliant?

"That's it for the day."

Backstage crew storms the set, clearing props and replacing markers. Juliet appears from behind the curtain and races to Ozzy. She wraps her arms around him and then grabs onto his face and says, "You were perfect."

Couldn't they have just skipped to the scene where she kills herself?

Mr. B gathers both actors in, one hand on each of their shoulders. A pep talk, quiet and serious. I can't make out what motivational drivel he preaches. I can only tell that he is thrilled with his leads. Afterward, Juliet helps clear the stage. Ozzy takes the stairs down to the front row and reaches for his bag. I sink deep into my seat and watch him pull out his phone. Slip, duck.

Finished, he types. *I did awesome!*

Awesome, I reply, *or perfect?*

He looks up but doesn't see me.

I'll be out in a sec. Just cleaning up.

Juliet climbs down from the stage. She grabs her bag from the front row and pulls her hair into a ginormous ponytail. She and Oz get into an animated conversation. Their faces glow like paper lanterns.

Are you coming? I type.

I watch him acknowledge the buzz of my text in his pocket. He doesn't respond.

Why don't you just get Juliet to drive you home.

This time he pulls out his phone. He looks up as I stand and leave. What Caspian described as *moving away.* I hear Ozzy's footsteps behind me.

"Rowan," he calls.

I exit the theater, dodging the mop streaks in the hallway, and push through the front door. Ozzy catches up, breathing heavily.

"What the hell? I said I was coming."

"You said you were just cleaning up."

"I was."

"You like her."

"It's acting!" He throws up his arms.

I take a deep breath and try to reel in my emotions, but they are heavy and tug at my mouth. I can't keep the words in.

"Well maybe you can act that way around me."

"What way?"

"Like you're still in love with me."

"I am still in love with you, Rowan. What more do you want from me? You're the one who's never around anymore."

"That's not true."

"Okay, then what's up with you training in some guy's house? Gym not big enough, you have to go to his basement or wherever it is you're training?"

"Sorry, what was it you said about Juliet? She was helping you because you were 'late to the acting game.'" I make air quotes. "Well, I'm late to the MMA game. Caspian is helping me."

"The MMA game? Since when are you into MMA?"

"It helps me with wrestling."

"The last time I checked, the NCAA wasn't giving out scholarships for head kicks and kimuras."

He knows what a kimura is?

The front doors open like a slingshot and a group of students pour out along with Mr. B. I don't look to see if Juliet's among them. Ozzy and I stop talking. We wait for the group to disband. A cacophony of beeps from cars and SUVs being remotely unlocked ricochets through the parking lot. Juliet climbs into the front seat of a RAV4. She pretends not to watch.

"You know nothing about the NCAA or what I'm training for, or how or why, or with whom. All you care about is acting."

"All you care about is yourself," he retorts, kicking at the ground. A rock launches into the air from his foot and bounces onto the grass leading to the football field.

I bring up my arm, my hand in a fist before I can even think about what I'm doing, and punch a No Parking sign, *right on the button* as Caspian would say. My hand throbs as I pull back and my mouth drops open in a reaction that is half pain, half awe.

What the hell am I doing?

Ozzy shakes his head. "Nice, Row. I can see how you're putting all that 'help' to good use. Good luck in New York."

He turns to walk away, but he has nowhere to go. I'm driving him home. Tall Dad is making Sunday dinner. The table will already be set for four. He'll have already pressed my favorite napkins with the little dots that look like stars. Short Dad will have already started mashing the potatoes.

"Wait," I say, blood trickling from my split knuckle. "I'm sorry."

"We can't keep doing this."

"I know."

He spits on his shirt and wipes my bleeding hand, and in the moment, it feels like the most romantic thing he's ever done. He pulls me in and when I look at his face, I see he's exhausted. He has bags under his eyes, his lips are chapped, and his hair is unwashed. It's like looking in a mirror.

"I'm sorry too," he says. "Let's just get through this. Okay? We made it through a pandemic. Surely, we can get through one play and one tournament."

"Yes."

He kisses my bloody knuckle, ritualistic and crude. We embrace in the parking lot, against my car, Ozzy pressing into me with the sort of force I'd expect from Caspian, until the janitor comes outside to empty the mop bucket.

CHAPTER 21

Short Dad unloads a toolbox from the back of his work van when we pull into the driveway. His shirt is sweat-drenched, and his work boots paint-splattered. He sets the toolbox on the lawn and wipes his brow.

"Ozzy, Rowan." Short Dad nods. "What's new in the worlds of wrestling and Shakespeare?"

"More like MMA and Shakespeare," Ozzy says.

Short Dad furrows his brow. "Whatever the worlds, I hope they've left you both starving." He turns to face Oz. "Your dad even brought out the gold-plated potato masher tonight."

Ozzy takes my hand and leads me up the stairs as Short Dad opens the garage door and organizes his tools. Inside, Tall Dad wears a screen-printed apron that reads *REAL MEN BAKE*.

"Well, if it isn't Romeo and Juliet," he says, a meringue pie centered on the island like a yoga pillow. Ozzy turns red. I ignore the flu shot sting of Tall Dad's greeting and go with it.

"I'm more of a Lady Macbeth," I joke, "but Ozzy's all Romeo."

Ozzy appreciates the banter. He squeezes my hand before opening a San Pellegrino and handing it to me. *Blood Orange.* Neither of us can handle any more drama today. I'm beginning to think relationships are just plays that go on too long, with everyone begging for the intermission, counting down the scenes until they reach the final bow.

I wash my hands with bergamot soap, whatever that is. Tall Dad asks Oz a million questions about rehearsal. He's obviously been helping Ozzy learn his lines as he recites an entire soliloquy while simultaneously scrubbing a roasting pan.

"Do I have time to take a shower?" Short Dad pokes his head in from the inside garage door.

"Dinner will be ready in twelve minutes," Tall Dad replies.

Short Dad grabs a beer from the fridge.

"I poured you a glass of wine."

"I'll have that after I shower."

Tall Dad wipes his hands on the apron and sips his own wine.

I take a seat at the island, across from the pie. A hint of lemon filling peeks from the crust.

"I hear you're going to miss the play." Tall Dad makes a sad face. "Though for a good reason. I'd kill to go to New York. We haven't been since Ozzy was six or seven."

"Yeah, it's a huge girls' tournament. NCAA scouts will be there. I'm hoping to get noticed."

"Well, if you're going to get noticed, New York is the place to do it." He winks.

Ozzy sits on the swivel stool next to me. We bump knees and I become aware of a bruise I didn't know I had. He slides an orange ticket across the granite.

"What is it?" I ask.

"Read it," he says.

"Admit One."

"Look at the date."

"This Friday?"

"It's our first dress rehearsal. Mr. B knows you're going to be away so he said you could come watch. You don't really need the ticket. I just made it up because I know you save all that stuff."

"This is awesome, Oz. I thought I was going to have to get Ike to tape it or something. I can't wait to see it."

And it's true. He was good today. Unlike anything I'd seen him do before. It's as if something has clicked in his acting. He wasn't himself on stage. He was Romeo.

We continue the small talk until Tall Dad summons us to the table. I spread one of the star napkins across my lap and pile my plate with roasted vegetables.

Short Dad talks about a new house they're flipping in the northwest, and goes into infinite detail about the basement wiring. I think about Caspian's basement with the unfinished ceiling, the faded mat, and the metal weight plates lining the wall like stacks of coins. I need more equipment to train at home.

Tall Dad passes the horseradish. "Will you see any shows in New York?"

"That's the plan," I reply, "but tournaments never end on time. Coach says we'll have to line up to get last-minute tickets. Unless he finds a good deal online."

"We should go back to New York," Tall Dad announces. "Maybe when Oz graduates."

"I was thinking of going there this summer." Ozzy pours a figure eight of gravy onto his plate. "If I don't get into the South Carolina program."

"By yourself?" Tall Dad asks.

"A bunch of people from school are going. Mr. B has some connections."

It's the first I've heard of Ozzy's backup plan.

"And what about you, Rowan? Your family have any big plans this summer?"

As soon as it comes out of Short Dad's mouth, he wants to take it back. Does he think we're going to take Dad on a cruise? Buy him a dolphin ride? Zip-line him through the jungle?

"We're staying home," I reply. "For the most part. It all depends on my dad."

"Of course." Tall Dad fills his wine.

"I may go to a camp in Colorado. It's by invite only, so we'll see."

Ozzy scrapes his plate clean. A thought soaks into my head. *What if Dad's gone by summer?* I think of our walk to the river and my father's indifference toward Sweden. *Does he know he's dying? What if he wants to die?* When he was first diagnosed, I found stories online of ALS patients who planned their own deaths. *Medical Assistance in Dying.* They threw funerals and parties in front yards and church halls, under pergolas, and gathered around fireplaces. There was always storytelling and comfort. Photos from lost trips. Favorite blankets. And music. Always music. Cellos, bagpipes, Leonard Cohen, Lynyrd Skynyrd, "Moonlight Sonata." Why *wasn't* my dad doing this?

Ozzy stands to clear the table.

Tall Dad slides dessert plates and silver forks into our vacated place settings. "This is my first lemon meringue pie," he declares. "So lie to me if it tastes bad."

"It looks delicious," Short Dad says.

Two weeks from today, I'll have just finished competing. Maybe I'll be posing in Times Square with Pia, medal in one hand, personalized M&Ms in the other. The naked guy who plays the guitar in the foreground. Or I'll be holed up in our

Airbnb, hating myself, while Coach drowns his sorrows in a pastrami sandwich. I take a bite of pie. No more junk after this.

"It's good, Dad," Ozzy says, helping himself to a second piece.

My phone chimes inside my pocket. Tall Dad looks up. He hates phones at the table. I silence the ringer and sip my water. It goes off again, buzzing against my leg. I excuse myself, slip into the bathroom, and dig out my phone. The makeshift ticket to Ozzy's play flutters to the floor. He's printed the date and time in fine-liner. I notice he's written on the bottom: *starring Ozzy Howard-Spencer.*

The text is from Caspian. *I got you a fight.*

My hand trembles and I nearly drop my phone. Oh my God. *When?* I reply.

Friday night.

Fuck.

This Friday???

This Friday.

I set my phone on the edge of the sink and collapse down onto the toilet. *Holy shit. What have I got myself into?* I imagine the pub's basement. Same dark wood as the upstairs, ground-level windows, filthy and barred, dirt floor, and suits. Hundreds of them: double-breasted, Italian, wool. I should be terrified. I'm going to miss the play. *What am I going to tell Ozzy?*

I get up from the toilet and stare into the mirror. Adrenaline zips through my limbs. I feel like I could fight right now. I can't wait until Friday. I grab my phone and rush back to the table.

"Thanks for dinner. It was awesome. The pie too. For real."

Tall Dad smiles.

"I gotta go."

"Is something wrong?" Short Dad asks.

"No, I just ..." I pick up my dirty plate and set it by the sink. "I have to train."

"Row?" Ozzy says. "It's Sunday night. Since when do you train on Sunday nights?"

"New York's in two weeks."

I have five days.

Ozzy rises from the table. Both dads look concerned.

"Are you sure everything's okay?" Tall Dad says.

"It's fine," I wave, making a beeline for the front door. "I just have to ..."

Be ready, Caspian texts.

Right. "Be ready," I say. "I have to be ready."

I race down the front steps to the car, leaving Ozzy at the door scratching his head. "Goodnight?" he says.

Yes. *A thousand times goodnight.*

CHAPTER 22

I text Caspian from the car. *Can you meet me at the gym?*

Axel will be there.

So? He only said he couldn't train me. He didn't say you couldn't.

Can you pick me up? I'm just finishing my shift.

I'll be there in fifteen minutes.

The commute to the university district is quick. Caspian's on the front stoop of the pub when I pull up. He smiles when he sees me.

"Rowena," he says, climbing into the front seat, his head brushing the ceiling. "We need to do something about that name."

"It's not even my name," I reply, checking my GPS for the quickest route to the gym.

"That's debatable."

"Oh my God, no it isn't. *Casper.*"

"What I mean is you need a fight name."

I contemplate this. Nothing tough or intimidating comes to mind. No interesting play on words, no savvy rhyme. *Rowan the what?* I turn left. Caspian reaches over. He tucks a piece of hair behind my ear.

"Who's my opponent?" I ask. "What's her background?"

"He's a kickboxer," Caspian replies.

I nearly crash the car. "You are not serious. *He?*"

"You can beat him."

"I'm going to die."

"You're not going to die."

"When I asked you to get me a fight, I meant with a girl."

"There are none. And for the record, you did *not* specify that. You just said you needed the money."

"Yeah, I need the money. But it's supposed to be for my dad's treatment, not *my* funeral."

"Relax, Rowena."

"Relax? Are you fucking kidding me right now?" *Oh my God.*

"You know how much you're gonna make fighting a dude? Double, triple, probably five times what you'd make if you fought a girl, which, as I already said, there are none."

I clench the steering wheel so tight I feel I could yank it off the dash. I park midway between the gym and the strip mall's KFC. *What the hell have I done?*

Caspian scrambles out of his seat belt and turns, practically kneeling in his seat.

"Look at me," he says, his voice authoritative. "You will win."

I will cry. Tears rise. Caspian grabs hold of my face, his massive hands cupping each side of my jaw, the faint scent of pub food and detergent soaked into his skin. His eyes are beautiful, the color almost unreal. He looks like every dreamy virtual character every girl has ever created. For a moment, I forget that on Friday I'm going to die.

"You're going to win," he repeats, and then he kisses me on the cheek, big and wet and absolutely not romantic. It's how I'd imagine Coach would kiss me if I won the Olympics. Fatherly, proud. Gross. Next, he's going to ruffle my hair and call me *squirt* or *champ*. Peach.

I wipe my face.

"Sorry," Caspian says. "I got a little carried away. I'm just excited. Let's go punch stuff."

I grab my bag and we file into the gym. Axel runs a striking practice. He looks up when he sees us kicking off our outdoor shoes in the lobby. He gives the small group of fighters he's training some instruction, and then comes over.

"Rowan," he says, nodding. "Caspian, what are you doing here?"

"A little side training," Caspian replies, fishing his hand wraps from his backpack.

"You know she has a big tournament in two weeks, right?"

"Uh huh."

"Be smart," Axel cautions.

"You're acting like I'm a high school dropout, or something," Caspian replies.

Axel faces Caspian but looks at me. "You good with this, Rowan?" he asks.

I nod.

"If your coach asks, I had nothing to do with this."

"I know."

He backs away, half shaking his head, and orders his athletes to do push-ups. I wrap my wrists and run a few laps. Caspian works through his own warm-up. We meet in the back corner, away from the front windows.

"You need to learn how to check a kick," he says. "If he goes in for a low kick, you gotta bend your leg and bring it up to your thigh." He demonstrates. "Ideally that'll make him smash your shin or knee."

"Wouldn't that hurt?"

"Yeah, it hurts. Like a motherfucker, but if you don't check his kicks he'll just chop away at your leg."

We go through the motions. Even with light kicks it hurts like a bitch.

"What about head kicks?" I ask. "Just block 'em?"

"Pretty much. You basically make a shield with your arm. Keep your guard tight, chin tucked, elbow bent, and face your opponent. You can also use the other hand to help absorb some of the force." He switches stances. "Kick me."

I step left and kick right. Caspian's elbow shoots up. I land somewhere on his forearm.

"Good," he says. "Again."

We alternate between offense and defense. Axel paces in the background.

"Why are you working head kicks?" he calls, setting the clock timer for sparring.

"My first pro fight's coming up," Caspian argues, brushing his hair from his face. "He might be a Muay Thai guy."

"He's not a Muay Thai guy. He's a wrestler. We've established that. Stick to the training plan."

"What if he doesn't make weight, and I get a Muay Thai guy in his place? Or a kickboxer?"

Axel looks me up and down, his eyes tracking the bruises on my legs as though they might form a constellation.

"Look at me, Caspian."

Caspian stops bouncing. Even though he is taller than his coach, Axel is intimidating. His eyes are wild. The same as Coach's when he decides I lost a match for not listening to him.

"We're talking about *your* fight, right?"

Caspian throws open his arms. "Yeah," he says, like me having a fight is a ridiculous possibility. "Why would she have one?" He gestures with a hitchhiker thumb.

"Keep it that way," Axel says, a finger in Caspian's face.

I'm right here.

"Come on, Coach," Caspian argues. "I don't do that anymore."

We square up and Caspian throws a head kick. I block it barely in time. His foot ricochets off my ear.

Axel can't help himself. "Who, whoa, whoa," he says. "Rowan, there are other ways to defend that. Not that you're ever going to get kicked in the head in a wrestling match," he mutters under his breath. "You can sway like this, just moving your head and body to the side. Or, when you see it coming, *if* you see it coming, counter with a low kick. It'll take him longer for his foot to connect to your head than it will for you to connect with his calf. Does that make sense?"

Caspian and I go through the motions. When he goes for my head, I step in and get the low kick.

"Even better," Axel says. "*Go in* to him. The kick will fail, and you can grab onto his leg and get a takedown." He is animated now, even though his fighters throw lunging overhands and lazy back fists, unsupervised, behind him. "It'll feel counterintuitive," he coaches, looking at me intensely. "The logical instinct would be to run away, but watch what happens when I go in."

Caspian attempts to kick Axel's head. Axel steps in, takes Caspian's leg, and gets the takedown he intended.

"Coach Axel," someone calls.

We look to see one of his athletes nursing a nosebleed. Blood drips, creating a Spirograph pattern on the mat.

"Excuse me," he says, rushing off to the bathroom.

Caspian and I train alone for the remainder of the practice. By nine, I'm exhausted. Everything aches. We leave the mat, and both slide down the wall beside the water fountain, our chests heaving, elbows resting on our knees.

"What's your fight name?" I ask, catching my breath.

"For my upcoming debut, it's Caspian 'The Crusher' Hughes."

It sounds like a *Game of Thrones* character.

"You have more than one?"

"Hell, yeah. Can't use my real name underground."

"So what's your name for that?"

"Dishboy."

"It is not." I laugh.

"I didn't pick it."

"So if I don't need to use my real name, then what should mine be?"

"Athena."

"No way."

"What's wrong with that? She's the goddess of war. Born from Zeus's forehead, fully grown and dressed in armor."

"It's terrible."

"What about Aphrodite?"

I shake my head. "No mythological shit. Besides, isn't she the goddess of the sea, or snakes, or something?"

"Of beauty," he says.

I blush and take a sip from my water bottle. "I'll think of something."

CHAPTER 23

I fall asleep in social studies, which is the best class to fall asleep in, because instead of getting pissed off, Mr. Williams recites the Dalai Lama: "Sleep is the best meditation." I wake up when the bell rings.

"Morning, Rowan," he says.

"Sorry, Mr. Williams."

"Happy dreams, I hope?"

I dreamt that Caspian asked my dad for my hand in marriage, except that both of my hands had been amputated. *What the hell?*

"I was dreaming about the political, social, and environmental responsibilities associated with global citizenship."

"I'm sure you were, Rowan. You're good?" he asks.

"I'm good," I reply, collecting my books. Students from his next class spill into the room.

"The notes from today will be posted online. Email if you have any trouble." He lowers his voice. "And get some sleep."

I excuse myself and text Pia: *Is it off yet?*

She sends a pic of her skinny bare arm.

OMG you have a cast tan lol

I know!!!

Are you coming back to school?

I want to tell her about the fight. I can never tell her about the fight because if she's half the friend I know she is, she'll do everything in her power to stop it.

I'm going straight to physio.

K, see u at practice tonight.

DON'T BREAK MY ARM, she types.

We have a sub in second period, which allows me to catch up on missed work. Afterward, Ozzy and I meet for lunch. He hands me the orange ticket he made for *Romeo and Juliet*.

"You left this in the bathroom the other night."

"Oh my God, *yes*. I've been looking for it everywhere." I didn't even know it was missing.

Tall Dad's packed Ozzy a gourmet lunch. Three-bean salad with sweet and sour dressing, homemade focaccia, and a brownie. I brought a PowerBar. We eat at a picnic table at the rec center across from the school and watch the traffic zoom by. City buses and work trucks and tiny sedans with car seats in the back. An accessibility bus stops at a red light.

"How's your dad?" Ozzy asks, plucking a piece of parsley from his teeth.

"Different," I say. "Almost like he's checking out."

"Like, *dying* 'checking out' or something else?"

"I dunno. Checking out from *living*. Like when you know you're not into something anymore: hockey, turtlenecks, K-pop …"

"Relationships," Ozzy adds.

Is he trying to tell me something? "Okay, sure. Relationships. Except in my dad's case, he's not into living."

Ozzy crosses his ankles. His socks have geometric patterns reminiscent of early video game graphics. "Maybe he's just tired."

"Maybe." *Tired of living.* I appreciate Ozzy's effort. Talking about death isn't easy, and Oz doesn't try too hard to be perfect about it. Not like Ms. Foy, who talks about grief and loss so precisely, sometimes it makes death seem like flying an airplane when it feels more like driving a go-kart with three wheels and a broken steering column.

A text chimes from my pocket, startling us both out of our contemplation.

Caspian: *Let's go for a run.*

"Who's that?" Ozzy asks.

"Caspian." *Dishboy.*

"What does he want?"

"He wants to go for a run."

Ozzy scoffs.

"What's wrong with that?"

"You run together now?" He shoves the brownie down his throat.

"Do *you* want to go for a run?"

Chocolate crumbs spew from his mouth.

"I'll take that as a 'no.'"

Ozzy watches my thumbs, waiting for me to respond to Caspian's text.

I type, *Yes. When?*

Now.

"Now?" Ozzy asks. "Does he not go to school?"

"He works," I reply.

"Sounds like a real winner."

"You're kind of being a dick right now."

"I'm being a dick?"

"Yeah, Oz. You are."

"I don't like you hanging out with this guy."

"I don't like you hanging out with Juliet."

A couple walks by, holding hands, laughing, loving. *Fuck off.* It's me and Oz two years ago. Ozzy sees it too: the love, encircling them like a valentine. We are the cold spot in the ocean.

"I'm not going to stop seeing Caspian," I say. "And you're not going to stop seeing Juliet. We both have to accept that, or …"

"Or?" Ozzy interjects.

"We move on."

Across the street, the school bell rings. We both rise. Ozzy stuffs his lunch container into his backpack. The foil wrapper from my PowerBar catches the wind, and sails into the parking lot behind me. I chase after it, failing three times before I finally stop it with my foot, and pick it up.

When I turn back around, Ozzy is gone.

* * *

The drive to the Havelock Park stairs triggers a million memories of Ozzy. I pass the theater where we saw some play with Tall Dad, and Ozzy kissed me in the coat check. The grilled cheese food truck that we both got food poisoning from; the drugstore where we first bought condoms, and Ozzy was so nervous he sort of threw the box, and it slid across the counter and landed on the clerk's foot; the school where he watched me wrestle my first university tournament. I bite my lip. *Why does love hurt?*

Caspian is stretching at the bottom of the stairs when I arrive. He wears jogging pants and a striped tank top.

"All right, Rowena," he says, beaming. "Let's see what you're made of."

I look up at the winding staircase, shielding my eyes from the sun. I can't see the top.

"On your mark," Caspian says.

"Get set."

"Go."

I blast forward. Caspian's back foot slides out on the gravel like a bike tire, fishtailing. I get to the stairs first, and press upward, taking the steps two at a time, arms pumping. He curses behind me, but his movements are heavy, reverberating through the wooden structure. One flight, then two.

My lungs burn. I imagine them smoking inside my chest, setting my whole body on fire, causing microexplosions in my calves, my heels, my brain. Another flight, a forty-five-degree turn, another step. Caspian closes in.

I push harder, my teeth clenched. I don't know if I look more like the girl being chased with a chain saw, or the guy wielding it. Run.

On the eighth flight of stairs, I trip. My shin drives into the wooden plank. *You have to check his kicks.* Blood. Caspian hurdles over me, grazing my shoulder. I push off the step and power behind him, my upper body barely upright.

Caspian turns, entering the final zigzag to the finishing platform. The sun stings my cheeks. My hair feels heavy. He stumbles. I gain. I think of wrestling when there are seconds on the clock, and I'm down in points, and I have to drive for one last takedown. Forward.

I collapse at the top, two seconds behind. Last. Lost. Caspian paces, hands on his hips, breathing in a way that would alarm a health professional. He falls onto a bench. I get back to my feet.

"You're crazy, Rowena," he says. "No one's come that close to beating me. Ever. The only person who can get up these steps faster is Axel. And he doesn't count." Hard exhale. "You're amazing."

I close my eyes and rest my head in my hands. I try to remember the last time Ozzy said I was amazing. I still want to be amazing to him, even if I don't know that I am. Even if I can't recall the last time I said it to him.

"How come you don't have a girlfriend?" I blurt.

"What makes you think I don't?"

A boot camp of runners trickles up to the platform in various states of exertion. They high-five each other, and check their times on giant GPS watches.

I shrug. "Do you have a girlfriend?"

"Hell, no."

"That's a bit harsh, isn't it? What's so horrible about the idea of being in a relationship?"

"Someone always loses."

"I just lost that race. Doesn't mean it wasn't worth running it."

He reaches for my leg and examines my shin, pressing his pinkie into the cut. "That's deep." He strips off his sweaty tank top and ties it around my leg like a tourniquet. "You sure it was worth it?"

I try not to stare at his bare, ripped chest and abs. "Well, I almost beat you, so yeah. But relationships aren't fights or races. You don't *win* or *lose* them."

"My mom's in jail because of my dad. Tell me that's anything but a loss."

I don't know what to say. Where's Ms. Foy when you need her?

Caspian wipes the sweat from his face. "Love is being ahead the whole fight and getting knocked out at the buzzer."

"Wouldn't fighting get boring if you thought you'd always win? Would it still be as satisfying if you never lost? If you never had to go back and train harder and try to get better?"

"Look, opioids may have taken my father, but love took my mother."

"Don't give up on love because it's hard."

"I've got enough *hard*," he says.

CHAPTER 24

Friday morning, I can't eat. My nerves are worse than they've been before any wrestling tournament. All of my movements are jittery and exaggerated. I pull the junk drawer right off the tracks and out of the cabinet while looking for the first aid kit. It crashes into my knee before flipping onto the floor.

"Rowan, what the heck are you doing?" Mom stands at the end of the hall. One side of her hair is curled. She's wearing one of those generic mall necklaces all middle-aged women use to dress up a boring outfit.

"You have a showing today?" I ask, righting the drawer and sliding it back into place. I collect a pile of old swimming report cards from the carpet and a braid of charging cables that probably don't work.

"Your father has an appointment with Dr. Patel," she replies.

"About Sweden?" I bend to pick up paper clips, stacks of expired coupons, and old fridge photos. Dad's ski pass from a hundred years ago slips out from the folds of a tattered recipe. Popcorn makes off with one of Mom's sales brochures. She looks way younger in the picture, even though it was probably only taken three years ago.

"Yes," she replies, straightening her shirt. "There's paperwork to fill out."

Once everything's been safely returned to the drawer, I ram it shut with my hip. Too hard.

"Rowan?" Mom says again, this time decidedly more irritated. "Stop slamming things."

"Sorry."

She turns to head back to her room.

"I won't be home tonight," I call after her. "I'm going to see Ozzy's play."

"What about dinner?" she asks.

Elbows and a side of jabs.

"I'll just go to Subway."

Ike and I drive to school. He smells like he hasn't showered since the weekend. A cold Pop-Tart with pink icing balances on his knee.

"What's a badass fight name for a girl?"

"Kayla."

"Frig off, I'm serious."

"Okay, Ava."

"Ike!"

"What? I dunno."

"Like who's a really tough woman."

"Beryl."

"I am *not* going by Beryl," I shout.

Ike looks at me, smirking. "What do you mean?" He makes fists and pretends to shadowbox the dash.

"I'll tell Mom where you hide your weed."

"You know where I hide my weed?" Ike says.

"The Nike shoebox under your bed."

"You found that?"

"Popcorn did. And don't smoke too much pot. It can fuck with your head."

I turn into the school parking lot. We are late and have to park at the back, near the professional center.

"You know what else can fuck with your head?" Ike says, gathering his backpack. "Getting punched in it."

Touché. I think of Degan. "I know how to block."

"I don't know what you're up to, Row, but let's hope that's true."

We get out of the car and cross the lot as the bell rings.

"Don't say anything to Mom and Dad." I spy Pia up ahead. "Or to anyone."

I follow Ike to his locker, waiting for a response.

"Don't do anything stupid," he says. His locker is stuffed with thousands of loose pages, textbooks, and unwashed T-shirts.

"I won't."

Ike sticks a mechanical pencil behind his ear and unearths a scientific calculator from the bottom of his locker.

"What are you doing tonight?" I ask.

"Probably hanging out with Jesse and Sean."

"Just do me a favor," I say quietly. "Answer your phone if I call."

"Don't be stupid," he repeats.

We head off in opposite directions. I sit in class but might as well be on a moon colony. I listen to nothing and hear no one. I go through combos in my head: one-two-three. One-one-three, one-two-one. I practice wrists locks and choke invisible opponents. At break, I walk by Ozzy standing near the auditorium with a group of castmates. I don't stop. I feel him watching me. Focus.

When Pia approaches from behind and tugs my ponytail, I nearly back fist her.

"Whoa," she says. "You're jumpy today."

"Sorry. I think I'm low on calories."

"Want my apple?" She digs through her bag.

As soon as the apple's in my hand I lose my appetite. Pia studies my face. Not a good thing. The longer she stares, the more she'll figure out every detail of what's going on, plus a few others.

"You okay?" she asks.

I take a bite of the apple and gag. "I'm good. Why?"

"Because you're in total fight mode."

I swallow. "No, I'm not."

"Yeah, you are. Hard. This is how you act before a tournament. Oh my God. Do we have a tournament and Coach didn't tell me?"

"There's no tournament. Oz and I just haven't been getting along lately."

"I saw him five minutes ago. He said you were going to his dress rehearsal tonight."

Ahmed walks by and nods at Pia. The biggest, most ridiculous smile lights up her face. She grabs my wrist. "We're going on a *date* date tonight."

"Where?"

"I don't know yet. We'll probably grab dinner somewhere. Maybe go to a movie." She glances at the apple in my hand. "You're not going to eat that are you?"

I shake my head.

"You gotta eat something, Row."

"I will."

"See you at practice tomorrow."

Caspian texts on my way to last period. *You got a name yet?*

Fuck. I scan the corkboards and SMART Boards. Mostly university recruiting posters and tutoring ads and summer school information.

I'm still thinking of one. What time should I be there?

You'll have to sneak in before eight. Text me when you get here, and I'll let you in the service door.

I narrowly escape Ms. Foy when the final bell rings. I have hours to kill before the fight. If I time things correctly, I can watch the beginning of Ozzy's play, race to the pub, fight, and maybe get back in time for the final scene. As long as he sees me there when the house lights are still on, he'll have no idea that I've ever left.

I drive to the river alone. I find a rock on the bank free of goose shit and sit. With my eyes closed and body still, I try to relax. Mr. Williams runs *learn to meditate* sessions at lunch and Ms. Foy forced me to take one. She said it might help me process some of my feelings around my dad. It never works. My mind usually wanders and I forget what I was supposed to be doing.

Inhale. Exhale. The whoosh of the river drowns out the noises of the city. Traffic moves like a silent film. I try to align my brain waves with the river's current. I have no idea if this is meditation, but a sense of calm anchors me to the earth. For the first time in weeks, my shoulders aren't cranked up to my ears and my hands feel like hands. Not weapons. I imagine myself floating.

A memory surfaces from the summer before grade three. Dad and I had gone camping together alone. Ike had gotten the stomach flu and Mom stayed home to look after him. Dad and I got lost picking blueberries. We spent hours trekking through the woods in search of our campsite. The sun had set by the time we found it, and we had to build a fire in the pitch dark.

Dad never once let on that we were in trouble. It must have been terrifying.

The problem with keeping the fight a secret is that I have no one to do my hair. I blindly part it into sections and attempt multiple French braids. My shoulders are sore from training, and I can barely keep my arms lifted above my head. I do a shitty job. Some braids are tight; others loose and bumpy, and I've missed a chunk of hair at the nape of my neck. I see my reflection in the water. *Oh my God, Medusa.*

I text Caspian my fight name.

At six o'clock, I order a sub and head back to the school. The ink on my ticket has bled, rendering the words illegible. Not that anyone is checking tickets. I find a seat near an exit. There are a few other people in the audience. A grandpa with an oxygen machine sits in the front row. Younger siblings. I text Ozzy to let him know I'm here.

Break a leg, I type.

I'm so nervous, he replies.

Me too, Ozzy. Me too.

Mr. B races back and forth onstage. The lights go up and down like horses on a merry-go-round. At one point the curtains open six feet, and then violently swing shut. A few sound checks later, Mr. B finds the spotlight. I check my watch. They are already ten minutes behind.

"Welcome," Mr. B says. "Thank you for coming to our dress rehearsal. As you can tell we're still working out some tech, but we are now ready to get started. May I present to you, *Romeo and Juliet.*"

Five people clap. The curtain opens on a bunch of weirdos. I wish I had a program to understand what's going on. *Prologue?*

They don't stay on stage for long before new characters arrive. I wish they wore *Hello, My Name Is* … signs around their necks. The first character I recognize is new Benvolio and that's only because of his line: *Part, fools! Put up your swords, you know not what you do.* I've heard Ozzy say it a hundred times before. New Benvolio is six-five. The green vest does not fit him the way it did Oz. Ten minutes in, and I have no idea what's happening on stage.

I nervously check my phone for the time. I have to leave in five minutes. Finally, Ozzy's part. He looks sort of regal and comical, the way he puffs his chest and commands his lines. Hot too. A smile sweeps across my face seeing this new Oz. I remember him telling me after watching one of my tournaments, that I looked like a different person when I wrestled. He'd used the word *nefarious*.

Ozzy looks out into the audience dramatically. "Farewell, thou canst not teach me to forget."

Thou canst not teach me what the hell is going on in this play right now.

Benvolio replies in a riddle, and they leave the stage.

Farewell, I whisper, easing out of my seat and crouch-walking up the aisle. I slip out a side exit and run, my braids whipping in the wind.

I park at a McDonald's and walk the few blocks to the pub.

I'm here, I text.

The back door flies open almost immediately. Had I been standing closer it probably would have knocked me out. Caspian drags me inside by my wrist with almost cartoonish violence, sending a strike of fear through my body.

"Is everything okay?" I whisper.

"There's a lot of money being exchanged down there."

"But that's a good thing, right?"

"Yeah, we're just at capacity. This whole operation only works if we can control it." He pauses. "What's up with your hair?"

I frown. "I didn't have anyone else to do it."

"Come." He ushers me into a tiny staff room with cinderblock walls and plastic chairs. Beer paraphernalia is scattered about. A Budweiser clock hangs on the wall. "Sit."

I slump in an orange chair, the plastic cracked so that it reclines unnaturally. Caspian yanks the elastics from my braids.

"What are you doing?" I ask.

"Fixing it."

"What matters about my hair?"

"Rowena, these braids are so loose someone's gonna get their fingers caught and rip them out."

He smooths and tugs my hair with reckless precision and creates, from what I can see in the dusty Heineken mirror, two perfectly symmetrical and tight French braids.

"What are you wearing?"

"Just a black shirt, these leggings, and my wrestling boots."

"Perfect."

"Did you bring my gloves?" I ask.

He freezes. "There are no gloves."

"What do you mean?"

"It's bare-knuckle."

"We never practiced bare-knuckle!"

"And why do think that is? You'd split 'em open and not be able to fight."

Oh my God, I'm going to have to wear gloves for the next week like we're back in the frigging pandemic.

"Get changed. You lock the door like this. I'll be back in a minute."

He leaves. I lock the door and change into a rash guard. My hands shake so much I can barely lace my boots. From below, the voices of men rise. They travel through the vents, an angry mob. The anticipation is palpable. They've come for blood. The whole building vibrates.

There's a small window on the back side of the room. It's probably never been washed. Dead flies line the space between the panes. The casing is blistered and warped. I look out onto the street. I don't even know what for. A sign?

I can just make out the side door. A pair of men walk up, inconspicuously. One wears a suit, the other jeans and a sports coat. Degan collects money from them and they disappear inside. I hear their footsteps on an invisible staircase. *I thought they were already at capacity.*

I take a deep breath and take one final look out at the street. There are no signs. No men in wheelchairs. Nothing to say *you must do this,* and no ambulances or caution tape to say *you must not.* All I hear is Ike. *"Don't do anything stupid." What the hell am I doing?*

There's a knock on the door. "You good?" Caspian calls from the other side, like a massage therapist.

I choke out a weak, "Yeah," and unlock the door.

He holds a tub of Vaseline.

"What's that for?"

"Makes your skin less likely to tear." He digs out a glob with his fingers and swipes it across my brows and cheekbones. Then he tapes my wrists, checks my fingernails.

"Are you ready?" he asks.

"I'm scared."

A text chimes from inside my bag. We both look.

"There's no time," he says, referring to my phone. "They've already introduced Stone."

"Stone? I'm fighting a guy named *Stone*? That his fight name?"

"That's his real name."

For fuck's sake.

"I'm scared," I say again.

"You should be scared," he replies. "You need fear to fight. I'm literally terrified every time I step into the ring, but I never show it. That's what makes you a fighter."

I think of my dad on that camping trip. *My dad is a fighter.*

Caspian thumps my shoulders and slaps my face a few times before cupping it tight and looking into my eyes. "You got this, Rowena."

The next thing I know, we're descending the crumbling stairs into the basement. The floor is dirt like a Victorian morgue. I keep my head down. Dust fills the leather-punched holes of fancy shoes and colors laces brown. The room smells like earth and cologne and cash. A splash of beer lands on the tip of my wrestling boot.

I hear someone yell "Dishboy" and then the chanting starts. A low, guttural hum: *Medusa, Medusa, Medusa.* The forest of men clears and I'm in the "ring." My opponent paces across from me, a pit bull. He has the same body type as Leo and a shorn head. An octopus tattoo stretches across his chest.

I'm all of a sudden aware of my teeth and my tongue. I don't have my mouth guard. My risk of concussion is likely higher than any payout. I can't get knocked down.

The ref is middle-aged and big as a basketball player. I take a second to scan the crowd as he reviews the rules. *What if someone recognizes me? What if someone I know is here watching?* Images of men flicker through my head. Short Dad, Tall Dad, Coach, Axel, Mr. Williams, all of my dad's therapists, Dr. Patel, Pia's dad, any of my parents' friends. Right now, I don't identify anyone. I just see jowls and stubble and muscle and ties.

The ref raises his hand, calls us both in. "If you want to touch hands, now's the time."

Stone refuses and goes back to his corner. I take one final scan of the crowd and find Caspian. He gives me a solid thumbs-up.

"Fight."

Stone charges. I raise my fists. *Don't retreat.* He circles, throws a jab, trying to find his range. Misses. I fake a shot. He kicks my thigh. Pain rushes my leg. I throw a hook, but it's wild, and only grazes his shoulder. Circle. Fake. High kick. Miss.

I don't see the jab that explodes like a grenade in my face. I only feel my neck torque, the spit on my cheek. My ears ring, the men shout. I stagger. He throws a combo, touches my shoulder with the jab. I duck away from the cross. I need to advance.

I hear Caspian yell, "Set it up." The takedown. Set up the takedown with a punch. We've been over this. Stance. Stalk. Jab, jab, hook. I hit him and he starts to waver, stumbles back. Level change, shoot. I get the single leg and take him down. Scramble. He's heavier than me.

"Don't let him get mount." I don't know who says this. My shoulder drags across the floor, the makeshift "mat" no thicker than a yoga mat. His knee digs into my liver, skims my rib cage. Escape. I am faster than him.

I get mount. Too high. I taste blood. A whiff of Gillette Cool Wave stings my nose. My father's brand. I adjust my position and start pounding. Blow after blow. Hammer fist, back of the ear. He bucks and I fly forward, nearly into a handstand. Knee on belly. Blood on my arm. I am partially back on my feet. An up kick buckles my legs. Stone attempts to get up. I duck under him and take his back. He fights my hands. Escapes. I narrowly miss a back fist.

He spits and we square up again. My ears buzz. My heart's on speed. He knocks me with a front switch kick. I teeter back, breathless, as though his heel is still there wedged into my rib cage like a stick in a storm drain. I gasp and go for a double leg. He spins out and I fall to my knees.

Everything slows and everything flashes before me. My dad, Coach, Ozzy, Popcorn, New York City. I need to end this. I get up and charge forward as if I'm going to shoot, but instead I jump, hands flailing, reaching for Stone's head. I drive upward and unleash a flying knee.

His head flings back and he collapses to the ground. The ref moves in, shoves me out of the way, protecting Stone from any more damage, and waves his arm. Over. I can't even raise my hand in victory. Mouths open and close, but I don't know what they say. I just want to get out. I search for Caspian. Blood is all I smell, all I taste.

From out of the crowd, Caspian emerges and wraps me in a feral hug, lifting me off the ground. Cheers and whoops ring in my ears. Men high-five each other. They make fists and punch the air in celebration. Someone drops a beer. No one is allowed to take pics.

"Get me outta here," I mumble, a thread of spit catching on my chin.

Caspian carries me down a narrow hallway, my head nearly scraping the low ceiling, dodging dungeon lights. I hear someone yell, "Medusa." We go up a different set of stairs. He puts me down at the top, brushes past, and beckons for me to follow. I can barely walk.

There's blood on my wrestling boot. I take a cautious step and wobble. I must look like my dad did when he started to lose his mobility. I remember the grief on his face every time he tried to take a step. The shock. I start to cry. Caspian leads me back to the small staff room, half-pushes me inside, and locks the door.

"Holy shit," he paces. "You did it. I knew you could do it." He is animated and wild-eyed. "But a flying knee, Rowena? We never even practiced that."

I learned it from watching Axel. It's how he ended his last fight in the UFC. Seemed an appropriate way to end my first underground one. My only one.

"Okay, we need to get you cleaned up." He presses a metal device onto my cheek.

"Ouch." I recoil. "The hell is that?"

"An enswell. Will help reduce the swelling."

He grabs a couple bags of ice from an apartment-size fridge in the corner and applies them to my neck and shoulder. He wipes my faces with a wet cloth, applies some sort of antiseptic spray, and ointment. So much ointment.

"How do you feel?"

Other than physical pain, I feel nothing. I feel like I've stepped out of body, out of my life, and I am someone else. *Who am I?* I shake my head.

"I'll be back," Caspian says, closing the door behind him.

I stare at the mirror on the other side of the room. *Do I dare look?* I take a deep breath, drag myself over. Monster. I am cut on my forehead and my cheek is swollen. A scratch marks the right side of my jaw like a bad makeup line. My leg and shoulder throb. *Holy shit. How am I going to cover it? What am I going to say? I got hit by a rogue Shakespeare prop?*

I lock the door and gently peel off my rash guard. My shoulder is red, but I can move it. The thought of changing any further in this testosterone-laced shit hole freaks me out. I keep my soiled sports bra and slip on a new shirt and switch my wrestling boots for sneakers.

The Budweiser clock says it's just shy of nine. I don't even know if that's the real time. *How long is a Shakespeare play?* I frantically search for my phone. There's a knock on the door.

"It's just me," Caspian says.

I let him in.

"You're never going to believe it, Rowena."

I think of Stone. "Please tell me he's okay."

"He's fine. Probably'll never fight again — at least not here — but he was likely already up walking by the time we hit the top of the stairs. He's already gone."

"So, what then?"

"Seven thousand, three hundred, and sixty dollars is what."

I brace my hand on what might be an umbrella stand. Adrenaline zips through me. I can barely catch my breath.

"Seriously?" I choke.

"New record."

"Oh my God."

"That enough to get your dad to Sweden?" Caspian asks. A spot of my blood stains his green Adidas jacket.

"It'll get him there, yeah. Don't think it'll cover all the treatment, but I think he can get some of the costs covered."

He hands me a drink.

"What is it?"

"A Shirley Temple." He smiles. "It's the best post-fight drink out there. Just don't tell anyone I said that."

I take a sip. The mix of carbonation and grenadine is a surprisingly soothing concoction.

"So, what are you going to tell your parents?"

"I'm not telling my parents."

"About the money. Aren't they gonna want to know how you randomly saved seven grand?"

My face drops.

"Oh my God, Rowena." Caspian's eyes grow. "You never thought about that?"

"I did at the beginning, but I kind of let it go because I never thought I'd actually get a fight and then when I did, I spent all my time focusing on not getting killed."

"Well, now that you're not dead, you should think about how you're going to handle that before your parents kill you."

"They will kill me."

I slump into the orange chair. *What was I thinking?* More accurately, *What the fuck was I not thinking?* Maybe I can tell them I started a new GoFundMe campaign. Or that Pia's family did. Or Ms. Foy. Axel. Someone less easy to track. Harder to thank.

I stuff my rash guard into my backpack. My phone flies out and lands on the stained linoleum floor.

"I have to get back to my boyfriend's play," I say. "Like right now. Before it ends."

"I'm not stopping you," he says, handing me a brown envelope of cash.

I feel like a drug mule. I check my phone for the time. 9:10. There's a new crack in my screen and one new message from my mom.

Sweden is not looking promising.

CHAPTER 25

My legs give way. Caspian stops my fall. "You okay?"

"Yeah, I just … can you walk me to my car?"

"We'll go out the back. Anywhere else they'll be lined up for autographs," he jokes.

The air has a pleasing edge that cools my stinging face. My left quad throbs. Outside the McDonald's, kids straddle bikes and lick late-night cones, and I long for the simpler times when the most complicated decision I had to make was what kind of sauce I wanted with my Chicken McNuggets.

We get to my car.

"So, I guess this is it," Caspian says. "You got your fight; you got your money."

I don't want this to be *it*. "But you never got your GED."

Caspian shrugs. "I can take courses."

"We can still train together. I mean, we don't have to work under hooks and uppercuts. We could just run the stairs, or whatever. And why take a course when I can help you study for free?" *Unless you'd rather take a course?*

"Thanks for the offer." He starts to back away. "I gotta go back and clean up." He crosses the street. I watch him go, my hand frozen on the door handle. *Bye?*

I'm about to leave when he stops. I wait.

"Hey, Rowan?"

"Yeah?" I reply trying to disguise the hope in my voice.

"You take your braids out and part your hair on the side, sweep it across? It'll probably cover up that cut on your forehead. You know, so your boyfriend won't see."

Ozzy.

"Right," I reply, unsure if I'm even loud enough for him to hear me. "Good idea."

He cuts through a yard and disappears. I climb into my car and yank the elastics from my braids. So many split ends. I tussle my hair with my fingers and notice a gash on the inside of my hand. The blood has dried, staining my love line a deep crimson. Pia went through a palm-reading phase last year and I can't imagine she would say this is a good omen. All my other lines left her flustered and confused. *What do they say?* I'd asked, and she'd gently lowered my hand to my lap and said, *I can't read them. Your lines are a jumbled mess. They don't make sense.*

There are still cars in the school parking lot when I arrive. A good sign. I pull into the fire lane, flick on my hazard lights, and hobble-run like Popcorn to the main doors. Locked. *Oh my God.* I go around the side of the building to the doors near the auditorium. Also locked. *Fuck.*

I check my phone. No texts from Ozzy. The play has to be still going on. Maybe the soundboard short-circuited or the curtains caught fire, causing a delay. Maybe Juliet fell off the balcony. I try another set of doors, pressing my face into the glass. Don't janitors work Friday nights?

Finally, I see kids. I recognize one from the beginning of the play, a restless younger sibling brought to the dress rehearsal because he'd never make it through the real thing. Case in point. Both are doing cartwheels and intermittently fighting over a high-bounce ball. When the ball rolls toward the door I'm standing outside, I motion for them to let me in.

When the girl approaches, I quickly brush my hair over my forehead so I don't resemble a haunted house. She is cautious. The boy swoops in, collects the ball, and opens the door. The girl punches him in the arm and tackles him for the ball. I step over the heap of them and race to the auditorium.

Light bleeds from the hallway as I open the theater doors. The stage lights are a hazy navy blue. Quiet. I hunch over and take the first seat I can find. Some guy from my math class performs a monologue. The set would indicate the *closing* monologue. That means Romeo is dead, and if Ozzy were such a great actor his eyes would've been closed when I snuck back in.

"For never was a story of more woe, than this of Juliet and her Romeo."

The lights dim and the theater melts into blackness. I hear the mechanical whoosh of the curtains being drawn. Woe. My grade ten LA teacher said *Romeo and Juliet* was "a tale of love and violence." I feel the ache in my cheek when I open my mouth, the tightness in my split forehead. My shoulder sulks and my heart grieves. I am a tale of love and violence. And woe. No wonder Pia couldn't read my palms.

The audience of five claps with the fervor of five hundred. Standing ovation. The curtains fly open like swirling dresses, and the cast steps forward to bow, all of them in a line, Ozzy and Juliet holding hands in the middle like figures on a wedding cake. Mr. B rushes the stage like a rogue fan, slaps hands with his cast, and shouts a barely discernible yahoo.

The full houselights come on. I stand in the back row, clapping. I wait for Ozzy to notice me, but his eyes are locked on Juliet. *Doesn't he know the play's over?*

One of the moms or aunts in the front row moves to the stage with her camera and motions for the actors to squish in for a photo. The grandpa with the oxygen machine waits with a cane at the end of the aisle.

A stage crew brings Mr. B the mic. "Thank you all for coming to our dress rehearsal," he says, slapping Oz on the back, but facing out. "You were a small but mighty audience, and we appreciate your support here tonight."

This time the cast claps and jeers before Mr. B turns and says something I can't hear. Students and stagehands scatter, clearing props and moving set pieces. Twin brothers wheel a crypt upstage. I wish Juliet was still in it. Ozzy still hasn't looked for me. *Why give me such a hard time about missing the show and then not even bother to come find me?* I could be sitting in the pub staff room counting money and sipping Shirley Temples with Caspian right now.

I step into the aisle. Finally, Ozzy looks up. He nods. *A nod?* It's the kind of gesture you give your mom when she comes inside the school to pick you up, and you acknowledge her, hoping she'll go away.

Fuck you then.

I turn to go.

He calls, "Row!"

Why does he always wait until I'm walking away?

He pounds up the aisle toward me in his buckled shoes and billowy shirt, face more bronzed than a California Barbie. I frantically move my hair to conceal my forehead.

"Hey," he says, eyes sparkling, breath heavy. "What did you think?"

"It was great, Oz."

"Even though I messed up my lines?"

Did he?

"Better now than messing up in the real show."

"I was kidding."

Silence. He stares at me curiously. At my forehead. Fuck.

"Come here," he says, reaching.

I bat his hand away.

"What happened to your cheek?"

My cheek? What's wrong with my cheek?

"Nothing."

"You have a bruise."

"Took an elbow. In practice."

"You didn't have practice today."

"In gym class."

He moves my hair. "Rowan, what the heck? Your frigging head is split open. What the hell happened to you?"

"I'm fine."

"Did he hurt you?"

"Who?"

"Casper. Caspian. Whatever the fuck his name is."

"No, he didn't *hurt me*," I say. "I told you I fell in gym class. I took an elbow and then hit my head on the volleyball net post."

"Why didn't you see a doctor?"

"I didn't want to miss your play."

He pulls me in for a hug. I'm probably covered in the scent of toxic masculinity. I don't hug him back.

"Are you sure he didn't hit you?"

"Yes, Oz. I'm sure." I raise my voice. The mother/aunt with the camera looks up and then uncomfortably starts fiddling with a lens cap. "Caspian's a good guy. He'd never touch me." Juliet leers in the background a few rows away. "Something I'm not sure she's capable of."

Ozzy looks back at Juliet. "Really, Row? You're gonna start this now?"

"You started it," I shout.

Mr. B looks up from the stage, a tattered script in his hand.

"You started it when you implied that I would hang out with someone who beat the shit out of me."

"A net post, Rowan? You think I'm stupid? The volleyball module was in January."

"Which is probably the last time you put any real effort into this relationship. Good luck, Oz."

I storm toward the door and stop. "Hey, Juliet."

She looks up, wide-eyed and flushed.

"Ozzy doesn't like a lot of tongue." I head out of the auditorium to my car, waving mosquitos from my face. By the time I crash into the front seat, the adrenaline from the day catches up and I break down, crying all over the steering wheel. I need to fix my face. I call Ike.

"'Sup?" he answers.

"What are you doing?" I sniff.

"Just chillin'."

"I need your help."

"Pick me up at Sean's. We're in the garage."

"I'll text when I get there."

Sean lives in our old neighborhood, three doors down from our old house. I wonder if it tortures Ike to see it every time he goes there, the house where we were both brought home from the hospital. Where we learned to walk and ride bikes and turn on the oven. Where families and fathers were intact.

I take a shortcut through an outdoor athletic park where men play soccer under floodlights. My head throbs. I pass my elementary school, with the red bricks and the windowed foyer plastered with art. Maple leaves, bison, inuksuks. The playground has been updated since Ike and I went there, the murder slide replaced with something blue and plastic.

At the end of the block, our old house. I park in front of it and roll down my window. Music and pot drift from Sean's garage three doors down. Our house looks the same. The steep front lawn that was a headache to mow but fun to roll down, the rock wall flanking the driveway that Dad helped me traverse when I was little, and the house number, four, whole and off-kilter. Only the door color has changed from my dad's favorite yellow to charcoal as if the new owner might've tried to snuff out any disease my dad could've left behind.

I'm in front of our old house.

K, coming.

A few minutes pass before I see Ike emerge, his hand lost in a bag of Cool Ranch Doritos. His hair looks like a conspiracy theorist's. He climbs in the front seat.

"Are you stoned?"

"What happened to your face?"

"I need you to fix it." I lift my hair from my forehead.

"Fuck, Rowan." A chip falls from his mouth. "What do you want me to do?"

"I don't know. Make it less obvious or something, so Mom and Dad don't see."

"Why didn't you get Ozzy to do it? Wouldn't he have, like, stage makeup or some shit?"

"Ozzy's busy."

Ike flicks on his phone's flashlight and examines my forehead, pressing the skin around the cut.

"Ow," I wince, elbowing him away. "That hurts."

"I think you need stitches."

"I can't go to the hospital."

"Did you at least win?"

"I didn't lose. Put your seat belt on."

Ike, still sitting sideways, tugs the seat belt so it stretches awkwardly over his body. I pull onto the street.

"Can you get my water from my backpack? I'm dying."

Ike reaches into the back seat. I make a U-turn and head out of the neighborhood.

"You think Mom and Dad will still be up?" I ask.

"Depends if there are new episodes of *Alaska Fish Wars*." He's pulled my bag onto my lap and rifles through it with his dirty cool-ranch fingers. My gear will smell like a senior's buffet.

I pull up to a red light behind a cop. I take a quick survey of my surroundings to make sure I'm not doing anything illegal. Seat belt on, lights on, no phone in my hand, license in my wallet. Good.

"Holy shit, Row!"

My pay-out is spread across Ike's lap. Hundreds of bills, some of them slick and straight out of an ATM, others crumpled and worn. The brown paper envelope balances on his basketball shoes.

He lets out a high-pitched, "What the hell?" and starts laughing maniacally.

"We're behind a fricking cop," I say through gritted teeth. "Put it away."

"How much is it?"

I haven't seen Ike this happy since the Easter Dad built him a bike jump. His eyes are as big as BMX tires. He fingers through the money, returning handful after handful to the envelope. When the light turns green, I follow the cop to the next set of lights and turn right. I can't risk getting pulled over.

"What are you going to do with it?" Ike asks.

"It's for Dad to go to Sweden."

He looks serious all of a sudden. "Didn't Mom text you?" A hundred-dollar bill is stuck to his shorts.

"She said it didn't look promising. That doesn't mean it won't happen. There's always just a bunch of stuff to sort through."

"Yeah," Ike agrees. "Like permits and waivers and shit."

Is that all it is?

We drive a block in silence. I don't even know where I'm going. We have no destination.

"Help me fix my face."

Ike shoots up straight like he's had an epiphany. "Turn right, here." He gestures.

"Home?"

"Close," he says, shaking his head. "Beryl's."

"Will she even be awake? It's almost midnight."

"She watches *Coronation Street* marathons on Friday nights," Ike replies.

I park a few doors down, away from our house, away from the possibility my parents are still up and spying out the window. I've only been inside Beryl's a handful of times. We cut across the lawn to a side door.

"It seems too late," I argue. "She's a hundred years old. Shouldn't she be asleep?"

"Ninety-six," Ike corrects. "And midnight is like ten a.m. for her. She did night-ops in the military." He gently raps on the door, one slow knock followed by three quick. A tap code. The porch light flicks on. And off. On. Off … On.

What the hell?

Ike smiles. "Morse code."

The door flings open. "Come in, soldiers," Beryl says. "Let me pause my show."

We follow Beryl through her galley kitchen with the camouflage backsplash to the living room. Built-in shelves wrap around the walls. They are covered in books and memorabilia and photos of men. Men with berets, men with pocket squares. Bearded men. Kilted men. All the men.

"What can I do?" she asks.

"Rowan needs stitches."

"Stitches?" Beryl and I say in unison.

"No, I don't," I say.

"I sure as hell hope not," Beryl replies. "Been years since I've given anyone stitches. What do you need them for?"

"Her forehead," Ike says.

"Let's have a look." Beryl shuffles across the carpet that is faded and thick as a battlefield. She turns on a desk lamp and cranks the moveable head to create a spotlight. "Come," she urges.

I step into the light, move my hair off my forehead. The smell of burnt dust seeps from the bulb.

"The hell happened to you?" she asks, pushing and pulling my skin with an "all business" touch. I wince.

"Fight." I don't know why I tell her the truth except that what's the point of lying to a woman who took out Nazis and collects men?

"Gotcha good," she says. "Hope you won."

She cups the back of my head and moves in for a better look.

"Probably could've done with some stitches, but I got something better. Ike," she calls over her shoulder, "get me some cotton from the bathroom."

He doesn't have to ask for additional information. He disappears down the hall, running his fingers down either side of the papered walls. Beryl wheels a desk chair into my heels and says, "Sit."

Ow.

I sink down and examine my Achilles for blood. From the kitchen, bottles rattle and drawers slam. I hear the suction and thump of the fridge door opening and closing. Sounds like a meth lab.

Beryl comes back with a mason jar of clear liquid in one hand and a tall brown bottle with a flip-top in the other.

"What are they?" I ask.

Ike sets a handful of cotton balls and wad of gauze on the mantle.

"Drink this first," Beryl instructs.

"Is this the same stuff you gave us last time? What you gave 'the living'?"

Beryl shakes her head. "Honey, this is what we gave the dying."

Lovely.

"Open it." She passes Ike the bottle.

He flips the top with his chewed thumb. His cuticles are shredded. He takes a sniff, shrugs, and hands it to me.

At first, I smell nothing. But after a second whiff, I detect some kind of alcohol and … ferns? Dandelions? Paint thinner? Kind of smells like Short Dad's work van.

"How much do I need to drink?"

Beryl measures a third of the bottle with her pointer finger. A ring with a nut cluster of rubies clings below her knuckle. Scars on her hand resemble barbed wire. Her veins glow blue.

I close my eyes and tip the bottle. The liquid glugs and floods my throat like Drano. Maybe it is Drano. I am drinking fire. I am drinking the allied invasion of Sicily. Stalingrad. I am drinking World War II. I am falling off the chair.

I hear Beryl say, "Get her to the couch," before I pass out.

It's 2:00 when I come to, IN MY OWN BED. *What the fuck?* I touch my forehead. Gauze, a bandage. My face and neck are drenched in sweat. A blanket resembling a fishing net is draped around my body. When I attempt to sit up, Popcorn, curled at the foot of my bed, raises her head.

I lie back down, my brain a mess of fuzz and jumbled thoughts. An iPhone gone through the wash. The ceiling stars blur. I shoot back up. *Where's my stuff?* I bend over the side of my bed and find my backpack. My phone is face down on the bed-side table. Am I wearing Beryl's gardening sweater? I'm going to owe Ike until he's twenty-one.

Popcorn circles at the end of the bed and relocates by my hip. I pet her head. She licks me. It is the first time she's slept with me and not my parents since I brought her home. It's as if she knows who in the family needs the emotional support, and when.

I check my phone. Two texts. From Caspian: *How r your injuries?* And from Ozzy: *We need to talk.* I check the time stamps. Sent within the last hour. I roll onto my side. Wrong one. My shoulder still aches from the fight. I shift and press my fingertips into the wound on my forehead.

How did I end up in a constellation of three? A triangle?

I remember the first time I met Oz. It was in gym class. He had the hairiest legs in grade eight. We'd been partnered for a fitness evaluation. I beat him in the beep test. He had the higher vertical jump. We tied for plank. He asked me out in the middle of a push-up. And Caspian. Dropout, knockout. The kind of guy who'd win the Hunger Games and shrug it off like it was a game of checkers. He'd never buy me a stuffed polar bear with pink heart lips. He'd be more likely to give me ringworm or rubbing alcohol or Bio-Oil. Only once in a while would he buy something totally cliché and impractical. A dozen red roses. A heart-shaped box of chocolates.

I stare at my phone. *We need to talk.*

One week until New York. I need to wrestle like my life isn't a meteor about to hit the earth's atmosphere and burn up. My relationship with Oz, my dad; I am losing people. The least I can do is win matches.

I text Caspian back first: *Not bad*, though I don't really know. When I touch my forehead it doesn't feel as spongy as it did before. I'm not exactly sure what Beryl did — seal it with a blowtorch and cover it with cement? — but it doesn't feel life-threatening. As long as I can keep it from Coach.

We need to talk.

Do we? Is that what we need? I wonder if Oz is still up, lying in bed with the scent of Juliet and crushed velvet and stardom on his neck. I stare at the plastic stars above my bed, wishing they would tell me what to do.

Pia once said Ozzy and I were star-crossed lovers. I loved that sentiment. It seemed romantic and superior. How could things go wrong when our love was celestial? When the stars themselves had brought us together? Only recently did I learn that it was shitty to be star-crossed. *Romeo and Juliet* is, after all, a tragedy. Their union *thwarted by a malign star*, not upheld by one. *Asshole.*

I start a text: *We need a break.* I stare at the words hovering in the message box waiting to be launched, waiting to become reality. The cursor flashes. I trace Ozzy's name at the top of the screen. *Is this what I want?*

Popcorn rests her face on my chest. It doesn't seem to matter what I *want* anymore. I'm down to needs. Basic and boring: a good night's sleep, Polysporin, and a trusty pair of wrestling boots.

Send.

CHAPTER 26

Mom flies into my room, her robe tied tight, and her hair in her face. "Rowan!" she hollers. "It's after nine. Get up, you're going to be late for practice."

I roll onto my face. Oh my God. My body hurts. My head feels like an astronaut helmet. "I'm getting up," I croak.

"I'll make you some food," Mom says, rushing away toward the kitchen. Popcorn follows, her nails clicking optimistically on the hardwood. Her limp is gone.

I don't want food. I fish an Advil from my bedside table drawer and swallow it down with week-old water. I touch my forehead. *What about my cheek?* I slide out of bed and examine my face in the mirror. *How can I hide my head in practice?* I can't cut bangs or I'll look like a frigging twelve-year-old. I'll just have to stick to the story: volleyball net post.

I alternate layers of concealer and foundation on my cheek, around the bandage on my forehead, my jawline. Anywhere my face screams street fight. Powder, blush, bronzer. Fuck it. *Why not add eyeliner and mascara too?* When I'm done, I look like a Spice Girl. *Grapple Spice.* Maybe Coach will play "Wannabe" and I can lead the team in a lip-synch.

My backpack stinks. I pull out my dirty shirt from the fight and hide it in my closet. The socks I throw in the laundry. My wrestling boots still have blood on them. I chuck them under my bed and grab my backup pair. At the bottom of my bag is the envelope of cash. I leave it there, tucked under my hoodie, and zip the bag shut.

"There's a bowl of oatmeal on the table," Mom says.

"I hate oatmeal." I don't mean to snap, but holy shit. I haven't liked oatmeal since third grade. Ike likes oatmeal.

"Rowan," Mom says. "You can't go to practice on an empty stomach. We've been through this a thousand times. It's not healthy."

Neither is drinking a bottle of wine every other night.

"I'll just take a granola bar."

"What do you think is in a granola bar? Oats."

Oh my God. Shut up.

She follows me down the hall. I have my boots, I need water. The oatmeal sits alone at the dining room table.

"What am I supposed to do with that?" Mom gestures to the bowl. There's a fleck of egg on her cheek.

"I don't know. Give it to Beryl. Can you just drive me? I'll get a ride home with Pia."

I'm too jittery. I snatch a plastic water bottle from the fridge. *Since when did she start buying water?* Mom exchanges her robe for a cardigan, her slippers for slip-ons.

"I'll be in the car," she says. "I wish you wouldn't waste food."

I wish you weren't so annoying.

I try to be nicer when I get in the car. I keep my hair down, concealing my forehead. I feel like I'm forgetting something. Boots. Water. *Nope, I'm good.*

"Why does Sweden no longer seem promising?" I ask.

Mom stops at a crosswalk. Kids on bikes tear through. The sky is dark and smells of rain. Perhaps they're racing the weather.

"Just stuff," Mom replies.

"Well, that's kind of vague."

"It's complicated, Rowan. ALS is complicated. You know that." Her tone bends toward hostile.

"Is it the money?"

"That's part of it."

The light ahead turns red. Mom doesn't seem to notice, pressing forward at a highway-merge speed.

"Mom! It's a red light!"

She slams on the brakes. Our bodies jolt forward and then back. She narrowly missed rear-ending the red Subaru in front of us.

"Shit," Mom whispers, her hands locked on the steering wheel, knuckles pale as milk froth. "That was close."

I stare at her profile. The amount of gray in her hair seems to have doubled since last week. Her skin is pallid. I don't remember the last time she went swimming or to the gym or did anything social.

The light turns green. I don't know whether to ask her what else it is besides the money that makes Sweden less promising. I worry she may have already told me in almost getting us killed. I don't know that I want her to say it out loud. That maybe my dad's not well enough to travel halfway across the world for treatment. That maybe it's just *too late*.

She pulls into the gym parking lot. The smell of fried chicken already wafts from the KFC. *Who's eating a Zinger for breakfast?* Probably Coach. I'm about to jump out of the front seat when a bone of loneliness pokes my heart, remembering all the times

I sat across from Caspian in the KFC, calculating square roots and cosines and whether we had enough ketchup packets to get through our meal.

I pause and tuck my hair behind my ear. I'm about to lean in to kiss my mother goodbye when she recoils, a disturbed look on her face.

"What happened to your forehead?"

Uh oh.

"I hit my head in gym class yesterday."

"The school never called."

"Because I'm not in grade two. It's fine. I just needed a bandage."

"I sure hope so," she says, her expression squeamish. "Don't let it get infected. The last thing you want to bring to New York is impetigo or ringworm."

"It's a tiny cut."

I get out of the car, one hand in each wrestling boot, water bottle tucked under my arm.

* * *

"Rowena," Coach calls from the corner where he's trying to plug in a speaker. "Got a call from the Athletic Director at York College. He was wondering what your plans are after graduation."

"Where's York College?" I ask.

"Kansas."

Not that. When I think of Kansas, I picture yellow brick roads and tornados. I couldn't even place it on a map.

"What did you say?"

"I told him to ask you in person. In New York."

Oh great. I lean against the girl's changeroom. "I can't wait."

Pia's at the mirror brushing her hair into a high ponytail. "I thought you were never going to get here."

"I slept in."

"Me and Ahmed. We're officially going out." She girly-squeals.

"Neither of you is allowed to date."

"Right, so don't tell anyone. He's so hot, and shit, he's smart too. Remember that calculus assignment that I was doing and it was taking forever and I kept screwing up the answers? He was the only one who was able to explain what I was doing wrong."

I smile.

"I love him."

"I told Ozzy we needed a break."

"What?"

I shrug.

"What did he say?"

"Haven't checked my phone."

"Oh my God." Pia slumps onto the bench, covering her mouth with her hands. "This is serious. Are you okay?"

"I need to focus. I want to do well in New York, and wrestling seems like the only thing I can control right now. Plus, Ms. Foy's been harassing me about the SAT. You know I was supposed to have already written it this spring?"

"Your makeup looks amazing."

I glance in the mirror. It does.

She stares at my bandaged forehead. "Do you have ringworm?"

"A small cut."

"Here, let me do your hair."

She sits on the bench and I sink down to the floor in front of her. The tile is cold and gives me goose bumps. This is her way of showing me she cares. It's always been her way. She gently parts my hair with the tip of her black comb and begins to braid.

"Hurry," I say. "Coach will freak out if we're late."

"I can't believe you haven't checked your phone. When did this happen?"

She tugs at a piece of my hair, twisting it into the braid. It hurts and I wonder if it's another bruise I picked up in the fight. For the most part, I blocked Stone's head kick, but some contact was made. It's why my shoulder hurts.

"Last night."

"But you and are Ozzy are like …" Her voice trails off.

Don't say star-crossed lovers.

"Soulmates."

"All we do now is fight."

Pia ties off the first braid and gathers the rest of my hair to start the second.

"I'm sad we can't go on double dates," she says.

"We can," I reply. "It'll just be with Ahmed's older brother."

Her mouth gapes and she shoves my sore shoulder. We both laugh.

Coach knocks on the door. "What, are you playing beauty parlor in there?" he says in his gruff voice.

Kind of.

"We're coming," Pia says. She hastily ties off the second braid.

I get a head rush when I stand up, and quickly lace my boots.

"Please say you're coming to New York."

Pia opens the door and bends and straightens her arm. "We're about to find out."

CHAPTER 27

Leo looks a bit dejected when Coach tells him to partner with Nate. After weeks of wrestling with me, he now has to wrestle up a weight class and Nate smells like an expired TV dinner. *Sorry,* I mouth to Leo.

Pia is lighter than me and I've forgotten what it's like to wrestle a girl. Her shots are quick. We work ankle picks from an underhook position and then from a two-on-one. I'm scared to take the two-on-one on her bad arm, but she assures me she's fine.

Midway through practice, Caspian rolls into the club and kicks off his slides at the front door. He wears the same red hoodie he wore the first time I met him. Minutes later, he's at the back of the gym and stripped down to his Spandex fight shorts. Pia and I watch as he steps onto one of the electronic scales. Axel records his weight.

"Holy abs," Pia whispers.

"Right?" I say. *And holy something else.*

Coach clears his throat. "And all this time I was worried it'd be you, distracting them. Am I going to start having to tell these fighters to wear baggy shirts and sweatpants?"

Oh my God, Coach.

Pia playfully rolls her eyes and shakes her head. I laugh and we square up for the next round of ankle picks.

As we near the end of the practice, I ask Pia, "Are you going to do live?" We've only been drilling at fifty percent. I don't want to reinjure her.

"Depends what Coach says," she replies. "I feel fine."

But Coach splits us up. I'm back with Leo, and Pia goes with some junior high kid with a mouth guard designed to look like a poop emoji.

Leo feels ten times heavier now. He gets my leg and drives forward. I spin as I'm falling so I don't land on my back, jamming my face into the mat instead. Leo climbs on top and tries to set up a leg ride. I defend, lifting my head, but notice my bandage is on the ground in front of me, along with a soiled piece of gauze. Blood starts dripping from my forehead. Leo abruptly stops. I scramble to my feet, cupping my hand over the cut.

"Did I do that?"

He passes me his T-shirt. Soaked. I press it into the wound. Coach begins crossing the mat toward us. From the corner of my eye, I see Caspian looking concerned.

Coach looks at Leo. "Elbow?" He takes away the balled-up T-shirt and tilts my head to the fluorescent lights humming above. "What the hell happened to you?" he says, no joke, no sarcasm. If anything, his gaze is marked with fear.

"I hit my head at school."

"On an axe?"

"A volleyball post."

"What are you playing volleyball for this close to a tournament?"

"It was just in gym class."

"Did you see a doctor?"

Define doctor.

"Jog it out," he yells to everyone else.

"No."

"I think you should have it looked at." He shakes his head in a disappointed father way. I start to cry. I don't know if I'm crying more because my head stings, because I've let Coach down, or because my own father can't shake his head in disappointment at me anymore. Either way, I'm a blubbering mess.

Coach hesitantly puts his hand on my back. He can do all the prep work in the world to have me physically ready for an important tournament. It's always the mental part that throws him off.

Another hand touches my back. Caspian's. He hands me a towel. I wait for Coach's reaction. His face is the red of a warning light. He's either going to lose it or let it go. The entire gym watches, in silence. Blood trickles down my face. I taste it on my upper lip. Coach withdraws his hand, says nothing to Caspian, and goes to the paper towel dispenser. Back near the heavy bags, Axel grabs the first aid kit.

"It's okay, Rowena," Caspian says. "The cut just opened up a little." He sweeps away the stray hairs, bloody and damp, caught in the wound. I bury myself into his chest. Axel peels me away. Caspian steps back into the small crowd of fighters as Coach and Axel take turns examining my face.

"You think it's too late for stitches?" Coach asks Axel.

"Hard to say."

"Rowan, can you get to the hospital?"

"No way," I protest. "Not right now. My mom's not in a good place."

I cannot go to the hospital. The hospital will ask too many questions. They'll call my mom. I'll be there all night.

"Do you have your health card?"

"I can't go to the hospital."

"There's a clinic on Eighty-fourth my guys use," Axel says. "Doctor's an old friend of mine. They do stitches there. If she needs them. Might be too late. I can get her in."

"Does that work?" Coach asks.

I nod. "Can you drive me though? I don't want my mom to worry right now."

"Meet me at my car."

Pia helps me to the changeroom while Leo starts mopping the blood.

"How bad does it look?" I ask.

"Pretty gross." She wets a paper towel and cleans my face. "You're trembling," she says. "Did you eat before practice?"

"I brought a granola bar."

"But you never ate it?"

Ugh, she sounds like her mom. She sounds like my mom.

I change out of my wrestling boots. There's a knock on the door. Pia gets up to answer and returns with Caspian's red hoodie.

"I guess so you don't have to walk around covered in blood?" She tosses it over. It smells like cheap detergent, chicken wings, and boy deodorant. Hard work. I slip it on over my head being careful not to swipe it against the cut. It is warm and worn. Exactly what I need right now.

"Good luck," Pia says. "Call me after. And let me know what happens with Oz."

Oz. Ugh.

My body starts to seize as I stand and make my way to the parking lot. All the damage I took in the fight magnifies. My ligaments, joints, muscles. All the invisible injuries begin to flare. Realistically, I probably need a week off to recover.

Caspian opens the front door for me. "If you need anything, text."

"Thanks for the hoodie," I reply, my boots under my arm and my hands tucked into the front pocket. "I'll bring it back tomorrow."

"No rush," he says. "And Dr. Volkov is great. He'll fix you up." He slides the hood over my head and I step outside into the rain.

Downpour. Water gushes off the eaves in glistening sheets. A man with a bucket of chicken fights with an umbrella. I duck and crawl into Coach's car. He removes a wrapper from the passenger seat. Sausage and Egg McGriddle. He's upgraded his sins.

"Eighty-fourth Street," he mumbles, switching the gearshift to reverse. "We're going north."

We drive in silence until we are out of the busy core and on the ring road. Same way to Caspian's house. Visibility is poor. The wipers move at a dizzying pace and Coach is constantly adjusting, moving his head like a boxer.

"You sure you got that cut in gym class?" Coach asks.

Does it matter?

"Yes."

"Because you know you can talk to me if there's something going on."

Oh my God. Ms. Foy 2.0. Robo-Coach edition.

I snap. "Why does everyone want to make such a big deal about it? It's just a stupid cut!"

"Don't give me a reason to call your parents."

I swallow.

"Some of these MMA characters are bad news."

"What's that supposed to mean?"

"It means they do stuff on the side. Stuff that sometimes leaves them with broken jaws and busted kneecaps." He pauses. "Cuts on their foreheads."

It's a moment where, if the rain weren't assaulting the windshield and blinding him, Coach would look me in the eyes. The same way my dad does when *we need to talk*. Fuck. I think about Ozzy and have a sudden longing for him. He'd know right now to say nothing. He'd know not to ask any more questions. He'd know to just let me be. I wrap myself tighter inside Caspian's hoodie.

We drive again in silence. Coach yells at a pickup truck, flips the bird at an SUV. The clinic on Eighty-fourth is inside a small professional center, a square red brick building with a central hallway, and a sketchy elevator. We take the stairs. The letters on Dr. Volkov's door are peeling. The only person in the waiting room, an old man, is asleep.

The receptionist summons us to the desk with a wave of her manicured hand. I *don't* have my health card. I don't even have my wallet. She disappears down the hallway and brings Dr. Volkov back with her. He is a giant. Bald as a baby, broad-shouldered and scarred. He has a limp like Popcorn once did. He looks like he may have escaped a gulag.

"Follow me," he says in a Russian accent so thick it seems fake.

We go into an examination room and he motions for me to sit on the black vinyl bed. He doesn't take my blood pressure or my weight or ask me any dumb questions. He tilts my head and comes at me like he's going to do my makeup with an otoscope.

"Not infected," he says after much poking.

262 / ALI BRYAN

Coach breathes a sigh of relief.

"Glue should seal it."

He washes the cut with gauze and antiseptic. I bite my hand. Next, he applies the glue. It takes only a few minutes for it to set. He finishes the job with adhesive tape.

"Don't get it wet," he says to me, his tone stern. "And don't touch it for twenty-four hours." He looks at Coach. "No fighting tomorrow. Day off."

"But she'll be okay to compete next weekend?" Coach asks.

"No problem." He turns back to me. "You win."

Is that a command or a prophecy?

"I'll try."

"No try. Win." He pulls open his lab coat, untucks his thinning pinstripe shirt, and shows off a scar the size and shape of a tire iron. "Win."

I have no idea what he "won," but I nod in agreement. "Win."

Coach shakes Dr. Volkov's grizzly paw. We both sanitize our hands on the way out, and take the elevator back down.

"Well, that was weird. And entertaining," Coach says, confused but happy. "So don't get it wet, and for God's sake, don't touch it. I just booked tickets to the Tina Turner musical. They're non-refundable."

We get back in the car and head south toward home. When his wife calls, I finally check my phone. Five missed calls, all from my mom. *Shit.* My ringer was off. That familiar sense of dread starts coursing through my veins, dragging down my heart, messing with my brain. The dread that asks, is this it? Is this *the* call? My father looked fine this morning.

I call her back. She answers on the first ring.

"Rowan, where are you?"

"Just in the car with Coach."

"Get home immediately."

She sounds angry. *Why would she be angry?*

"Is everything okay? Is Dad okay?"

"Your father's fine."

Huh? I don't ask any more questions. "I'll be home in a few minutes."

I hang up, puzzled. Coach finishes his own call.

"Everything okay?" Coach asks.

"Yeah," I shake my head. "I just forgot to take out the garbage this morning."

"I did too." He smiles.

I half-smile back, distracted. *Why is she so mad?* I'm almost scared to go in the house when Coach pulls into the driveway.

"Thanks, Coach," I say, collecting my boots from the floor of the passenger seat. "Guess I won't see you tomorrow."

"Recover, Rowan," he says. "I need you healthy. Maybe spend some time with your family."

I'm scared too. I close the car door and take the wheelchair ramp. When I finally get inside, Mom is on the couch crying, my dad beside her with a serious expression on his face. *Him too? God, what did I do?*

My oatmeal from breakfast is still on the dining room table, untouched. Popcorn sits on her bed next to my dad. Her ears are pricked, alert. *Where's Ike?*

"What?" I say, dumbfounded. "What did I do?"

My mom pulls the brown envelope of cash from behind her back.

Fuuuuuccccckkkkk.

"That's what we want to know, Rowan." She sobs. "What exactly did you do? How did you get this money?"

I get a text from Ike.

"Put away your phone," my mom yells. Dad says the same thing with his eyes.

I look at the screen. *Say it was Beryl.*

"I said put away your phone."

I shove it inside the pocket of Caspian's hoodie. "It was from Beryl," I say.

"You expect me to believe that Beryl just gave you *seven thousand dollars*?"

"How else did you think I got it? Selling crack? Hooking?"

"Rowan!"

"What?"

A hint of calm relaxes my mom's shoulders. Dad's brows twitch.

"Why would Beryl give you all this money?"

"Why do you think, Mom?" I shout. "To help get Dad to Sweden."

At least that part is true.

Mom drops the envelope on the floor and covers her face with her hands. After a quiet minute she starts massaging her temples. Dad looks … relieved? I can't interpret his expression.

"It's a lot of money," she says.

"She wanted to help."

"She already has." Mom gestures. "The bathroom renovations, Ike's tournament fees. It's too much."

My phone continues to buzz in my pocket. I take it out, not caring how my mother will react. The text is from Ozzy.

Maybe a permanent break.

"Practice was hard," I say. "I'm going to lie down."

I hear my mom say to my dad, "What are we going to do with seven thousand dollars?"

I slam my door and flop on my bed. A permanent break? *Fuck you, Ozzy.* I don't respond.

* * *

The next day, I sleep in. Even my internal clock is off. It's weird to be home on a Sunday, and not be going to practice. Mom believes me when I tell her Coach said to take the day off as part of the training plan for New York. *Periodization*, I'd said.

A therapist I've never seen before works with Dad in the living room. I sneak by, covering my chest because I'm not wearing a bra. Probably not necessary, given I still have on Caspian's hoodie. I dump the oatmeal from yesterday into the compost, and make coffee. It tastes bitter, so I add two extra scoops of sugar. Popcorn watches me curiously.

Mom follows me to my room. "Can we talk?"

At least she's asking.

I sit on my bed cross-legged, cradling the mug.

"I want you to give the money back to Beryl."

"Why?"

"Dr. Patel doesn't think your father's well enough to travel."

"Is he dying?"

"We're all dying."

"You know what I mean, Mom."

"Not specifically," she says. "Not medically. At least not in the obvious ways. It's just a lot." She places a hand on my shin. "But there's a similar treatment coming out of Toronto. It may be even better than this one."

"I don't want to go to New York if he's dying."

"Your dad wants nothing more than for you to go."

Does that mean he is dying?

"You've worked really hard to get here, Rowan. You've given up school dances and sleepovers, and sugary drinks."

Not all sugary drinks.

"You don't have time for a part-time job. A scholarship to a school in the US would be a really big deal for you."

"I need to win."

"Do your best."

"No, I *need* to win. For Dad. Every time I win, he seems to get stronger. When I fight, he fights."

"Oh, Rowan," Mom says. She lies back on my bed with her arms outstretched, her hair fanned across my quilt. "Wrestling isn't going to save your dad."

"I want to make him proud."

"He'll be proud no matter what. You could come last in New York, and he'd still think you were the moon."

I curl up beside her. She turns to look at my face. "Do you remember your first track meet? You were nine and you competed in a whole bunch of different events. Hurdles, high jump, running, some throwing one. Anyway, you were just terrible …"

"Mom!"

"You were. You threw the shot or the discus — no it was definitely the shot put — sideways and nearly hit the judge. You ran into the high jump bar and knocked it off before you even got airborne, and you kicked over every single hurdle."

I cover my face. "How do I *not* remember that? I must have blocked it out."

"You don't remember because your dad never made a big

deal about it. Believe it or not, you'd worked really hard at that competition. You never gave up. And when the meet was over you asked your dad if you could stay behind and practice a few more throws because you wanted to do better. You dad was so proud."

She gets up.

"Where are you going?"

"I need to get something."

I gather Caspian's hoodie, and bring it to my nose. I try not to think about what Ozzy's doing right now. Whether he's on stage or having brunch or knocking down a wall. I suddenly miss his dads too.

My mom returns a few minutes later with a picture of my dad and me standing outside a field house. My cheeks are sunburnt, my pigtails lopsided. I have no trophies, no medals. Not even a purple participation ribbon. My dad stands with his arm around me, giving a thumbs-up. He looks like he might burst. I forgot how tall and fit he used to be. How happy.

Mom lies back again, so we're both staring at the ceiling.

"It's that spirit that makes your dad proud, Row. It's what makes you a champion. You might've got it from your dad, but that spirit doesn't depend on him, and it won't make him better."

I dab my eyes. I can't get the adhesive wet.

"But God, were you ever terrible at shot put. Once you threw it backward and it hit the safety cage." She starts to laugh. Lightly at first and then full body heaves. My whole bed shakes. I laugh with her; both of us with our mouths wide open, unable to speak. We sound like animals. Ike comes to my door and stares.

"What are you guys doing?" he asks.

Neither of us replies. We laugh until we cry, until we *cry*.

Eventually, my mother hauls herself up and off my bed, wiping her eyes as she goes. I stick the picture in a book on my bedside table.

"You should probably start packing," Mom says. "At least dig your suitcase out of the garage."

CHAPTER 28

From the air, New York City looks like the intro to one of my dad's *National Geographic* shows. *Megastructures* or "feats of engineering." Pia leans into me to get a better view. Coach is somewhere a few rows in front of us wearing a Yankees jersey and working on his third bag of pretzels.

We touch down half an hour late. This is why Coach never lets us check luggage. Everything is meticulously planned. We clear customs with relative ease and assemble into a long line of irritable travelers waiting for cabs. Pia hangs off my arm.

"I can't believe we're here." She takes a selfie with a yellow cab in the background. Coach stands too close to the guy in front of him as if he's worried someone might jump the queue.

"We have to go straight to the weigh-in," he mumbles.

"I'm nervous," I say to no one in particular.

The line moves quickly. Our cabbie is a woman with a Brooklyn accent and a smoker's cough. Her hair is sprayed into a complicated updo. Bobby pins poke from her scalp. She honks, and swerves, and tailgates. Pia hangs out the window, taking pictures and talking about as fast as our cabbie is driving. Coach braces himself in the front seat, one hand splayed on the window.

We pull up to the tournament venue, where weigh-ins are already in progress.

"You have your singlet?" Coach asks.

Of course I have my singlet.

"Yep."

We pile out of the cab and climb the steps to the center. Neatly printed signs and directional arrows are posted in the entry. I find my age group and weight class and follow the markers down a wide hallway toward a changeroom. Coach goes in the opposite direction. I pull on my singlet and a pair of slides.

"I'm sorry," I say to Pia, fully dressed across from me. "I wish you could wrestle."

"Next year," she sighs. "At least I'm here."

I know that's partially because of me: moral support, warm-up partner, roommate — Coach and I can't exactly share a room — but she has her own agenda. We are standing in the Pratt Institute. Somewhere on this campus is the legendary School of Design and within it, the fashion wing. I imagine classrooms with mannequins and machines and 3D printers, closets stockpiled with vintage fabrics, a makeshift runway. And Pia will show an academic advisor her burgeoning portfolio, which includes, amongst other creations, her collection of original cast sleeves. If I believed in the stars, I might think her broken arm happened for a reason.

We exit the changeroom and follow the WEIGH-IN signs.

Holy shit. We join a line a few hundred deep. Girl wrestlers. Some wear national team jackets: France, Italy, Japan, a few from Canada. One girl I beat in Greco last year. Team Washington, Nevada State Wrestling. South Carolina, Pennsylvania. Texas. *Maine?*

I try to determine which of them are in my weight class. Short girl with big ass and pink singlet. Possibly. Tall girl with a floating rib and rosacea. Unlikely. Girl with ripped upper body and resting bitch face. Bring it on. The line moves rapidly, expanding into six chutes where personnel conduct skin checks. Behind them, a row of electronic scales. My palms sweat. Music pumps from overhead speakers.

When I reach my assigned chute, I hand Pia my phone and backpack. A gloved official examines my fingernails and skin. He stares at the scar on my forehead, the glue dissolved and wound healed.

"You got a doctor's note?" he asks like it might've been ringworm.

Frig. If I did it would probably be in Cyrillic.

I take a chance. If I lie and say "yes" he's more likely to let me pass without asking to see it. There are probably fifty wrestlers behind me. If I say "no" he might get a second opinion, holding things up.

"Yes."

He moves to get a better look at my forehead and then waves me forward to the scale.

Phew.

"Rowan Harper," I say to the wide man behind the plywood table.

He mutters my name back to me and hammers the keyboard with round fingers.

"Go ahead and step on the scale," he urges.

I kick off my slides and step on the metal platform. I should have at least got a pedicure. Flecks of baby pink paint from last month speckle the tips of my toenails.

"One thirty-seven point six," he says, entering the number into his spreadsheet. "Next."

"Done," Pia says. She hands me back my stuff and we meet Coach up front. His accreditation pass dangles from his neck like a cattle tag. Merch tables line the hall behind him. *Maybe I'll buy a new singlet.*

I text my mom. *Arrived safe. Tell Dad I weighed in at 137.6.*

When he was still able, my dad entered all my stats into a spreadsheet.

We head outside. The air is humid, unlike home. My cheeks are flushed, and Pia's hair looks like coconut fiber. Coach wipes his brow with a fast-food napkin from this pocket. Trees form canopies over the sidewalks. The women we pass have impeccable skin and bold glasses in exaggerated shapes, like Beryl's. They dress in mustard yellow and fuchsia and olive green. The odd wrestler weaves through in sport socks and slides and tight hair.

We stop in front of a brown brick building with an arched doorway and brass detailing. Air conditioning boxes jut out from apartment windows.

"This is it," Coach says, charging through the door. He lines up to check in. Pia and I wait on a worn but expensive cream leather sofa. She traces the grommet trim with her fingertips. Vintage *Vogue* magazines and art books line the wooden block coffee table. A picture book of Western film posters sits beneath a vase of white flowers.

Our room is nothing like the Holiday Inns we normally stay in. A queen bed with a swirly white metal headboard that reminds me of a carousel. High ceilings, ornate furniture, a bearskin rug.

"It's fake," Pia assures me, stroking the rug with her foot.

She lies on the bed. I peek out the window. We look onto another building, the same brown brick, with squashed balconies covered in milk crates and pigeons. Tiny pots of herbs. Pia loves it here. Ozzy would love it here.

I strip off my plane clothes, throw on Caspian's hoodie, and join Pia on the bed. Both of us pull out our phones. I search Instagram for activity that might involve Ozzy. Nothing. He'll be cramming for opening night. I wonder if my parents will still go. If Mom will force Dad into a pair of chino pants and dress socks and wheel him into the front row. I don't even know how well he'll be able to see the stage with his head tilt. If the tournament runs late, they'll stay home, crowded around Mom's phone, waiting for updates.

Pia shows me a video clip of Ahmed scoring a goal with a bicycle kick. Huge celebration. His hair doesn't move through the entire shot. I check my texts.

Coach: *Be ready in fifteen minutes to go for dinner. Meet in lobby.*
Ike: *Do u know where my wallet is?*
Caspian: *Good luck in New York. Take some bitches down.*
Mom: *Thumbs-up*
Ozzy: *I miss you*

I drop my phone on my chest, unable to reply to any of them. I don't know where Ike's wallet is. He loses it three times a day. I want to take bitches down. I don't want to admit that I miss Oz too. That as much as he's made my head spin and my heart ache, I crave to see his childish smile. To get infected by his chronic optimism. To feel his stubbled face press into my neck.

Pia puts on an asymmetrical dress she's sewn from lace tablecloths. She's brought a dress for me, as well. Simple, blue. A gift from a new clothing brand out of Toronto. She films a quick Tik-Tok and we meet Coach in the lobby.

"You're late," he says. "Nearly ate the entire contents of the snack bar."

You probably did.

He takes us to an Italian restaurant for a signature post-weigh-in meal. Something we can only do when there are night-before weigh-ins and more enjoyable when we're on the road and can choose a restaurant other than Subway or a crappy chain with a sprawling kid's menu. This one is halfway between fine dining and microwaving a can of Zoodles.

The servers wear floppy bow ties, chic white shirts, and aprons. One side of the restaurant has been painted to look like Venice. The other side is a cellar. Bottles of wine are stacked in curious patterns. Mom would love it here.

I order spaghetti and meatballs because they're predictable. Coach orders something with eight pounds of cheese, twice baked, and Pia gets a dish she's never heard of. She can take a risk when she doesn't have to wrestle.

The bread arrives at the table, swaddled like a baby. Coach unwraps it and tears a piece off.

"Saw a few recruiters in the accreditation room," he says. "There's a fella here from King University in Tennessee. And I spoke with a trainer wearing McKendree team gear."

"Where's that?" Pia asks.

"Lebanon, Illinois."

I don't know where half these places are. I text my mom, *Where did Dad do his Master's?* I know it was somewhere in the US.

"Some of these coaches have ins with their state schools. Just go out there and wrestle hard. You'll naturally put on a show."

My meal consists of one giant meatball and noodles. Pia and I laugh. It looks like something a kid imagined, all the meat lumped in the middle. It tastes amazing. Coach takes a forkful and dips it into his dish, while Pia schools us on the history of the bow tie.

"People *think* the bow tie originated in the nineteenth century, and with the French, but it was really invented by Croatian soldiers during the Thirty Years' War. That started in 1618."

So did Pia's story.

I tune out and begin running leg attacks through my head, twisting the spaghetti into oblivion around my fork. I need to work my speed, perfect my fakes, take clean shots. Single legs, high crotches, ankle picks.

I scroll through the tournament registrations on my phone, something Coach will be pissed about if he notices. *Shit.* One of the top Fargo girls from Washington is up a weight class and in my bracket. I bury my phone under my napkin.

When the bill arrives, Coach's eyes are glazed over and his stomach is practically resting on the table. He's pushed his chair back. The bow tie story has reached the 1920s when it finally jumps genders.

"Both Katharine Hepburn and Marlene Dietrich made them popular," Pia says, grabbing a striped spearmint candy from the bill tray.

Maybe I'll wear a bow tie with my singlet tomorrow.

On the walk back, we separate from Coach. He gives us a lecture on getting a good night's sleep, reminds us of the time change, and then shuffles away, Google maps on his phone, in search of antacids.

"We should go for cheesecake," Pia says.

"Cheesecake? How do you have room for dessert?"

"We can eat it later."

The streets are lined with brownstones and pedestrians. Fire escapes zigzag atop the awnings of pint-size shops: bookstores, bagelsmiths, check-cashing depots. Pia finds a café and orders cheesecake from a little take-out window. We turn the corner in the direction of our hotel. I freeze at a storefront. *Brooklyn MMA.*

"No way," Pia says. "Keep walking."

I stare through the window at the men sparring. The jabs and hooks and kicks. My body buzzes with adrenaline. I feel it zip through my limbs, bending my hands into fists.

"Let's go." Pia tugs my arm, as a man in a sleeveless T and glossy shorts leans from the doorway.

"You gonna come in and try it?" he says, all biceps and teeth. He's a darker, older version of Caspian, has an identical scar on his left eyebrow.

"Nah," Pia waves. "We're just out for an evening stroll."

An evening stroll? *Okay, Beryl.*

"Yes," I say.

'You're wearing a dress," Pia whispers.

"I tell you what, you come in, take a few shots, and I'll give you the gloves off my hands." He raises his arms, flipping his wrists, front to back. His gloves are bulbous and gold and mottled with bits of duct tape.

"Serious?" I ask.

"No, he's not serious," Pia says.

I'm already inside the door. I hated my basement fight. The nausea was intoxicating and there was something sinister about all those men with their gaping mouths, pumping fists, and sloshing beers, the smell of past fights: blood, vomit, and broken souls saddening the already dank air.

Old Caspian tosses me a pair of gloves. The other fighters watch with curiosity. Pia stands against the gym's mirror, the Styrofoam container of cheesecake balancing in her hand. *What the hell are you doing, Rowan?* her expression says.

I strap on the gloves while Old Caspian outfits himself with protective pads. Before he utters a word about stance or technique, I throw a jab.

He nods. "What else you got?"

The fighters who'd continued to spar stop.

Jab, cross, hook, knee. I can't throw a kick in a dress. We reset to the middle of the mat. He throws, I duck. Jab. Upper.

The spectators whistle. I feel good. A similar high to wrestling but without the pressure to win. It's all pleasure. I throw a few more combos, each with more power, each gaining more applause.

"You tricked me!" Old Caspian says after I unleash a punishing hook to the body. "But I am a man of my word." He drops the training pads and retrieves his gloves from the glass front counter. He gets down on one knee, to the amusement of the room, kisses each glove goodbye, and presents them. *At least I'm guaranteed to come home with something gold.*

I slip on his gloves. Warm and wet. Molded. The small crowd of fighters, there might be twelve at most, clap and cheer. My people. I punch the ends of the gloves together.

"Next stop the UFC," Old Caspian jokes.

Next stop hotel. We bump fists. I slip on my shoes and step back out onto the sidewalk. The men talk animatedly in the window.

"I can't believe you." Pia shakes her head, a smile on her face. "Are you going to take those off?" she asks, nodding at my hands.

"No way."

Blue dress, gold gloves. This is what Tall Dad meant when he said, *If you're going to get noticed, New York is the place to do it.*

In the hotel, we see Coach in the lobby, a pharmacy bag gripped tight in his hand. We take the stairs to avoid him, and flop on our bed.

"I'm so full," Pia complains.

I'm tearing off one of my gloves when my phone rings. Face-Time. My mom. I climb off the bed and curl up in the chair beneath the window.

"I'm taking a shower," Pia mouths. What she means is *I'm going to give you privacy.*

My phone connects. Both my parents are on the screen. *Uh oh.* A streak of panic hijacks my breath. *Is this a goodbye call?*

"How's New York?"

Phew. Smiles.

"It's awesome," I say. "We just ate dinner at this Italian place and Pia bought cheesecake."

My mom frowns. "What are you wearing?"

"Pia loaned me a dress."

"On your hand."

I drop my fist from view and yank off the glove. "Nothing."

Serious tone. "Your father and I were talking about the conversation we had before you left, and he just wanted to say a few things." Mom focuses the camera on my dad and leaves. He types into his device.

Don't feel you have to win for me.

"I know, Dad."

I don't want you to feel added pressure. You know I'll be proud of you no matter what happens tomorrow. Just do your best.

"I know," I say again. Tears well. My dad's face looks gray, but there's still so much life in his eyes. A thousand stories. A thousand bits of advice. A thousand *good jobs* and *I love yous*. A thousand *don't-step-on-the-backs-of-your-sneakers-because-you're-ruining-thems.* He can barely move his face.

Popcorn jumps up onto Dad's lap. She rests her head on his chest.

"Did Mom take her to a groomer?" I ask.

Things go quiet. For a moment there's only the whir of the shower pipes and the faint thrum of traffic below. My dad resumes typing.

Rowan, fight for yourself. Please, don't fight for me.

I stare at my father. I touch the screen, light-years away.

"Dad," I muster, through a broken throat. "The same goes for you." Swallow. "Please. *You* don't fight for *me*."

Tears roll down my cheek, turning Pia's dress into a deeper shade of blue. Dad blinks. His eyes change, almost like a sigh of relief.

Mom reappears and whispers, "You should probably get some sleep. Big day tomorrow. And don't forget to eat breakfast."

"Mom!"

"Sorry."

"Night, Dad."

He types, *Go get 'em Pea.*

Peach. The screen turns black.

CHAPTER 29

Morning barrels me over like a double leg. The time change. *Ugh.* Sunlight streams through the window and warms the back of my neck as Pia braids my hair, nearly lulling me back to sleep. When she's finished, I fish through my bag for the right thong and tug on my singlet.

Coach knocks on the door and drops off smoothies for me and Pia. Mine is green. God knows what's in it. The juice of one kiwi, an avocado, the grass of one lawn mower. Whatever, it goes down. My socks are striped. A pair Ozzy gave me last Christmas. I don't check my phone.

We meet Coach in the lobby. He's extra feisty, leaving us in his wake as he lumbers down the sidewalk in his new sneakers and nineties tracksuit. Pia looks gorgeous with minimal makeup and navy jogging pants. I crack my knuckles with each step.

Inside the venue, lights strobe and music blasts. They don't play the Spice Girls. The mats are set up to precision, like a Lego wrestling set. Girls warm up. Laps, arm circles, shadow shots, sprawls. So many braids.

Pia and I dump our gear in the stands. Her portfolio juts out of her backpack. We find a central mat to warm up on. Every girl looks intimidating. Even the ones with lip gloss. *Especially* them.

I feel good still. A minor ache in my shoulder from the pub fight, but strong. Ready. Instead of the paper bout sheets we use in Canada, matches here are posted on an electronic board. I'm up first on Mat 16, match 1605. *Fuck.* I scan the crowd for Coach as the tournament host delivers opening words. *Do your best!* Blah blah blah. Neatly dressed refs with bayou beards and gray pants converge on the mats. Officials gather behind scorekeeping tables. The American anthem plays over speakers.

Pia's gone, relocated to find an adequate place from which to film my matches. Matches my dad will no longer be able to download, categorize, or file. I pull my headphones over my ears and pace the perimeter of Mat 16.

I can barely breathe. I drank too much smoothie. The first match ends in a thirteen-second pin. Pace. The girls in the next match shoot at the same time and headbutt each other. The one in the Colorado singlet splits her head open, the other gets a bloody nose. Her coach hands her a tampon to shove inside her nostril. The clock stops for injury time.

By the time the match resumes, Coach has made his way to the mat. My music cuts out. *Why didn't I charge my headphones?*

1603.

Two matches out. I peel off my hoodie, check my laces, and instinctively look for my dad in the stands. This is when we find each other. This is when our eyes connect. Two matches out. This is when we nod.

He's not there. And even though I knew he wouldn't be, his absence is profound. Where is his yellow pencil? His glasses for distance? His comfortable shoes? There are only girls and empty seats.

1604.

I am alone.

I have only me to fight for.

My father's seat in the stands will always be empty.

1605.

"Rowan Harper and Bonita Rodriguez."

I walk onto the mat, Coach in my corner like the Terminator. Skin checks, handshakes.

The ref brings down his arm. "Wrestle."

Hand fight. My opponent is strong. I barely get out of a two-on-one.

Coach yells, "Circle."

We untie and reset. Fake. Sweep single, two points. I fail to get a leg lace. The ref blows his whistle, stands us up. She goes for a hip toss. Misses. By the end of the first round, I'm still up by only two.

At the beginning of the next round, I blast a double leg and pin her. The ref raises my arm. One down, God knows how many more to go. I shake my opponent's hand, and her coach's, and exit the mat.

"She almost had you on that hip toss," he says. "Way to defend." He pats my shoulder and disappears. I sip from my water bottle and head to the monitor to find out when and where my next match is. Names scroll across the screen. It takes minutes before my weight class appears and my next match flashes in blue letters. 1628. Against Fargo girl. *Oh God.* Headphones up.

I find a corner near Mat 16 and adjust my music to shuffle. Low battery. I watch the matches in front of me but don't really see. Takedowns. Tears. Gut wrenches. Faces in the mat. Black, white, Latina, brown. Made-up, bare, fierce, frustrated, frightened.

When 1626 is called, I don't look to the stands, but I hear my father's words. *Don't fight for me.* A man in an Adrian College golf shirt hovers by the bout sign. Breathe.

Fargo girl snaps me down hard. *Asshole.* She takes my back and gets two points. Coach turns red. We get into a clinch. I feel her setting up a throw, but I trip her. Four-point takedown. We stand. She shoots an angry single leg. Sprawl.

Fargo continues to drive forward, her arms still wrapped tight on my leg. I press my body weight into her. It's like wrestling Leo. Pia films from the side of the mat. I free my leg, take front head position, and think of the first time I drilled with Caspian, this exact move. How he called me Rowena and wouldn't tell me he'd dropped out of school. Later, the way he washed the dishes, hunched over the sink in his yellow kitchen, using too much soap, the delicate way he rinsed his grandma's teacups.

I drag Fargo's face to the mat, circle, and take her back for two. Gut wrench, times two, four points. The clock runs out, and the match goes to a decision. I win by points. Fargo looks like she wants to eat someone's baby. She rips off her headgear and storms off the mat.

I win my next two matches. One by pin in the first round, though I think she was injured, and kind of gave up. The other, against Resting Bitch Face, resembled my pub fight. She'd get a takedown; I'd get a takedown. She'd get cautioned for "striking"; I'd get cautioned for striking. She squeezed my wrist, I squeezed hers harder. I won by a single Hail Mary push-out point in the last three seconds. We both left behind blood spots and nests of hair. I vomited half my smoothie into a mat-side trash can.

During intermission, the mats and tables clear. Officials, coaches, and referees move to back rooms loaded with sandwiches and sodas and bags of chips. Tiny cups of black coffee. I buy an energy bar from the canteen and pick out the almonds. It tastes like honeyed sawdust.

I check my bracket online. Quarter-finals. If I win my next match, only the semis and the final are left to wrestle. If I lose, I'll have to battle through the back side of the bracket.

My phone balances face down on my knee. I rest my feet on the back of the curved plastic chair in front of me. I debate whether to check my texts. Still twenty minutes until intermission is over. Spotify plays a song Ozzy and I used to lip-synch to, every time we drove home from the mountains. It's the only country song on my playlist. Skip. Pia should be in her meeting now.

My phone chimes. Coach asks, *Where are you?* I tell him my location and scroll through the rest of my messages.

Pia: *Holy shit that was close.* Definitely referring to my last match. My heart skydives, just thinking about it.

Ike: *Popcorn peed on Dad's pillow.*

No texts from Ozzy or Caspian. Nothing from Mom and Dad.

I see Coach approaching below with a woman wearing a uniform and a severe ponytail. I sit up straight and remove my feet from the seat in front of me. He waves me down. She introduces herself as the assistant coach at Baker University.

Is that in California? Why haven't my parents texted?

I nod and smile. She stares at me. Coach stares at me. Expectantly. Like one of them has asked a question and is waiting for a response.

"She asked what you planned to study," Coach says.

"Study, yes, sorry. I was still thinking about my last match. Um, physics."

"A science major. I studied biology at Texas Tech," the woman says, her lips thin and serious.

Are my parents trying not to distract me? Are they just following my results online? Are they literally trying to ignore me so I have to fight for myself?

"Maybe we can talk after the tournament is complete."

I grab her hand, probably too roughly. "Yes," I say, apologizing again. "I'm just trying to focus on my next match."

"She's very focused," Coach adds.

"On something else," the woman replies. "I can see that."

Coach sees her off. They exchange quiet words. *Her Dad's sick*, he'll explain. *She's too focused in the middle of a tournament. Sometimes, she's a little ditzy.* All would be true.

Referees and officials lumber back to the mats. Matches are called. Some bitch who broke my collarbone is up on Mat 15. I hope she loses. 1680.

"Rowan Harper and Monica Calder."

Monica is tall, like me. Her mouth guard is black, singlet plain as pavement. She smells like fruit salad when we tie up. We are violent. Her hand on my head feels like a concrete glove. I want to tell her to *fuck off*. I stumble during a fake and she shoots. I scramble away, but she gets me out of the circle for one point. My legs tremble.

In my peripheral, Coach gestures wildly. My headgear is twisted. Can't hear him.

I get a four-point throw, but she reverses the position and gets two. She traps my arm, puts pressure on my body, turning me for another two. *Bitch, come on.* The ref stands us up. Coach yells for the two-on-one, but I feel a throw. Boom. I get her into a pin. She fights, bridging her hips. Tries to turn left. Right. I make myself heavier.

The ref lifts his hand, about to call the match. My opponent explodes up, momentarily knocking me off. We grapple. I get back on top. Pressure. I feel her body give, sinking, drowning into the mat. The whistle blows. On to semi-finals.

"What were you doing?" Coach says, disappointed.

"What do you mean?" I pull off my headgear. "I won."

"You were flailing all over the place. You didn't listen." He wipes spit from the corner of his lip. "Felt like I was coaching a zoo tiger that'd escaped her cage. Pay attention."

"My parents haven't texted."

"Why are you checking your phone? This is the biggest tournament of your life, Rowan."

"They usually text. For updates."

"They're getting the results online."

"How do you know?" How do you know my dad's not on a ventilator right now? How do you know the minister with the superblond hair, who married my parents, isn't sitting beside his hospital bed right now singing songs about Jesus and everlasting life? This tournament is everlasting.

"Because I sent your mom the link to Trackwrestling this morning."

"Mom can't even order groceries online. There's no way she can figure out Track."

"Turn off your phone," Coach says. "Two more matches. When you win, we'll call your parents. You're up next, 1693."

I hand Coach my phone.

"Stay hydrated," he says.

"Hydrated, right." I leave the mat area and wander down a back hallway to an exit door. I need fresh air. I need to clear my head.

I step out into a parking lot. The sun is high and hot. A man locks his bike to a rack, his sideburns waving in the breeze. I sit on the edge, where the pavement crumbles into the grass. Dandelions bend around me. Everything aches.

In sports movies, the main character never wins. They come second. But they act like it doesn't matter because they learned something greater than the victory, something intangible: perseverance, the true meaning of friendship, the value of hard work. I don't want to learn anything today. I don't want a teaching moment. I don't want to build character. I just want to win and go home.

When I get back inside, Coach is standing on Mat 16.

"Last call for Rowan Harper," a voice booms from a loudspeaker. I race to the scorekeeper's table, practically dumping my stuff at their feet.

"The toilet wouldn't flush," I say, fumbling. *What the hell?* They don't care. They don't want an explanation or excuse. A red-haired official points me to the mat. "Next time you'll be disqualified," he says.

Coach takes a chair, his hands knotted into a fist.

"Wrestle."

Adrenaline shoots out of my pores. I can barely sink into my stance. My opponent is slow and methodical, waiting for me to shoot. She is the kind of wrestler who scores only from defense. Earns points from other girls' shitty shots. *Fuck it.* Two can play that game. Circle, fake, retreat. The clock winds down. Her coach yells at her in French. *Attaque!* She doesn't. I snap her down and go behind, my arms wrapped tight as a corset around her waist. She tries to strip my grip. I throw her down. I crush her. Make her question her life choices. She sobs. One more to go.

Coach grabs my arm as I walk away to collect my stuff.

"You okay?" he asks.

His face is pale. I should be asking him the same question. I nod, numb.

"Let's sit."

I follow Coach to the stands where Pia is back, eating noodles from a take-out container.

"How was your meeting?" I ask.

She drops her fork. "He said some of my work was immature."

"What an asshole. Like what?"

"My sleeves."

"Did you tell him you sewed those with one arm?"

"Didn't matter. He was talking about the concept."

This is why I hate art. It's never *right*.

"He told me to take more risks, but that my portfolio was 'strong' otherwise."

Maybe she should have made bow ties. I change the subject. "Do your parents know how to use Trackwrestling?"

"They watched our Vegas tournament," Pia replies.

"Coach, did my parents text?"

"No, Rowan. One more match," he says. "Let's get through that."

"Would my parents call if my dad was in the hospital?"

"I'm sure they would."

I don't tell Coach I feel my dad's presence. That I thought I saw him in a cloud outside or eating a burrito by the first aid station or in the body type of the man refereeing on Mat 4. Exact same, pre-ALS. The long limbs and square neck and big hair. I don't admit my fear that my dad might be dead and that's why my mom won't text, and why I keep seeing him here. A ghost.

Two hours pass before final matches are called. My last opponent has a black eye. Californian. She comes at me like a frigging natural disaster the second the referee starts the match. She almost pins me in the first ten seconds. I have to fight off my back. I dig my heels into the mat and bridge my hips to the ceiling. The overhead lights are suspended from cables. I suck in a mouthful of my opponent's chocolaty hair. *Get off me.*

The ref is on his knees. The ref is in my face. I roll up onto the back of my head, lifting my shoulder blades off the mat. He can't call a pin if they are floating in the air. I manage to roll onto my stomach. Bitch mounts my back like a dolphin trainer at Sea-World. She tries to tie up my legs. I escape.

As soon as the ref stands us up, California attacks. This time I sprawl and take her back. I can't roll her. Up. I take her down but it's deemed outside the circle. Instead of four points, I collect one.

At the halfway point I can barely breathe. I can barely stand. I'm down by four points. Down by ex-boyfriends, and sick dads and confused moms and sad brothers, and whatever Caspian is. Depleted.

Coach rubs my arms, pours water down my throat. I stare across at my opponent, who's circling her wrists, breathing heavily. *Which one of us is the main character? Who gets the win today and who gets the lesson?* The ref calls us back to the mat. Screw scholarships to colleges I can't locate. Screw medals that'll one day end up forgotten in the bottom of a filing cabinet drawer. Screw ALS and Ozzy and the last shitty eight weeks of my life. Fuck lessons.

I explode and take her straight to her back. A ridiculous scramble ensues. I feel like I'm wrestling a reptile on one of

Dad's shows, *Last Feast of the Crocodiles*. We tussle, point for point, takedown for takedown. I glance at the clock. Ten seconds remain. We're tied. I'm about to shoot when she drives forward. I start to fall but use her momentum to get under her hips. I yank down on her arm, hoist her up, and drop her with a shoulder throw. The ref flashes four points, the clock ticks, ticks. My mouth opens. I don't know what comes out. Something animalistic. Something guttural and ugly and completely embarrassing. Grief.

I can barely get off my knees for the ref to raise my hand. An official dumps a gold medal shaped like a stop sign around my neck. My mouth guard is on the mat in front of me. I don't recall losing it. There's blood on my elbow, salt on my upper lip.

My opponent is gracious in defeat. She shakes my hand, smiles. Coach hugs me. A fatherly one, proud and affectionate. My body feels exhausted. I drink half a bottle of Gatorade. A man approaches as I head for the stands. A coach from Utah. He introduces himself as a friend of Axel's, waxing on about graduation rates, and rankings, and Salt Lake City. I nod. Take his card.

I slip outside to the parking lot where I disappeared earlier and almost missed my match. Only a few cars remain angle-parked under the evening sun. A lone pigeon wobbles by, the green and purple of its wing shining like a church window. I did it. I got the win, but I realize I also got the lesson.

CHAPTER 30

I change and get my phone back from Coach, call my parents on the walk back to the hotel.

"Congratulations," my mom answers. "We watched everything on Trackwrestling."

"Oh, Mom," I sigh. "You didn't text and I thought maybe Dad wasn't well, and I didn't think you could figure out how to watch it online."

"Rowan," Mom says, offended. "I might be a bit slow with technology, but I'm not an idiot."

"Did you see my last match?" I ask.

"Of course we did. We watched all of them. The wifi isn't great in the hospital, so it was all pixelated for a bit, but that was for only twenty seconds or so."

"Hospital?"

A pause.

"Mom? Is Dad in the hospital?"

"We had a little breathing scare this morning, but that's all it was. A scare. Your dad's perfectly fine. Scott, say hi to Rowan so she knows you're fine."

My dad's computer: *Hey, Peach. I'm good. You were dynamite today.*

"See?" Mom says. "We should be out of here shortly. We're waiting for the nurse to discharge us. Ike's already gone to pull the van around front."

"You'll pick me up from the airport tomorrow?"

"We'll be there. Coach says you're seeing Tina Turner."

"Kill me."

"Rowan. A little live theater will be good for you."

Isn't that what life is? Live theater? Comedy. Tragedy. Standing ovations, missed lines, failed props, and wardrobe malfunctions?

"I don't even know who Tina Turner is."

"Well, you will after tomorrow. We'll see you at the airport, good and late."

Inside the hotel lobby, Coach says he's going out for beers with some wrestling people. Pia and I are on our own for dinner. He sets a curfew. Gives us a safety lecture. Tells us when to be ready for breakfast in the morning.

We take the elevator to our room. Pia tosses her portfolio on the bed. "We should go out," she says. "Our last night in New York."

"Look at me," I say. "I look like shit."

"Take a shower. You'll feel better." She pulls her hair off her face. "Ahmed said he misses me."

So did Oz. I still haven't responded.

I shower and we go for pizza, then hit up the few straggling second-hand stores open late on a Saturday night. Pia buys original bell-bottoms, a tweed jacket, and a hideous T-shirt. She doesn't have enough room in her bag for all of her purchases and forces me to pack the jacket when we return to the hotel.

"What did you think of the recruiters?" she says. "Now that things are kind of off with Oz, where do you want to go?"

"No idea. I can't decide if I should go big, like Texas or California, or pick some tiny college on the East Coast where the leaves turn bright orange in the fall and everyone watches football."

"I'm going to apply to Pratt," Pia says.

"What about your parents?"

She shrugs. "They'll have to deal. I don't want to be an engineer. Or a vet." She looks out the window at the tiny balconies I'd admired earlier. "I want to be here." She points. "I want to be that guy up there watering his rosemary and airing out his spin shoes."

"Maybe you and Oz will both end up here," I say.

We crawl into bed, still in our day clothes, and turn out the lights. The air conditioner rattles. Children run up and down the hall outside. I fall asleep but wake just after three. Sirens. Somewhere below an ambulance cuts through the night, the back lit up like an electrical panel, paramedics saving someone's life.

* * *

The actress who plays Tina Turner is beautiful. We have third row seats. Pia and Coach sing through the entire first act. I want to kill myself. I eat handfuls of M&M peanuts hidden in my bag, and periodically check my phone.

A character in the second act could be Ozzy in ten years. I look him up in the playbill. He's Greek, lots of facial hair, a new-car smile. Dance background. He moves with conviction.

Coach is the first person in the audience to give a standing ovation. Pia is quick to join him. They look like besties at Coachella. It's kind of endearing.

We have to go straight from the theater to the airport. Coach hails a cab and we pile into the back with our luggage, which the theater begrudgingly held for us in their box office.

I fall asleep on the plane, my leg stretched across Pia's lap, despite turbulence and a daycare of screaming babies. Pia's over-stuffed carry-on barely fits under the seat. I get up once to go to the bathroom and catch Coach ogling the playbill. I can't tell if he's mourning his lost calling as a chorus boy or his coming-of-age crush.

When we touch down in Canada it's after ten o'clock. Pia gets held up at customs. Coach and I wait patiently by a cowboy statue. I flick my phone off airplane mode.

"Finally," Pia says. "They wouldn't quit asking questions."

"You girls both good?" Coach says, yawning.

"Yeah," we say in unison.

"My dad's in the cellphone lot," Pia says.

"My parents are picking me up."

"All right. No practice tomorrow. See you Tuesday."

Pia hugs me goodbye and drags her bag toward the exit. Her hair blows as air rushes in through the door. I check my phone.

From my mom: *Bentley is picking you up.*

Bentley? Why Bentley? I scan the arrivals for Tall Dad. He stands beside a Starbucks, a cup in each hand, brown paper bag tucked under his arm. No sign of Oz.

"Weird." I go to him.

"Hi, Rowan," he says. "Sorry it's me and not your family," he apologizes. "Hope you're still into Frappuccinos." He hands me a cup. Most of the whipped cream has dissolved. It looks like sea foam.

"Thanks." I take a sip. "Where are Mom and Dad?"

Tall Dad's expression changes. He is Ms. Foy.

"I'm taking you to the hospital," he says, kindly. "Your whole family's there."

I drop my bag. He catches it midair, swings it over his shoulder. We get to the car, Ozzy's car. I slide into the front seat where I've sat a thousand times before. Vents I've flipped opened and closed, footprints on the dash, the seat belt that always catches when I pull it too hard. I always pull it too hard.

Ozzy's spring jacket is bunched in the center console. I bring it to my chest. A child's blanket. Bentley pulls away from the airport. Away from the streak of cabs bringing people home. Away from the reunions and meeting points. He doesn't know what to say. Tall Dad always knows what to say. All he does is swallow. I watch the rise and fall of the lump of cartilage on his throat. His eyes look like it's going to rain.

I watch the city flit by like an old slideshow, frame by frame. A McDonald's Dad took me to for a milkshake after I had a tooth pulled. The downtown core where my father worked and occasionally dragged me on weekends to pick up a file or send an invoice. The parking lot near the old stadium where he taught me to ride a bike.

The hospital comes into view, benign and ordinary. It doesn't look like a place of miracles or hope. No colorful stained glass or dazzling lights. Tall Dad pulls into the parkade.

"You don't have to walk me in," I say. "I'll know where to find him."

"I don't mind," Bentley replies.

"I'm good." What a thing to say. *Good.* As if he's dropping me off at the mall. He loops around the lot and pulls up to the emergency department. I haul my bag out of the car, wear Ozzy's coat.

"Thanks," I whisper.

"We're here for you, Rowan. Anything you need. Just call."

I pass through the ER, past bodies sick and slumped on gray chairs, their caregivers scrolling their phones, staring up at the clock, willing a nurse to call out their loved one's name.

The elevator quivers en route to the seventh floor and stops with a jolt. I head to palliative care. Before I even pass through the door, I see Ike in the hallway in his jersey and shorts, his hair a big top. The laces of his court shoes are double-knotted. He's come straight from a game.

"Ike," I say.

He gestures toward the room, Dad's room.

I ask, "Will you come with me?"

Ike nudges me forward. The lights inside are dim. Mom is half in a chair, half draped across my dad's chest, holding on. Popcorn sits at the opposite side of the bed. She licks Dad's crumpled hand, her leash winding in loops under a chair.

Mom looks up. "Row," she whispers. Her face is pink and yet simultaneously colorless. I fall into my dad at the foot of his bed. Hug his legs. It's not enough. I crawl in beside him and I hate myself for being 62 kilos. All the traits that make me a good wrestler — my broad shoulders and strong quads and ever-thickening neck — crowd the narrow hospital bed built for one.

I cry into his gown. Dads should not wear gowns. They should wear athletic shirts and hiking boots and work gloves and bow ties. I touch my father's hand. I kiss his cheek. His eyes are closed, but something in him wakes, infinitesimal and quiet as if he knows I'm here.

Ike cries at the end of the bed, his headband wrapped around his wrist, goose bumps on his bare shoulders. Mom cloaks her arm in my dad's. The same way she did in their wedding picture, taken in a canola field. Popcorn lies down.

* * *

My dad passes at midnight. The start of a new day. It's messy. The flurry of nurses moving about the room. The machines and wires and tubes. The beeping. Mom adjusts my dad's blanket, tucks it securely under his chin, tight around his shoulders, no gaps. Just as she'd done when he was alive.

I hug my brother who smells of cold sweat and uncertainty. He idolized my dad, and though Ike's considerably bigger than me now, he feels small in my arms.

In the corner of the room, my father's wheelchair looks foreign and out of place. An empty shopping cart in the middle of the street. I gather his shoes from the cupboard, his favorite magazines.

The last nurse leaves to give us some final time before they take Dad away. Why can't the morgue be on the roof? Why does it have to be so literal that they put the dead in the basement? Underground.

We each take turns saying goodbye. Mom goes last and when she turns away for the final time, my brother and I receive her, one of us on each side. She can barely stand. But it's Popcorn who tells us when it's time, standing at the door. Mission complete.

Mom can't even put the key in the ignition. Ike and I load Dad's empty wheelchair into the back, where it will probably stay until someone else's dad loses the feeling in his legs.

We pull into the driveway as the sun starts to cast a melon-orange glow over rooftops, swing sets, basketball nets. On the front steps, at the end of the wheelchair ramp, two figures are sitting. Ozzy and Caspian, separated by six feet, their hoods pulled over their ears. I don't even remember texting them.

Short Dad's van is parked on the street. Caspian would have walked for miles through suburbs he may have once played in to get here. Mom and Ike go around back with Popcorn. Beryl's light turns on. Off. On.

When I get to the top step, Caspian and Ozzy both stand. I drop to my knees. I feel each of their hands, distinctive, on my back. Ozzy's light, Caspian's firm and commanding. Tears fall, dampening the deck boards. It's Ozzy who speaks first.

"We got you," he says.

We?

"Whatever you need," Caspian adds.

Whatever, or whoever?

I pull myself onto my feet and study them both. Ozzy with two dads, Caspian and me with none. I don't know who to hug first. They don't make me decide. They lean in at the same time. As close to me, but as far from each other as they can get. And right now it's exactly what I need. All the men. Caspian, Ozzy, Leo, Tall Dad, Short Dad, Axel, Coach. It will take an army to fill my dad's empty chair.

CHAPTER 31

Ms. Foy sets a Ziploc bag of cookies, homemade, in front of me on her desk. For once she doesn't make me talk, and she doesn't say anything. She just lets me sit. It's my first day back at school since the funeral. I stay for half an hour before Pia comes to get me. We go to the gym locker room, where she wipes the stains from my cheeks and fixes my makeup.

Later that week, I drive Caspian to a vocational college on the east side of town, where he writes his GED. I pay for it with my fight money and wait for him in the parking lot, Popcorn curled in the back seat. The next night he wins his first professional fight. I watch from the front row, behind Axel. G-Ma takes us all to KFC to celebrate.

The high of New York wears off. Recruiters send flashy emails to Coach, but I still have another year. More girls join wrestling. It gets harder. I have to train more. I have to mix it up to stay on top. Coach lets me train with Axel twice a week. I wear my gold Brooklyn MMA gloves without telling anyone where, or how, I got them.

A local promoter offers me an amateur fight. I turn it down.

Once a month, I go to Ozzy's for dinner. Tall Dad cooks and talks about feelings, while Short Dad teaches me things. How to replace the rubber seal on a tap, fix a running toilet. Tape a room so the paint doesn't drip on the baseboards. My dad could never figure that one out.

Ozzy and I kiss when he leaves for theater camp in South Carolina. It's a weighted kiss. A *Romeo and Juliet* kiss. We are forever star-crossed lovers. Still on a break.

Summer is punctuated by record temperatures. Heat rises from the pavement in mind-bending waves. Ike mows lawns for cash and weeds Beryl's garden. On Canada Day, her ninety-seventh birthday, we set off fireworks in the backyard. Ike fills a piñata with Mardi Gras necklaces, Ring Pops, and water guns.

Mom pours her grief into running and selling houses. In August, she sells more houses than any other realtor in the city and comes second last in her first marathon. We cry at the finish line.

I spend a lot of time at the river, visiting the bench where I last sat with Dad. I study for my SAT. Sometimes Caspian joins me for a run or a Zinger. Sometimes we hold hands. Sometimes we kiss.

On the last day of summer vacation before the chaos of grade twelve, I dig out the brown paper envelope of cash buried in my bottom drawer, beneath the singlets and lucky socks, playbills and ticket stubs, Polaroids and gold medals.

I tuck the envelope into my gym bag and usher Popcorn into the car. We drive with the windows down, the last holdback of summer dwindling. You can see it in the shrinking lawn sprinklers and fading flowers, the discarded bikes, their chains off and tires deflated. In living rooms, parents clip tags off new backpacks.

Popcorn and I arrive at our destination. A small farm just outside the city near Pia's mom's clinic. It's a cheery place with an almond-shaped pond, and big sky. A dog run wraps around the house. We meet Amanda on the front deck, as planned. She stands beneath a calligraphed sign for *Valley Therapy Dogs Society*. A shaggy retriever wags its tail at her feet. It looks just like Bitzy.

I hand Amanda the envelope. She says thank you. Her mouth continues to move. She says something about changing lives, but I tune out because I already know. I stare out beyond her property, at the relentless fields and hills, the trees thick as fortress walls, the Rocky Mountains, sharp and majestic. Places my father loved and lived, and roamed. I feel him in the wind.

ACKNOWLEDGMENTS

A huge thank you to my daughter Pippa Bryan, my first child, my first reader, and the pulse of this book. I couldn't have written it without you. Nothing — no one — can wrestle away your spirit. And to my other children, Hugo and Odessa, watching you play has always brought me joy, no matter the sport, the tier, the size of the tournament. Most importantly, I honor all three of you outside of sport. The *who* of you. Your big, beautiful beating hearts.

Thank you to my agent, Stacey Kondla, the entire team at DCB, and my thoughtful editor, Barry Jowett, who understood the book's heart from day one and worked to guard it.

This books could not have been completed without the generous support of Calgary Arts Development.

To my writer friends, my best friends: Bradley Somer, Leanne Shirtliffe, paulo da costa, Sandra McIntyre, and Judith Pond. Thank you for being in my corner.

To my husband, Dave, even if we never did figure out the "over-under" drill, we've done okay. I'm happy we're ringside together. I'll never tap.

Mad love to all of my family, friends, teammates, and readers. You are the fuel.

In memory of Alfie. Lemon senses your presence. I do too. You are deeply missed.

Lastly, to any athletes out there who've been taken down by a shitty sport experience, may you recover, may you rise, may you play again.

Isaiah 54:17: no weapon formed against you shall prosper

Ali Bryan is an award-winning writer. Her debut YA novel, *The Hill*, was longlisted for the 2021 Wilbur Smith Adventure Writing Prize. She is also a Lieutenant Governor of Alberta Arts Awards Emerging Artist recipient. Born in Halifax, Nova Scotia, she currently lives on Treaty 7 Territory, in Calgary, Alberta, where she has a wrestling room in her garage and regularly gets choked out by her family.

We acknowledge the sacred land on which Cormorant Books operates. It has been a site of human activity for 15,000 years. This land is the territory of the Huron-Wendat and Petun First Nations, the Seneca, and most recently, the Mississaugas of the Credit River. The territory was the subject of the Dish With One Spoon Wampum Belt Covenant, an agreement between the Iroquois Confederacy and Confederacy of the Ojibway and allied nations to peaceably share and steward the resources around the Great Lakes. Today, the meeting place of Toronto is still home to many Indigenous people from across Turtle Island. We are grateful to have the opportunity to work in the community, on this territory.

We are also mindful of broken covenants and the need to strive to make right with all our relations.